KINETIC

OTHER BOOKS BY ANNA DURAND

Willpower (Psychic Crossroads, Book One)
Intuition (Psychic Crossroads, Book Two)
The Mortal Falls (Undercover Elementals, Book One)
The Mortal Fires (Undercover Elementals, Book Two)
The Mortal Tempest (Undercover Elementals, Book Three)
The Janusite Trilogy (Undercover Elementals, Books 1-3)
Obsidian Hunger (Undercover Elementals, Book Four)
Unbidden Hunger (Undercover Elementals, Book Five)
The Thirteenth Fae (Undercover Elementals, Book Six)
Cyneric (Undercover Elementals, Book Seven)
Echo Power (Echo Power Trilogy, Book One)
Echo Dominion (Echo Power Trilogy, Book Two)
Echo Unbound (Echo Power Trilogy, Book Three)
Passion Never Dies: The Complete Reborn Series
Banished in the Highlands (A Hot Scots Prequel)
The Notorious Dr. MacT (A Hot Scots Prequel)
The British Bastard (A Hot Scots Prequel)
The MacTaggart Brothers Trilogy (Hot Scots, Books 1-3)
Gift-Wrapped in a Kilt (Hot Scots, Book Four)
Notorious in a Kilt (Hot Scots, Book Five)
Insatiable in a Kilt (Hot Scots, Book Six)
Lethal in a Kilt (Hot Scots, Book Seven)
Irresistible in a Kilt (Hot Scots, Book Eight)
Devastating in a Kilt (Hot Scots, Book Nine)
Spellbound in a Kilt (Hot Scots, Book Ten)
Relentless in a Kilt (Hot Scots, Book Eleven)
Incendiary in a Kilt (Hot Scots, Book Twelve)
Wild in a Kilt (Hot Scots, Book Thirteen)
Lachlan in a Kilt (The Ballachulish Trilogy, Book One)
Aidan in a Kilt (The Ballachulish Trilogy, Book Two)
Rory in a Kilt (The Ballachulish Trilogy, Book Three)
Brit vs. Scot (A Hot Brits/Hot Scots/Au Naturel Crossover Book)
The American Wives Club (A Hot Brits/Hot Scots/Au Naturel Crossover Book)
A Novel Secret (A Hot Brits/Hot Scots/Au Naturel Crossover Book)
The Dixon Brothers Trilogy (Hot Brits, Books 1-3)
One Hot Escape (Hot Brits, Book Four)
One Hot Rumor (Hot Brits, Book Five)
One Hot Christmas (Hot Brits, Book Six)
One Hot Scandal (Hot Brits, Book Seven)
One Hot Deal (Hot Brits, Book Eight)
One Hot Favor (Hot Brits, Book Nine)
One Hot Bash (Hot Brits, Book 10)
Natural Obsession (Au Naturel Nights, Book One)
Natural Deception (Au Naturel Nights, Book Two)
Natural Passion (Au Naturel Trilogy, Book One)
Natural Impulse (Au Naturel Trilogy, Book Two)
Natural Satisfaction (Au Naturel Trilogy, Book Three)
Fired Up (standalone romance)

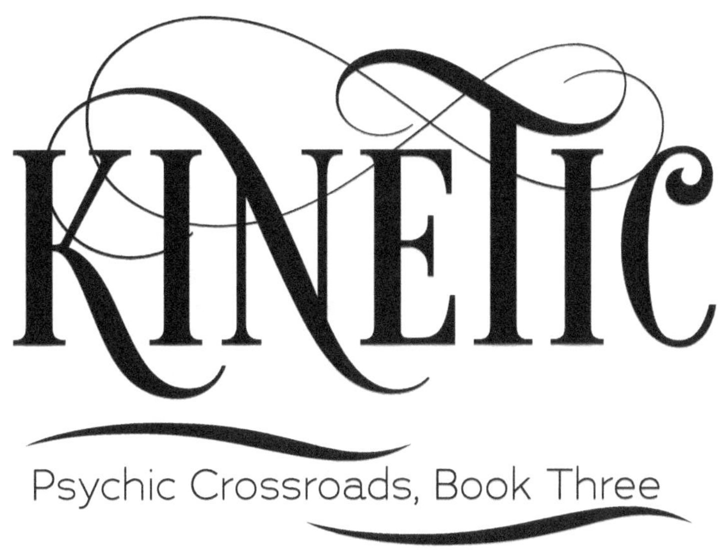

KINETIC

Psychic Crossroads, Book Three

ANNA DURAND

JACOBSVILLE BOOKS JB MARIETTA, OHIO

KINETIC

ISBN: 978-1-934631-83-6 (pbk.)
ISBN: 978-1-934631-84-3 (e-book)
Library of Congress Control Number: 2018956255

Manufactured in the United States.

Jacobsville Books
www.JacobsvilleBooks.com

Publisher's Cataloging-in-Publication Data
provided by Five Rainbows Cataloging Services

Names: Durand, Anna.
Title: Kinetic / Anna Durand.
Description: Marietta, OH : Jacobsville Books, 2018. | Series: Psychic Crossroads, bk. 3.
Identifiers: LCCN 2018956255 | ISBN 978-1-934631-83-6 (pbk.) | ISBN 978-1-934631-84-3 (ebook)
Subjects: LCSH: Psychic ability--Fiction. | Psychokinesis--Fiction. | Mental healing--Fiction. | Family secrets--Fiction. | Man-woman relationships--Fiction. | Romance fiction. | BISAC: FICTION / Romance / Paranormal / General. | FICTION / Romance / Suspense. | GSAFD: Love stories. | Occult fiction. | Romantic suspense fiction.
Classification: LCC PS3604.U724 K56 2017 (print) | LCC PS3604.U724 (ebook) | DDC 813/.6—dc23.

CHAPTER ONE

HEAL, *DAMMIT.* SEAN VANDENBROOK COMMANDED HIS PSYCHIC powers to activate, but got a big zippo in response. He hunched over the table, one hand lying palm up beside his empty lunch plate, and ran a finger of the other hand along the seam of the cut he'd gotten this morning while slicing open a well-taped box. Too bad he couldn't get rid of the stupid cut. What was the point of having the power to heal if he couldn't fix his own injuries? Psychic powers totally sucked.

"Did you hear me, Sean?"

He glanced up from his hand.

David Ransom was staring at him with narrowed eyes the way he did when he was in surrogate-father mode. Like David was old enough to be his father. Annoying big brother, maybe. Not a father. Why the hell did Sean care what David thought about him, then? He shouldn't. He wouldn't. Not anymore.

Sean felt nothing these days, by design. Maybe psychic powers didn't *totally* suck after all.

He leaned back in the white-painted, wrought-iron chair that matched the legs of the mosaic-tile table. His black leather jacket was making him a little too warm, but he didn't want to take it off. Maybe the jacket was his armor. Maybe he needed armor these days.

Elsewhere in the outdoor cafe, people talked and laughed and munched on trendy sandwiches. Sean barely noticed them, and he sensed nothing from them. No pain. No fear. Not even joy. He sighed at the relief of not knowing what other people felt. His first public outing in a couple months was going okay except for David's pestering.

Never mind that niggling uneasiness in his gut. It meant nothing.

"I heard you," Sean said. "Just don't have anything to say about it."

"Grace is worried about you," David said, slanting forward on the other side of the table to study Sean. "What have you been doing for the past two months? You don't call us. We only talk to you if we call you, and then it's brief and uninformative. You skipped your college graduation. Even dyed your hair brown."

Sean instinctively ran a hand through his hair. He'd let it grow out a few inches, and yeah, he'd covered up his red hair with brown coloring. So what? "I can change my hair without your permission."

"You're sitting there like a robot, like nothing affects you. What's wrong?"

Sean hiked up one shoulder and let it fall again. "I'm fine. Busy, that's all."

"Too busy to see your niece? Abby asks for you all the time."

"Your kid's not my niece."

David frowned. "You're her honorary uncle."

Sean snorted. "Honorary uncle? That's not a thing."

"At the time, you thought it was 'wicked awesome.' A direct quote from you."

"Gimme a break." Sean rolled his eyes. "I was eighteen and stupid. Maybe I don't need an honorary family anymore. I'm a big boy now, and you are not my dad."

Blocking his empathic powers might've made him a little…testy. No choice. He had to keep his powers in check for the sake of everyone else in the world.

David sat back, one hand on the table, fingers tapping. He fixed his blue eyes on Sean, and the irises began to glow with a preternatural fire.

Sean sensed the prickling pressure of David's mind trying to tunnel into his own. He gave it a psychic swat.

Across the table, David winced.

"What are you doing?" Sean asked, his voice low and dark. "Trying to read my mind? Grace told you to never, ever, ever do that. Better listen to your wife. You wanna go bat-shit crazy?"

Mind reading was the biggest no-no in the world of psychic powers. Grace had done it once and swore she'd never try it again. She'd made David and Sean both swear they'd never do it either.

Why the hell was David attempting it?

"You've left me no choice," David said, almost as if he were answering Sean's thought-question. "We know something's wrong with you. This hard-as-nails, don't-give-a-damn-about-anything attitude is a cover for whatever's going on with you lately. What happened to the boy who loved his powers and loved his honorary niece?"

"He grew up and grew a pair. I can take care of myself. Don't need my wannabe daddy giving me a heart-to-heart."

David watched him for a few seconds, then braced his elbow on the table and let his forehead fall into his raised hand. The energy seemed to flood out of him, sagging his shoulders. He drew in a long breath and raised his head to pin Sean with his gaze. "We care about you. You're a part of our family, and we won't give up on you no matter how much you act like a knucklehead. Do you realize how your behavior hurts Grace?"

Her face flashed in Sean's mind. Grace, with hazel eyes and auburn hair. Grace, with that kind smile and teasing manner. She liked to tousle his hair, even now, like he was still a kid. She'd encouraged him to get his GED and go to college. She'd saved him from torture of the most literal, physical kind—and of the psychic variety. If not for her...

A pang stabbed through his chest.

No, no, no. His shields had slipped. He slammed them back into place, shutting out all the emotions inside and outside himself.

Blessed emptiness.

"Not trying to hurt anybody," Sean said. The exact opposite, in fact. "You're all better off without me around, trust me."

The unease he'd experienced since entering this cafe resurfaced, tugging on his metaphysical senses. Movement caught his eye, and he glanced at the courtyard archway, the entrance to the cafe a dozen feet away. A young woman stood there, shoulders bunched, tension evident on her face. She'd tied her raven hair back in a long ponytail, the locks glistening in the sunshine. The light also glinted in her eyes, igniting the lighter highlights in her deep-blue irises. She was beautiful.

And for the first time in two months, despite his shields, he felt something. A twinge of what he could only describe as...longing. A bizarre impulse to wrap her in his arms. She seemed so lost, almost afraid. Of what?

"Sean," David said, with an uncharacteristic sharpness to his tone.

Blinking rapidly, struggling to shake the...whatever the girl had incited in him, Sean returned his attention to David. "What?"

"I'm glad you're still interested in girls," David said, "but we were having a serious conversation. Why would you think we're better off without you?"

"Because—" His gaze inexorably traveled back to the girl. She was fidgeting and scratching her arms, exposed by the short-sleeve shirt she wore. Her jeans had trendy slashes in them that gaped open around her knees, complete with fashionable threads dangling from them.

The girl lowered one hand, her arm straight at her side, parallel to her body. She flexed her fingers.

"For Christ's sake, Sean, pay attention."

He flicked his gaze to David, but his focus was pulled back to the girl by an inexplicable sensation of impending danger. Sean's body went rigid. He stared at the girl, not blinking, not moving, racking his mind for the source of this dread.

"Grace thinks you're suppressing your powers," David said. "Is she right?"

"What if she is? It's my business, not yours."

"Sean, suppressing your powers is dangerous. Not to mention bad for your health, mental and physical."

"I'm fine."

Sean couldn't look away from the girl. She'd closed her eyes, her face pinched. The power of her anguish battered his shields, but only a trickle penetrated them. It was enough, though. Even a taste of her pain left a bitter tang in his mouth. He shouldn't care, goddammit, but something about her…

He jumped up. "Back in a minute."

Before David could protest, Sean stalked toward the girl, weaving his way around tables and chairs.

Eyes squeezed shut, the girl curled her fingers into her palm.

Sean reached her just as she snapped her fingers straight.

The building exploded.

CHAPTER TWO

THE FORCE OF THE DETONATION THREW SEAN INTO THE GIRL. THEY tumbled to the stone-paved floor of the entrance with her pinned beneath his body. Debris rained down around them, and something large whumped to the ground nearby, sending shock waves through the floor. Sharp fragments of debris clawed at his skin. Dust surged into his nostrils and mouth, making him hack and spit mud.

As the debris cloud settled, he made out shapes. His ears rang, though behind the noise, he detected muffled voices shouting and screaming.

Sean looked down at the girl.

Her blue eyes, enlarged by shock, stared up at him. Powdery debris turned her face a muddy, mottled shade of pale. Her entire body trembled. Her lips parted, and he could tell she was speaking, but the ringing in his ears drowned out her words. She pounded her little fists on his biceps, shouting loud enough he barely made out what she said.

"Get—off—me—can't—breathe!"

Sean rolled to the side, onto a sharp metal object. It stabbed into his hip. With a snarled curse that sounded far away even to his ears, he pushed up onto his knees. His chest heaved with every breath, his eyes burned, and cuts on his arms and face stung like the devil. He started to wipe at his face with his shirt but stopped when he realized the fabric was coated with dirt and spattered with blood. His blood? Her blood?

His heart thudded.

Not enough blood to suggest a major injury. He prayed neither of them had anything more serious than cuts. But the other people in the cafe...

The girl was struggling to get to her knees, hindered by the top of a table that had come loose from its legs and slid onto her feet. Sean grabbed the tile tabletop and heaved it off her. The thing crashed onto a pile of rubble, shooting up a plume of dust. He grasped the girl's hands and pulled her up with him as he clambered to his feet. His knees quivered. The rest of him seemed okay, but she was still shaking from head to toe.

He leaned in close, bent to level their gazes, and spoke in loud, precise syllables. "Are you okay?"

She nodded shakily. Her eyes remained wide, her pupils large. Her skin, what he could see of it through the dirt, looked ashen.

No, she didn't seem all right.

He frisked his hands over her body to check for obvious wounds but found none. When he closed his fingers around her wrist, feeling her pulse, it was fast and fluttery. She swayed a little, blinking slowly. Jeez, she needed a doctor. He took her upper arms in his hands to steady her.

Sirens ululated in the distance.

Or maybe they were close, he couldn't tell for sure. The ringing in his ears was lessening, but he hadn't regained normal hearing yet.

David.

The thought slammed through him, and his hands fell away from the girl. He swung his head around, zeroing in on the table where he and David had sat.

It was gone.

No. His heart pounded so hard it seemed like his ribs might crack from the pressure. He should never have left David. If he'd been hurt or worse—

The girl bolted.

Sean took a step to follow her but froze. She'd sprinted out the entrance and out of sight down the sidewalk. He had no time to worry about her, though, and had to hope the EMTs would find and help her.

He barreled across the remains of the cafe, vaulting over debris piles. He stopped once to help a woman who lay dazed amid the wreckage, but she needed aid he couldn't give. Since she wasn't bleeding too badly, he told her to wait for the EMTs and not move. Then he raced the last short distance to where the table should've been, the one where he'd left David.

A pile of bricks slumped where the table had stood.

One foot, covered by a brown sneaker, stuck out from beneath the pile.

No, God, no.

Sean seized one brick, tossed it aside, grabbed them two at a time and then three at a time. He hurled them away, praying he wasn't burying another victim he couldn't see. *Save David.* That single thought consumed him. He uncovered one of David's legs, then the other, and with agonizing slowness he freed the rest of the man who'd been like a brother and a surrogate father to him. His best friend.

David lay limp on his stomach, his arms and legs askew, his head bent to the side. His eyes were closed, his mouth open. Blood oozed from a wound on his head, etching red trails through the dirt on his skin.

Falling to his knees, Sean felt for a pulse in David's throat. Faint, but there.

The sirens had gone silent.

Sean glanced toward the entrance, what remained of it, and saw the pulsing lights of emergency vehicles. A fire truck had pulled up right in front.

"Help!" Sean hollered. "We've got injured people here."

While EMTs wended their way through the debris, Sean sat vigil beside David, unwilling to leave until he knew his friend would be found and treated.

The explosion. It replayed in his mind over and over. What had happened? Something caused this, someone caused this, but who and why?

Sean gritted his teeth. The girl. She'd done this. He had no idea how or why, but when she'd flicked her fingers, the whole place had erupted.

A psychic attack?

He didn't give a damn right now. Until he knew David was okay, nothing else mattered. If David died…

Sean would find that fucking girl and murder her.

———

KIRA MAGNUSSON STUMBLED AROUND THE CORNER ONTO ANOTHER street, avoiding the EMTs by running in the opposite direction. Maybe she needed medical attention, but she couldn't risk it. Nothing seemed to be broken, so she ought to heal okay—eventually. On the outside. Inside…

A memory seized her mind, a nightmare come to life. Choking. Gasping. Lungs burning. Crawling on her stomach across the floor, desperate to escape. She deserved what they'd done to her that day. Compared to the horror of what she'd just done in the cafe…

Her stomach lurched.

She doubled over and vomited on the sidewalk.

Oh God, what had she done? *What you had to do*, a voice whispered inside her. Had this been her only option? They'd said it would be a smoke bomb, not—not—this.

Her stomach heaved again.

She staggered into an alley, knowing she couldn't make it much farther. At least in an alley, no one would notice her. Everyone was distracted by the…disaster. She sagged into the wall of a building, its concrete blocks cold against the bare skin of her arms. The disaster? She'd caused it. What if someone had died? She couldn't think about that, not now. Tears burned in her eyes, but she sucked in a breath and tried to stave them off. *Stay strong, for Caleb.*

Her phone rang.

She jerked at the sound, then dug the phone out of her pocket. With trembling fingers, she answered the call—no name, no number on caller ID. But she knew who it was.

"Well done," the familiar, electronically altered voice said. She couldn't tell if the speaker was a man or a woman, but the voice had an odd lilt to it.

"You told me it would be a smoke bomb," she hissed into the phone, sounding far stronger than she felt. Her knees quivered, threatening to buckle. "If anyone died, I'll—"

"Do exactly what we say, nothing more and nothing less. If you wish for your brother to live."

She absently flicked her thumbnail against her forefinger. A tiny spark flashed on the pad of her finger. She clamped her hand into a fist. "Let me talk to Caleb."

A scuffling noise suggested the kidnapper was handing his phone to someone else. "Kira? Are you coming to get me?"

Kira choked back a sob, clutching her stomach with her free hand. "Soon, sweetie, I promise. You be strong for me, 'kay?"

"I don't like it here."

"Won't be long, I promise." Lying to her eight-year-old brother? She had no choice. Telling him the truth, that she had no clue when the kidnappers might release him, would only escalate his panic. "I love you, Caleb."

"Love you too, Kiki."

She swallowed another sob when he spoke his nickname for her. Caleb was in this mess because of her. If she'd been more careful…But how could she have been? She didn't know how these evil bastards found her, much less how they got Caleb three days ago, sometime between school ending in the afternoon and Kira arriving to pick him up. In a matter of minutes, they'd taken her brother. She'd gotten slowed down by traffic and showed up three minutes late. *Three minutes.*

More scuffling. The altered voice of the kidnapper growled in her ear. "I suggest you find a place to hide and await further instructions."

"No, dammit, I will not—"

"Do you wish for your brother to die?"

The hand over her belly fisted, twisting her shirt around her fingers. She didn't dare speak, her emotions too wild to be trusted.

"I didn't think so," the kidnapper said. "We will be in touch."

Click. The call ended.

Kira stuffed the phone in her pocket. Pulled in a deep breath. Shoved a hand through her hair, filthy with dirt and who-knew-what other substances. Caleb had no one else, not since their parents ran away to another continent. To get away from her. She could almost understand that, but abandoning Caleb was unforgivable.

He had no one else, which meant she had to save him.

By whatever means necessary? Her conscience prickled at the thought.

She pushed away from the wall and hurried to...anywhere but here.

CHAPTER THREE

HOSPITALS SMELLED LIKE THE AFTERMATH OF DISASTER AND DEATH as embodied by the odor of disinfectant used to clean up and cover up the catastrophes that brought people here. Sean hated the smell, hated the sterile colors and the hospital beds, hated sitting in a chair that barely fit his frame and made his tailbone hurt. The medical types had taken David into the ER, and though Grace had gone with him, they wouldn't let Sean accompany her. He wasn't family, not technically.

So, he slouched in an awful chair in the waiting room. And he waited. And waited.

Being in the hospital niggled at his memories, the ones he'd repressed for so long with so much effort. Now, the memories unreeled in his mind's eye. Screeching tires. The explosive bang of metal slamming into a wooden pole. Smoke. Flames. A blur of noise and movements, sirens and ambulances. When he'd finally had time to process the event, he was sitting in a chair like the one he occupied today. Just like then, his stomach churned and acid scorched up his chest into his throat. His muscles ached from the tension stretching them taut. His jaw ached too, thanks to his gritted teeth.

Someone entered the waiting room, but Sean noticed the figure only peripherally until a hand settled on his shoulder. He lifted his eyes to the newcomer.

Gabriel Amador gazed down at Sean with a tight smile.

Though his fingers crooked toward his palms, Sean maintained an outward calmness when he spoke to Amador. "Why are you here?"

"Grace called me," Amador said in his slightly accented voice. He skimmed his gaze over Sean, his brows tightening. "You are injured?"

"Some cuts, nothing major."

"You can relax," Amador said. "I am here to assist."

Oh how awesome, we're all saved. Sean kept the thought to himself.

Why on earth Grace trusted this man, Sean had no clue. Five years ago, Amador had drugged her and tried to convince her he had psychic powers when he had none, just to gain her cooperation in his nutjob scheme for revenge. He'd held a teenage girl hostage too. Grace had forgiven him, though, because Amador had a great sob story. His young son had been taken by Sean's grandfather, the wacko Karl Tesler, and tortured until he died. Then Amador's wife had committed suicide, broken by the loss. By Amador's own admission, he'd gone loony tunes after that.

Sean's nails dug into his palm. Good old gramps had tortured him too, but nobody caught Sean doing wacky things because of it.

Amador squeezed Sean's shoulder. "How is David?"

"Don't know yet."

The ER door swung open, and Grace shambled into the waiting room.

Sean jumped up, hands jammed in his jeans pockets, shoulders hunched beneath his leather jacket.

Amador hurried to her, clasping her in a quick hug.

Disgust slithered through Sean. He couldn't like Amador, no matter how "nice" the guy pretended to be. Cari, the girl Amador had abducted and abused, was one of Sean's closest friends.

Grace looked ashen and tired, dark circles under her eyes. She tried for a small smile, but her lips quivered, and the expression disintegrated.

"David?" Sean asked, his entire body as rigid as concrete, his feet heavy as concrete too. He awaited her response with his pulse racing and a coldness washing over him.

"He's alive," she said. "They put him in a medically induced coma, so his body can heal."

A coma? David must've been seriously injured, more even than Sean had realized when he pulled his friend out of the rubble. "How long—I mean, do they think he'll be okay?"

"The doctor says he's optimistic, but only time will tell." She hugged herself, rubbing her upper arms. "Abby's going home with her great-grandfather. I'll stay here until visiting hours are over."

Amador took her hand in his, a smarmily concerned look on his face. "What can I do?"

"Nothing. But thanks for coming."

Sean wanted to tell Grace to go home, get some rest, because she couldn't do anything for David right now. He couldn't form the words. Grace and David had the kind of relationship Sean had thought only existed in romance novels. Their love had saved their lives and the lives of countless others—and that was no metaphor. The psychic bond they shared imbued their love with real power, the kind that could save the world. Sean knew he couldn't hope to find anything even close to that.

"David's still in there," she said. "As long as I can feel him, there's hope."

"Of course there's hope," Sean said. He raised his hands, intending to hug her, but let them fall back down. She'd let Amador hug her, but did she want comforting from Sean? He decided to try expressing his support with words instead. "You and David are like…I don't know, like Cinderella and that prince guy. You're meant to be together. Nothing can get between the two of you, not even this."

"Cinderella?" Grace almost smiled, though it dissolved into a downward curve of her lips. "Our relationship has never been a fairy-tale romance. We survived two psychos who wanted to destroy us, not to mention my amnesia. Maybe this is how it ends."

"No way." Sean grasped her upper arms, bending his knees until he could look her in the eye. "You're freaking out right now, that's all. David will get better. He *will.*"

"Yes," Amador interjected, "he will."

The urge to smack the man seized Sean, but he restrained himself. He hated the way Amador had insinuated himself into Grace's life over the past five years. Still, it was her choice whether to trust him.

She nodded weakly, unshed tears shimmering in her hazel eyes. Never one to let the tears roll or let life knock her down, she swiped them away with the back of her hand, then hauled in a breath and straightened. "We need to find out who did this and why. They need to pay."

A steely edge gave her voice a sharpness Sean had never heard before from Grace. Sure, she could be tough when necessary. But she had the kindest heart of anyone he'd ever known.

If she wanted vengeance, he would mete it out for her and for David.

For everyone who'd been caught in the explosion.

"Revenge will not help," Amador said. "You're upset, Grace. Make no decisions now. I'm certain the authorities will apprehend whoever is responsible."

Yeah, sure. Once again, Sean wanted to deck the guy.

The ER doors opened, and Edward McLean trudged out with four-year-old Abby Ransom in his arms. The little girl had her teeth clamped down on her lower lip, her eyes red and her cheeks stained with the tracks of tears now dried. Her great-grandfather carried the little girl over to Grace but kept Abby in his arms.

"I talked to my friend at the police department," Edward said. "There were no fatalities from the explosion, but fourteen people were hurt. David has the worst injuries."

Grace struggled to stay calm, Sean could see it, but the tears won out. She sagged against her grandfather, wrapping her arms around her daughter. No sobs, though. No, Grace wouldn't do that, not with her child right there. Sean knew tears must be streaming down her cheeks, yet from this angle, she seemed to be simply hugging her daughter.

Edward's lip curled in disgust—not for Grace's reaction, but for someone else entirely. "Who could've done this?"

Sean realized the older man wasn't asking a question. He was expressing what all of them felt. Fear. Frustration. Confusion. Anger.

Abby stuffed a thumb in her mouth, something the four-year-old hadn't done in a long time.

The coldness that had infiltrated Sean, once borne of fear and shock, transformed into a tight, iron-hard ball of dangerous resolve. Vengeance? Yeah, he could do that.

"Don't worry," Sean said, hands clenching into fists. "I will find out who did this, and I will make them pay for it."

Edward shook his head. "Sean, let the police handle this."

"Police? Screw them. They can't help with psychic attacks. I saw a girl right before the bomb went off. I think she caused the explosion."

"How?" Edward stared into empty space for several seconds, his lips tight. "My friend said the bomb consisted of two substances that are harmless when found alone, but when combined they're explosive. Each was held in its own glass container. There must've been a trigger to shatter the glass, but they haven't found the trigger itself yet or detected any evidence of how it worked."

Like a frigging cartoon character, Sean sensed a light bulb popping on above his head. No one else noticed his epiphany, of course, since it was contained inside himself. Suddenly, though, the facts of what he'd observed fit together to form a coherent picture.

The girl. The bomb.

She'd flicked her fingers and then—*boom*.

A trigger? Hell yeah, he knew what it was. The girl had used a psychic ability, maybe telekinesis, to shatter the glass containers and set off the bomb.

"Cops won't find a trigger," he said to Edward. "But I know exactly what it looks like."

Grace's head sprang up, her bleary eyes trained on him. "What are you talking about? You saw the bomb?"

"No." He flattened his lips into a line, recalling the anguish he'd sensed from the mystery girl. "The bomb was triggered by a psychic. And I'm beginning to think it was no coincidence the girl who set it off picked the day when David and I would be there."

"How could anyone have known," Edward said, "when the two of you would be there?"

Grace pushed away from her grandfather. "Psychics have a lot of ways to spy. I think Sean may be on to something here, but I can't leave David to go investigate." She glanced up at Edward. "And I need you to look after Abby."

"I'll get it done," Sean said. "Trust me, I will track down the girl and find out what the hell is going on, one way or another. All of us have pissed off plenty of bad guys over the years. The ones we know about are long dead, but they had facilities all over the world. Could be cronies who escaped. Either way, I'll root out the truth."

"This is a mistake," Amador said, his tone oddly sharp. "Grace, please do not encourage Sean. This is a reckless idea."

"Sean will be careful." Grace rushed forward to clasp Sean's face with both hands. "Don't do anything crazy. Promise me, Sean. I can't lose anyone I love, not again."

Grace didn't mean David, though all of them worried for his fate. Grace meant her parents who'd died at the hands of the lunatic Jackson Tennant seven years ago.

"I'll be careful," he assured her. "You won't lose anybody. Not David, not me, not anyone. We all will get through this safe and sound, you have my word."

He'd make sure nobody harmed his family, even if he had to take extreme measures to ensure it. After all, he'd promised he wouldn't get himself killed—not that he wouldn't take out the bad guys.

Sean understood Grace's fears of losing the people she loved. He feared for the same thing.

No one would die. No one except the scumbags who'd brought it on themselves.

Amador eyed Sean with a strange expression, almost curious, almost annoyed, but not really either one.

Well, the jerk had spent a good chunk of the past five years in a psychiatric clinic, off and on.

"I should get going," Sean said. "I know exactly where to start investigating."

The last place he'd seen the girl. The cafe.

THE STENCH OF SMOKE PERMEATED THE AIR, AND SLENDER TENDRILS OF it curled up from the blackened remnants of the cafe. The sallow glow of the streetlamps outside the entrance wall, which stood mostly intact, illuminated the smoke trails with a ghostly effect. Kira hunched in the entrance on the exact spot where she'd stood ten hours earlier. Though yellow police tape was strung across the entrance, she'd ducked under it. No one had been around to stop her since the cops seemed to have gone home for the night. She supposed they saw no need for guards. Only an idiot would sneak back into the scene of the crime she'd perpetrated.

Nighttime lent the devastation an eerie, almost otherworldly aura.

Cuts and bruises, that's all she had. But the victims in the cafe...

She fingered the strap of her little purse. The strap hung over one shoulder on a diagonal across her chest, the purse itself positioned over her hip. Inside the bag, she had chocolates and cigarettes. Her mouth watered, though not for candy. A smoke, that's what she needed. Even the toughest person would fall off the wagon in these circumstances. Who cared about wrecking six smoke-free months? She'd caused a catastrophe.

Biting down on her bottom lip, she tried not to think about cigarettes. But her thoughts came back to the bomb, the detonation, the screams. Carrying a pack of cigarettes in her purse to test her willpower had sounded like a good idea a month ago. Now, she craved a smoke so badly.

A chill skittered down her spine. She had done this. If anyone had died...

They said it was a smoke bomb. No excuse, and she knew it. For the rest of her life, she would live with the knowledge of what she'd done.

For years, she'd feared the possibility of anyone discovering she had powers, feared what the wrong people might do to her if they knew. Her nightmares had come true, more horrifying than she'd ever imagined.

"I knew you'd come back to admire your handiwork."

Kira jumped and spun around. Her heart thudded so hard she couldn't breathe for a second.

There, backlit by the streetlamps, hunkered a manlike silhouette. Shadows obscured his features. He seemed huge, like a demon straight out of Hell sent to drag her into the bowels of eternal torment.

The man surged forward to clamp his big hands around her arms. "Don't even think about running."

His voice snarled, like she'd always thought a demon's would.

"Who are you?" he demanded.

No voice. All she could do was gasp.

The demon spun them both until they stood sideways to the entrance, facing each other, his grip on her never easing up even the tiniest bit. His fingers pressed into her flesh, eliciting pains that webbed out into her shoulders.

And at last, she saw him.

The man who'd landed on top of her after the bomb went off.

His green eyes seemed luminescent in the spooky glow of the streetlamps. He must've been six feet tall, maybe a little more, with arms corded with muscles she could see even through the leather jacket he wore. His biceps bulged from the effort of holding her. His V-neck black T-shirt clung to his body, and so did his jeans, accentuating his every muscle.

This man could crush her with his bare hands.

"You detonated the bomb," he growled, "and I want to know why. Scratch that. You are going to tell me why if you want to keep all your limbs."

She started to scratch her thumbnail across her forefinger but tamped down the nervous instinct. Had he known someone who died here? Had she killed a human being?

No, God, no.

Kira didn't think about what she was doing. Panic gripped her in its icy talons, and she lashed out with all the power inside her, flinging it at the stranger.

He flew backward. With a thud and a grunt, he smacked down flat on his backside.

Run. The instinct propelled her. She barreled out the entrance, swerved left down the sidewalk, and—

Powerful arms latched around her torso and hauled her to a stop, her arms pinned to her body.

She yelped as the stranger hoisted her up, her feet dangling inches above the cement.

"You can talk here," he hissed into her ear, "or I can take you somewhere more private and find ways to motivate you to tell me what I want to know."

Was he threatening to abduct her? Like hell she'd let that happen.

"Don't," he said, and squeezed her so hard she couldn't breathe. Letting off the pressure just enough she could gulp in sweet oxygen, he told her, "I know you have powers, and I'm sure you want to use them on me again, but don't bother. Wherever you go, I'll find you. Someone I love is in a coma because of you."

What could she say? People had been injured—died, for all she knew—and maybe she deserved to be crushed to death by an avenging angel.

If she died, Caleb died too.

Kira marshaled all the energy she had left, tapping into her powers to the point of draining them, and willed his body to fly backward.

He jerked but held his ground. Held his grip on her too.

She was too weak to fight. Tears burned her eyes, but she refused to let them flow. Showing weakness in front of a man bent on exacting vengeance on her seemed like a really, really stupid idea.

"You've got a tell," he murmured into her ear.

"I've got a what?"

"A little movement you do right before you activate your powers. It gives away the game and gives me time to get ready for the attack." His lips were hot and dry against her ear. "You caught me off guard once. It won't happen again."

Wonderful. She had a tell, and he knew what it was. She didn't.

"I won't tell you anything," she said. "Either kill me or let me go."

"Nice try." He straightened, his arms still buckling her to his hard body. "But I'm not letting you out of my sight until I have all the answers I need."

Why oh why hadn't she bought a gun? A knife, even. Hell, a Taser would've done the trick. She'd never needed to defend herself until a few days ago, and by then it was too late.

She couldn't fight back against an invisible enemy.

The man grasped her wrists and yanked her hands behind her back, cuffing them in one of his hands. Something like hard plastic or nylon, a thin but strong cable of it, closed around her wrists. A zip tie? Her captor cinched it tight, though not so tight it would dig into her skin. Just snug enough to restrain her.

"I notice you're not screaming for help," he said, his strong hand holding onto the zip tie, his fingers between her wrists. "More proof you're guilty. Innocent people pray for help, fight to get away until they're bloody and beaten, scream for help until their throats are raw and they can't breathe."

The way he said those words, with a roughness and a slight break on the last syllable, she got the weirdest sensation trickling down her spine. He sounded like he knew people fought and screamed because he'd been in their shoes. He'd been a victim.

Oh no, she would not feel sorry for the man abducting her.

For all she knew, he was the world's greatest actor, conning her into empathizing with him as a means to break her will.

The stranger tugged on the zip tie. "Time to go."

He dropped a burlap sack over her head, plunging her into darkness.

She couldn't scream for help because she was guilty. She couldn't fight either because she was exhausted and powerless.

The stranger hauled her down the sidewalk. She tripped when they veered off the curb into the street. He kept her from falling down but dragged her onward until they halted, and she heard the distinctive sound of a car door opening. He shoved her into a bucket seat, shoved her feet inside too, and then strapped her in with the seatbelt. It pinned her to the seat with her hands bound behind her back, the strap at a diagonal across her chest. The lower portion of it banded her pelvis.

The door slammed shut.

Another door opened—the driver's door, she assumed—and slammed shut a moment later. The engine growled to life. The car shot forward, swerved right, rocketed ahead.

The momentum of each movement thrust her first backward into the seat, then sideways, and finally backward again. The zip tie dug into her wrists with sharp, stinging pain. She winced, gritting her teeth.

"Where are you taking me?" she asked.

"Not telling. Why do you think I put a hood over your head?" The car swung around a corner, and the engine roared as he floored the accelerator. "So you can't see where we're going."

Her wrists burned. A warm liquid oozed down from her wrists to her palms. Every wild movement of the vehicle shifted her position until the diagonal section of the seatbelt pinched her throat.

"Slow down," she said, her tone rife with a disquieting, almost pleading tone. "My wrists are getting rubbed raw, and the seatbelt is about to choke me."

Her captor let out a soft, harsh laugh. "This is a kidnapping, princess, not a spa vacation. You're probably lying, anyway. Criminals like to do that."

"Not lying," she grated between her clenched teeth. "Blood is running down my wrists. Look for yourself if you don't believe me."

Silence. Kira counted the seconds. One Mississippi, two Mississippi, three Mississippi.

The man in the driver's seat muttered, "Shit."

He swerved the car to the right, stopping with a suddenness that threw her forward. The seatbelt cut into her throat, choking her.

With a click, the seatbelt sprang free and withdrew into its housing with a *zzzt* sound.

The release of pressure made her haul in a deep breath, but that brought on a coughing fit.

He waited until she'd stopped coughing, then clasped her around the waist and angled her to the side. Large fingers felt around the zip tie. He muttered another oath. She heard him moving around, followed by the sharp sound of nylon snapping, and her wrists were free. Air wafted over them, making the scrapes sting and her eyes tear up from the pain. She gasped, partly from the pain, partly in relief.

Noises indicated he was rooting around in the backseat.

He wrapped a smooth rope around her wrists and cinched it tight enough to bind her without the rope cutting into her wrists. Once he'd knotted the rope, he secured the seatbelt around her again, leaving her hands free of the waist strap.

"There," he said. "You can't escape, but I don't have to listen to you whine about the zip tie anymore. No sneaky shit, understand? If you try to get away, I'll zip-tie you from head to toe. Besides, I turned on the safety locks which means you can't get out of the car. No sneaky—"

"I get it." What choice did she have? She leaned back into the seat, her bound hands in her lap. "The safety locks are only for the backseat, you know."

"Stop talking."

Considering that she had nowhere to go anyway, she complied with his orders. The rope irritated her raw skin, but that was the least of her worries. Blinded by the hood, she shut up and prayed this wasn't part of a plot devised by the people holding her brother. What they wanted her to do next, she had no idea. Their endgame remained a mystery too, one she needed to figure out but feared uncovering.

No way out.

CHAPTER FOUR

S EAN PARKED IN THE SPACE RIGHT IN FRONT OF THE DOOR TO THE
motel room he'd rented earlier. Yeah, okay, he'd planned on kidnapping the girl. Goosebumps prickled his arms and raised the hairs on his skin. Kidnapping. He was a kidnapper. Christ, that made him almost as bad as Bomb Girl and her cohorts.

Almost. But not quite.

He hadn't killed anyone.

Not yet, a voice whispered in his head, *but you're awfully close to hurting this girl.* Anything to get what he needed from her. That's what he'd sworn to do, though he'd promised himself he wouldn't go too far. Trouble was, he didn't know what "too far" meant anymore. Every time he considered untying Bomb Girl, he flashed back to the explosion and the injured people—and David crumpled under a pile of rubble. David in the hospital, comatose. Grace crying. Little Abby crying.

Sean yanked the key out of the ignition. He twirled the keyring, and the metal keys jangled each time he caught them in his closed fingers, only to swing them around again and again.

"What are you doing?" Bomb Girl asked, shrinking away from him.

"Planning how to torture you." He cringed at his own voice. Was that him growling like a bastard bent on revenge? Well, he supposed he was. Only a bastard would tie up a girl and drag her off to a motel. And vengeance was what he craved. Retribution. Bad enough to lose his mom when he was fifteen and just coming to terms with his powers. Worse to find out the mad scientist who tortured him had been his grandfather. But he'd be damned if he'd lose his new family, the people who'd saved his life and taught him to understand and appreciate his psychic gifts.

David and Grace had no idea how whacked he'd gotten. His powers…He caught the keys, fisting his hand around them. His powers weren't gifts anymore.

Sean had already hurt one girl. So what if he hadn't meant to? He'd done it. If he could hurt an innocent girl, one he'd cared about, he could sure as hell do whatever it took to wring the truth out of the terrorist in the passenger seat.

"Listen up, Bomb Girl," he said, "you've got two choices here. Walk into the m—the room I'm taking you to, or I tie up your feet, gag you, and throw you over my shoulder to haul you in there."

"Gee, let me think." She bobbed her head side to side as if considering the options. "I'll walk, Un-incredible Hulk."

"I'm not green." He thrust the driver's door open. "I'm red, with horns and a forked tongue."

She scoffed.

He almost smiled at her defiance. She had spunk, a quality he liked in women.

Not that he liked her. The terrorist.

As he climbed out of the car, he said over his shoulder, "You sure talking back to your kidnapper is such a bright idea? Getting sassy won't earn you any leniency."

He shut the door before she could talk back some more. Striding around to the passenger door, he swung it open and bent down to unhook her seatbelt. She flinched. He stepped back.

"You wanted to walk," he said, "so get your butt out of the car."

Bomb Girl swung her legs out first, testing the ground's solidity with her toes before setting her feet flat on the pavement. She struggled to get up, hindered by her bound hands.

Watching her flounder made his throat tighten. When she bumped her head on the car's roof, he grimaced and took hold of her rope-tied hands to help her stand.

On her feet at last, she shook her hands free of his.

Sean rested a hand on her back to guide her to the motel-room door. He warned her about the curb, but she stumbled over it anyway. When she fell backward into him, he couldn't help noticing the firm roundness of her buttocks.

He held her to his body and hoisted her over the curb.

Naturally, she scrambled away from him—and nearly smacked into the wall.

With one hand on her arm, he halted her inches from disaster and redirected her to the door. She sniffed, as if annoyed that she'd needed assistance. He felt a near smile tugging at his mouth again while he unlocked the door with the keycard.

Once he had her inside the room, with the door shut and locked, he pushed her down onto the bed. "Sit there."

He whisked the hood off her head, tossing it onto the table by the windows. Thick curtains blocked the view through the windows. He shed his leather jacket, draping it over a chair.

"No sneaky shit, remember?" he said as he dropped into the nearest chair and draped his arm over the table.

She speared him with her midnight-blue gaze. "Now what?"

He shrugged one shoulder. "You could tell me everything I want to know and save yourself a lot of trouble."

Save him from doing things he didn't really want to do.

Of course, she had to be contrary about it.

"I can't tell you anything," she said. "Might as well kill me."

"What kind of kidnapper offs his victim before getting what he wants?" Sean leaned back and propped one ankle on the other knee, feigning a casual attitude he didn't feel. His gut burned with acid, and his jaw ached with tension. "What's your name?"

She lifted her chin, those blue eyes shimmering in the harsh light from the bedside lamp.

He tapped a finger on the tabletop. "Guess I can keep calling you Bomb Girl."

"Whatever."

"Or I could come over there and search you for ID." Sean let his gaze wander over her body. Lush breasts. Narrow waist. Womanly hips. She had a body made for sin but a face worthy of an angel, with a small mouth and a perky little nose. The idea of frisking her made his blood heat up and his skin tighten.

She said nothing, just glowered at him and tossed her raven hair.

"All right," he said, and rose to stride toward her. "Body search it is."

He fought to ignore the excitement that rushed over his skin like an electrical current. What kind of creep got turned on by the girl he'd abducted? Well, she was a terrorist after all.

A beautiful, sexy one.

Sean gritted his teeth and slanted down until his face hovered in front of hers. The feminine scent of her surrounded him. Her eyes went large, and her lips parted. He tore open her tiny purse, the one she'd slung around her neck so it hung at a diagonal across her torso. Searching with one hand, he found no ID, just lipstick, a compact, a cell phone, a bag of candy, and a pack of cigarettes. Tossing the phone on the table, he settled his hands on her thighs, trying not to notice the soft curves of them, and slid his palms around her hips to her backside. When he found the hip pockets of her jeans, he thrust his hands into them.

Eureka.

He pulled out a thin, pink wallet.

Bomb Girl's mouth popped open on an irritated gasp. She clapped her jaw shut and glowered at him some more. Pissed because he'd found her wallet.

Or maybe because he'd kept his other hand in her hip pocket, pressed against her behind.

He withdrew that hand, straightened, and flipped open the wallet. He couldn't stop the triumphant laugh that chuckled out of him. "What kind of terrorist carries her ID with her when she's committing a heinous crime?"

A faint blush tinged her cheeks, and she averted her eyes.

The driver's license photo didn't do her justice, but at least it gave him a bit of information about the suspect seated in front of him.

"Nice to meet you," he said, "Kira Magnusson of Walnut Drive, Topeka, Kansas. A local girl, huh? Got a funny way of showing your community spirit."

She pursed her lips, glaring at the ugly carpeting for a change.

"I love having the upper hand," he said as he sat down at the table and slapped her wallet down on its surface. "I know a lot about you now, and you don't even know where you are."

She glanced around, her focus landing on the bedside table, then her lips kinked in a haughty, closed-mouth smile. "I know exactly where I am."

He gave a harsh laugh. "Yeah, you're my hostage in a motel room. But you have no clue—"

"We're in the Home Sweet Motel in Lawrence."

Sean froze. Slowly, he rotated his eyes until he spotted the telephone on the bedside table. It featured a big sticker emblazoned with the information she'd recited. "Crap."

"You suck at kidnapping."

He ran a hand over his face. "Yeah."

She studied him with measured interest. "What do you hope to gain from holding me hostage?"

"The truth." His voice had grown rough, and a pain gnawed at his gut. "That bomb put my best friend in a coma. I want to know why you blew up the cafe."

"I had no choice."

"Everybody has a choice."

Kira chewed on her lower lip, and her gaze turned assessing, like she was sizing him up.

"Fine," she sighed. "You want the truth? Some very bad people took my eight-year-old brother and threatened to kill him unless I do what they want."

Sean narrowed his gaze on her. "Let me get this straight. To save one kid, you blew up a whole building full of innocent people? Why didn't you call the cops?"

Kira stared down at her lap where she wrung her hands. "I tried, but they basically laughed at me because I couldn't say who these people are or where they're hiding. I had no proof they'd taken my brother. My parents are in Uganda, and I was supposed to take care of Caleb—"

Her voice choked off.

Sean hated the twinge of sympathy he experienced when he saw her anguished expression.

"They swore," she continued, "it was a smoke bomb, nothing more."

"Bad guys always tell the truth."

She shot him a hard look. "You should know, being a bad guy yourself."

"I'm not a villain." He squirmed in his seat. "And I never set off a bomb."

"Maybe you don't believe me, but I'm telling the truth." She inhaled a shaky breath. "They showed me what they'd do to Caleb if I refused to do what they wanted."

"They—hurt the kid?"

"No." She bowed her head, and her shoulders slumped. "They hurt me."

He clenched his fist, itching to punch something, anything. Why did she have to say that? He hated anyone who hurt kids or women, which explained why he hated himself these days.

"I couldn't let my brother suffer," she said, "because of me. I believed the device was a smoke bomb and no one would get hurt. This was the final test of my powers, they said. I'm guilty of being an idiot, but I am not a terrorist."

"How the hell did you set off the bomb? Can you use your telekinesis from a distance?"

Mouth tight, she flicked her thumb against her index finger, and a tiny spark ignited.

Telekinetic *and* she could make electricity? *Damn.*

As the spark fizzled out, she said, "I didn't know I could until three days ago when these people took my brother and ordered me to practice setting off the smoke bomb. They told me to get two glass bottles and place them inside a metal box with a gap between them, close the box, and break the glass with my powers. I had to do this repeatedly, moving the box farther away each time. When I could break the bottles while the box was in another room, they said I was ready for the final test."

"Detonating the bomb at the cafe."

"Yes." Her thumb raked across her finger again, setting off another, bigger spark that floated down to the floor as a miniature ball, sputtering out just as it touched down. "I've done everything they wanted."

"Where have your parents been this whole time?"

"Gone."

"Oh jeez, I'm sorry. When did they—"

"They're not dead." She caught her bottom lip between her teeth. "I don't want to talk about them. Like I said, I'm an idiot and maybe a coward. But I am no terrorist."

Should he believe her? He didn't trust his intuition right now because the battle between his anger and his need to squelch his emotions had him tied up in knots.

"Can't let you go," he said. "Not until I've got proof of what you're saying about your brother and these mysterious bad guys. If you help me find that proof, it'll go a long way to showing you're not evil."

"Fine, I'll cooperate." Kira lifted her bound hands to him. "Untie me. Please."

"Please?" Sean raised one brow. "Playing nice won't make me let you go. I still don't trust you."

"I know." She stood, hands held out to him. "The rope is rubbing on my wounds from the zip tie. I won't try to escape, you have my word. Please untie me."

He mulled the situation for a moment, fingers drumming on the tabletop.

Then he removed the rope.

THE SECOND THE ROPE FELL AWAY FROM HER WRISTS, KIRA BOLTED for the door. Two feet from it, she was yanked backward by a pair of powerful arms that snared her around the waist and hoisted her off her feet. Pinned to her captor's body, she flailed her feet but couldn't kick him. He'd pinned her arms too, and she couldn't reach any part of him to bite. *Trapped.*

Her heart hammered, her breaths came shallow and fast. Caleb needed her. She could not let this jackass waylay her. When the next call came…Would she obey their commands?

No choice.

The man restraining her in his vise-like embrace set her feet on the floor. His arms stayed belted around her. His lips scraped the shell of her ear as he hissed, "I'll cooperate, you said. I won't try to escape, you said. That one was a promise. I was nice, and you took advantage."

She swallowed hard. A cold sweat broke out on her forehead, and her palms grew clammy.

"Can't trust your word," he snarled. "You brought this on yourself."

He dragged her toward the TV stand near the foot of the bed. A black duffel bag slumped on the floor there, its zipper undone. He forced her to kneel with him, so he could dig items out of the bag. She couldn't see what he was doing, but she heard the rustling and felt his muscles flexing around her as he maintained his iron grip with one arm.

She ought to be able to wrestle free of him. He held her with one arm. But struggle as she might, she failed to gain any leeway. Holy cow, he was strong. He'd said she brought this on herself, but what exactly did he plan to do with her?

He leaned sideways, the heat of his body retreating, and pulled her hands together in front of her belly. While he held her wrists in one hand, with the other he wrapped something soft around them. Soft? She glanced down and saw he'd folded a length of fleece in half. Once he had the material around her wrists, he secured them with a zip tie again. The thick fleece protected her skin from the sharp edges of the nylon restraint.

Confusion made her brows draw together and her lips fall open a crack. Why would he bother cushioning the zip tie? The action implied he cared about her well-being. He wanted to spare her any additional pain? It made no sense.

He'd cut the first zip tie back in the car, when she'd complained it bit into her flesh. And he seemed more desperate than psychotic. What had he said about his best friend? She winced a little, her stomach lurching. He'd said the bomb put his friend in a coma. The bomb she'd set off. What had she done? Someone might've died. Maybe this guy had a point about her risking dozens of lives to save one little boy.

But he was her brother. She couldn't forsake him.

Her captor secured another zip tie around her ankles, cushioned with fleece.

"Did anyone die?" she asked, her throat constricting. "From the explosion. Did anyone—"

"No." The gruff reply rasped in her ear, because he'd slanted in again. His lips grazed her skin. "People got hurt, though, so don't go feeling better about yourself because nobody kicked the bucket."

People like his best friend.

Her gut twisted as if a fist had clamped around it. "I'm sorry. About your friend."

"If he dies, you die."

Despite the nastiness of his tone and his words, she had the oddest feeling he didn't mean them. Pain drove him, not rage. *Yeah, right.* Like she could know that from his voice. She'd never been empathic or had any mind-reading ability. She couldn't divine his emotions or intentions, and yet she sensed he…What? Meant her no real harm?

She couldn't know that. This prickly sensation, the way she sensed she understood him in some small way, it was probably the onset of Stockholm syndrome.

He swept her up in his brawny arms and dropped her onto the bed. Her body bounced a little, but her head landed on a pillow with a *whuft* sound. He scanned her body, his lips compressed, towering over her from his position beside the bed.

"You cold?" he asked.

Once again, he sounded gruff but evinced concern for her comfort. *Weird.*

"I'm fine," she said.

His fingers worked as if he were considering doing something with them. His gaze flitted around the room. "Better gag you."

A chill raced through her. "Please don't. I promise not to scream."

He flashed her a scowl. "Like I can take your word for anything."

"I'm sorry for lying." Hey, wait. Why was she apologizing to him? "But you kidnapped me. What did you expect? You're lucky I didn't nail you in the balls."

She swore his lips quirked the tiniest bit.

"Being feisty won't get you anywhere," he said. Then he hesitated, eying her with a strange expression. "Why didn't you hit me with your telekinetic powers?"

Goosebumps raised all over her arms. She wouldn't tell him she'd exhausted her psychic reserves. "What makes you think I have powers?"

He snickered, the sound rife with derision. "You got amnesia? We've been through this already. I know because you walloped me with your powers back at the scene of your crime."

"Excuse me for getting forgetful when I've been abducted."

"Or maybe you were hoping I'd forgotten."

The statement he'd made earlier about knowing she had powers actually had slipped her mind. Everything had unfolded so fast, with him hauling her away in his car, that she couldn't recall the exact sequence of events when he'd found her at the destroyed cafe.

"Most people," she said, aiming for an even tone despite her rapid pulse, "would dream up a so-called rational explanation for something like that. They wouldn't jump to 'she has psychic powers' like you did."

He lifted one shoulder in a half shrug. "I trust my perception."

What an odd way to phrase it, she thought. Rather than saying he trusted what he saw or what he felt, or even what he experienced, he'd said he trusted his perception.

A new wave of goosebumps erupted on her skin, lifting every fine hair. *Perception.* The meaning of that word finally struck her. "You have powers."

He jerked his head back, eyes flaring wide for a split second.

"I'm right," she told him, enjoying a spike of victorious pride. "What's your gift?"

Jaw clenched, he shot her a hot glare. "Shut the hell up."

What had she said that set him off? He hadn't gone all Terminator until she asked what his gift was.

She bit the inside of her lip but plowed ahead. "Why are you sensitive about discussing your powers?"

"I'm not." He tunneled his fingers into his hair, molding his hand to the back of his head. "Don't want to talk about this with you. Shut up or I'll gag you."

He spun away and stalked past the foot of the bed, then stalked back up the length of the bed. While he paced like a caged lion, she lay there bound but not gagged. Maybe she should've been grateful he hadn't silenced her with a sock in her mouth or a length of fleece tied tightly.

Fleece. She glanced at her hands. The fabric he'd padded the zip tie with prevented her raw wrists from hurting. Her abductor took care not to hurt her, yet he held her prisoner. He seemed desperate, and she knew his friend had been injured because of her. Considering the frantic actions she'd taken to save her brother, she had no right to criticize his behavior. She understood the panic induced by learning a loved one was endangered by a criminal act.

Her criminal act had harmed innocent people.

What he'd done had harmed no one, not even her.

Oh no-no-no, you will not empathize with the kidnapper.

She couldn't help empathizing a little, though she would not trust this man. No way. Never.

Her phone rang with the silly ringtone Caleb had picked for her. It was the theme song to some cartoon show.

The man pacing the length of the room whirled around to stomp toward her. He halted at the bedside near her hip. The phone rang a second and a third time. He snatched it up and frowned at the screen before tilting it toward her. "Unknown number? This your cohort?"

"It must be them, but they're not my cohorts." She tried to sit up but fell back onto the bed. "If I don't answer, they'll hurt my brother."

He waited for a fourth ring, then swiped the screen to answer and tapped the speaker-phone symbol. As he held the phone near her face, he mouthed, "No tricks."

She raised her head. "Hello?"

"It's time," said the altered voice she'd come to know too well. "I will text you the address. You know what to do."

"You said you'd let Caleb go if I did what you wanted. I set off the— bomb."

"No, child," the distorted voice said, "we told you we would release the boy once you completed your mission. This is phase two."

She opened her mouth but couldn't speak. Phase two? How many phases did this mission have? How many crimes would she have to commit to free her brother? How many innocent people would suffer this time?

Her skin crawled. She wanted to scratch her arms, but the zip tie constrained her. She would've settled for a smoke.

Neither smoking nor scratching could eradicate the burning itch in her soul.

"Please," she said, "let Caleb go. He's just a kid."

"Trigger the device," the caller said in an eerily calm voice. "You have until one-fifteen a.m."

Click. The call was terminated.

She tightened her trembling fingers around the phone.

It made a tinkly noise, indicating a new text message.

"They're sending the address," she said. "I have to—"

"You have to what?" Her captor bent low over her, his green eyes luminescent with the spooky glow of psychic powers ramping up. "You have to hurt some more people?"

"They have my brother." Tears pooled in her eyes, stinging and hot. "I don't want to do this, not again, but I have no choice."

"Don't you get it?" He slapped the phone onto the bedside table and punched his fists into the mattress at either side of her pillow. "They will never let him go."

Against her every hope, she knew he was right. She'd known it for a while, maybe all along, but couldn't make herself face up to the truth.

"The only way you save him," her captor said, "is if we track down those bastards."

"I don't know where they are." Tears poured from her eyes, streaming down the sides of her face to trickle into her ears. "Please believe me, I don't know."

He stared at her, his face unreadable, for so long her tears morphed into sobs. All the fear and anguish she'd repressed since the moment three days ago when those people took Caleb was unleashed in a torrent of scorching tears that flowed down her face to drizzle onto the pillow. Her body wrenched with each sob. The salty liquid dampened her hair. She couldn't see her abductor through the watery haze.

"Shit," he growled.

And then he shoved his arms under her torso and pulled her up—into his waiting embrace.

CHAPTER FIVE

SEAN INHALED THE SWEET FRAGRANCE OF HER HAIR, OR THE SHAM-poo or whatever. It smelled feminine and delicate, the way she felt in his arms. Kira's body sagged into him, and her face was buried against his neck while she wept softly. He had his arms around her, cradling her soft and curvy body against him.

Why the hell had he pulled her close like this?

Because she'd started crying. That was the simple answer, but the simplicity was deceptive. The second he saw those tears and the anguished look on her face, he'd been overwhelmed by the need to soothe and protect her. Protect the woman who'd nearly killed David? *Crazy.*

The shields he'd erected to contain his powers had cracked. He sensed it. Like the sun peeking between the halves of closed drapes, he'd begun to experience…things seeping in through the cracks. The sharp and bitter tang of her fear. The hot and wrenching pain of her guilt and shame.

"Caleb," she moaned against his neck.

A cold spike stabbed into his chest, knocking the breath out of him. It wasn't his pain, though. It was hers.

His empathic ability had surged to life again, with only a sliver of an opening to sneak through. He wasn't really feeling bad for her, she was making him feel this way. Her emotions had crept into him, poisoning his psyche. Hell, maybe she did it on purpose. Other than her obvious telekinesis and that weird sparky thing, he had no idea what powers she might wield against him.

He pushed her away.

Kira blinked at him slowly, confusion clouding her eyes.

Sean slammed his shields down again, reinforcing them with every shred of psychic energy at his command.

Fresh tears rolled down her cheeks.

"Cut the tears," he said. "I'm not falling for your sob story. Everybody's got problems and past traumas. That's life, Bomb Girl."

His deliberate and snarling emphasis on the moniker made her cringe for half a second. But then she set her jaw and lifted her chin, those blue eyes catching fire. "Go to hell."

Sean gave a derisive laugh. "That's my home address, babe."

Kira bristled, her lips tightening into a slight pucker.

He'd pissed her off. Good. The last thing he needed was her getting under his skin again, literally, with whatever voodoo she had in her arsenal. No more cracks in the armor.

"What's your deal?" she asked. "You act like a creep most of the time, but then you care if these bindings hurt me."

Not anymore. He didn't care. He wouldn't care.

Emotions were weakness. Emotions were dangerous.

"Don't worry about my deal," he said. "Start worrying about how you'll convince me not to kill you along with your phone buddies."

Whether he *could* kill someone, he had no idea. In self-defense, for sure he could. But for vengeance?

An image flashed in his mind, of David in a hospital bed with needles and tubes stuck in him.

Yeah, he could kill someone.

But a woman? One who cried and swore she hadn't meant to blow up innocent people?

A thread of doubt wound through him. What if she was telling the truth? If someone had taken Abby and threatened to hurt her unless Sean did what they wanted, would he have said no? If they'd fed him the same story they fed Kira, about the device being a smoke bomb to test her powers, maybe he would have agreed. If he'd known it was a real bomb, maybe he still would've agreed. To save someone he loved, to save a kid…

Maybe he wasn't so different from Gabriel Amador. The man had committed terrible acts because losing his family had ripped him apart. Now Sean had kidnapped a woman for reasons not unlike Amador's.

Sean's gaze landed on Kira's wrists and the zip tie binding them. Why had he padded the tie this time? He shouldn't have cared if it rubbed her skin raw.

"I can't do what they want," Kira said, her tears finally subsiding, though her gaze had gone bleak. "But if I don't go to the address they texted me and set off another device, Caleb will die."

"You'd risk more lives for your brother?"

"No, I can't, I won't. But I have no way to find him and save him before the deadline." She sniffled, wiping her nose on her sleeve. "If I don't do this, they'll probably get someone else to set off the bomb. Caleb will die, I will die, and it won't save anyone."

Yeah, he'd figured as much. But still…

An idea burst in his mind like a firework in the sky. The flare of hope, he realized, however puny it might be. He had to try.

"There may be a way," he said, "to track down these creeps."

Kira perked up, though her eyes were bloodshot and puffy. "How? GPS or something?"

He slid off the bed and straightened. "Or something. I have to go talk to somebody."

She swung her legs off the bed. "Take me with you."

"Oh no," he said, shaking his head. "I don't trust you. After that little escape attempt earlier, I can't risk you getting another chance at it. You stay here, tied up and gagged."

Kira puckered her lips again. "Don't gag me. I won't scream."

"Yeah, sure, like you wouldn't try to run away either. If I could generate an EM field, I'd know for sure you can't use your powers on me. Even then, I wouldn't know you won't try to escape. You tricked me once."

"A what field?"

"Electromagnetic," he said with exaggerated precision. "Set to the right frequency, an EM field can dampen psychic powers."

"Oh."

He snagged a sock and another length of fleece from his bag, returning to the bed with the items. "I didn't do this, you did. If you hadn't broken your word, I wouldn't have to gag you."

Why was he explaining himself to her?

Her gaze darted to the fleece strip and then to his face. "Where'd you get these long, narrow pieces of soft fabric?"

"I had a girlfriend who liked to be tied up."

"You had a girlfriend? Was she the Unabomber's granddaughter?"

He balled up the sock, shoved it in her mouth, and secured it in place by tying the fleece around her head. He knotted the fabric at the back of her head.

She could get out of the room, even bound like this, if she really wanted to.

Another restraint ought to do the trick. He rushed back to his bag, dug out the rope he'd used to confine her earlier, and tied it to a rail in the headboard. Once he'd secured the other end to her zip tie, he nodded, satisfied.

"There," he said. "No more snarky comments from you, and you won't be sneaking out while I'm gone."

Her eyes narrowed, and he knew she was itching to snap a scathing retort.

But she couldn't. *Hah.*

As he strode out of the motel room, he wondered if he should have given Kira a drink of water before he gagged her. No, he decided, she'd forced him to do this by betraying his trust. An annoying little voice whispered in the back of his mind. *You kidnapped her, genius, what did you expect?*

No time to think about that. He needed a hand from someone he shouldn't be asking for help right now. He needed Grace—or more specifically, he needed her powers. He knew of no one else on earth who might have a snowball's chance of finding these terrorists.

Grace could do almost anything because she could tap into the greatest source of psychic energy in the universe. The Golden Power offered omnipotence, but it came at a hefty price. Last time, it had nearly killed her.

Sean stopped at the driver's door of the car, his fingers hovering over the handle.

Yeah, Kira was right about him. Only a cold-hearted bastard would ask a woman whose husband was in a coma to tap into a power that scared the hell out of her on a good day. Only a villain of the first order would bind and gag a woman, then leave her alone in a motel room. Kira seemed genuinely afraid and genuinely horrified by what her actions had caused.

He smacked his palm on the car's roof. He had become as narcissistic and rotten as Gabriel Amador. Would he wind up in a mental hospital too? Pushed over the edge by his own need for revenge?

That was no way to help Grace and David. After everything they'd done for him, they deserved so much better.

Sean spun around and stormed back into the room.

Kira jumped, her eyes wide.

He stalked to the bed and removed the gag.

She eyed him like he was a rabid wolf circling her.

Teeth gritted, he hissed a breath out his nostrils. Scaring girls had never been his goal. After what he'd done to Bree…God, he had so many sins to atone for that it might take his whole life and then some.

With a long sigh, he dropped his butt onto the bed's edge. "I'm sorry."

She started, her eyes flaring wide again. "You're sorry?"

"Yeah." He pulled out his pocket knife, turning it between his fingers. "I shouldn't have done this to you. I believe what you told me about your brother."

Her mouth opened, but she said nothing.

Flipping the knife open, he sliced the zip ties around her wrists and ankles.

She drew her knees up, massaging her wrists.

He heaved his body off the bed, scuffled to a chair, and collapsed onto it.

"You can go," he said, waving toward the door.

Sean dropped his face into his hands, elbows on his thighs. The weight of a hundred buildings seemed to have settled on top of him.

"I thought you had to talk to someone," Kira said.

He heard shuffling as she moved around on the bed. "Just go. I can't help you or anybody."

What had he thought he'd do? Save everybody. Punish the bad guys. Groaning, he ducked his head, his fingers plowing into his hair. How full of shit he'd been.

Delicate fingers closed around his wrists and tugged gently.

Sean lifted his head just enough to peek through his fingers at Kira. "What are you doing?"

"No idea." She tugged again, and he relented, letting her lower his hands to his knees. "But I think we should stick together. I can't do this alone, and neither can you."

He scrunched up his face. "Why the hell would you want to help me?"

"Because you're all I've got." She smiled bitterly. "Crazy, isn't it? The terrorist and the kidnapper joining forces."

Kira didn't mean it as a jab at him, he knew that. But the statement pierced his chest like a rusty nail. He had become a kidnapper.

"I'm sorry," he said again, helpless to think of anything better to say.

She sat back on her heels. "I'm sorry too. Your friend got badly hurt because of me."

"Because of them." He leaned back in the chair. "How long do you have to do the next thing for them?"

Kira snatched her phone off the bedside table and swiped her thumb over the screen. "Three hours. I'm supposed to go to this address and—" She swallowed hard, looking sick. "I'm supposed to set off another device."

"What kind of target is it?"

She bowed her head, shoulders caving in. "A movie theater."

At this time of night on a Friday, a theater would be packed.

They had to stop this, somehow.

———

KIRA SLAPPED THE PHONE DOWN ON THE TABLE. THREE HOURS. THE seconds drained away one by one, siphoning minutes and soon hours from their timeline. Their timeline? Well, it was theirs now. She needed help, and this guy was all she had.

She didn't even know his name.

The man in question slumped in his chair, eyes closed.

"Who are you?" she asked, wriggling around until she sat cross-legged on the floor.

He cracked one eyelid. "What?"

She drummed her fingers on her knees. "Who are you? What's your name? You know mine, but I have no idea what yours is. If we're joining forces, don't you think I should know what to call you?"

Both his eyes opened, and he peered at her with a blank expression. "Sean Vandenbrook."

Kira held out a hand to him. "Nice to meet you, Sean."

One of his brows quirked, along with one side of his mouth, but he took her hand. "Yeah, it's a monumental honor to meet you too."

His hand enveloped hers, big and warm and rough. She should've pulled away, but the contact fired an electric shiver through her. Sean. His name was Sean.

She let her gaze wander over his body, over the muscles partly concealed under his T-shirt and jeans. His biceps were thick and corded with muscles, his thighs strong and muscular. Though he had brown hair and tanned skin, she spotted a smattering of well-hidden freckles beneath the bronzing. His eyes were a striking green, and those lips…They were wide and thick, the kind of lips that could strip away a woman's inhibitions if she pressed her mouth to them.

Not that she would. He may have plucked her sympathy strings and stopped acting like a total dick, but she would not succumb to Stockholm syndrome.

Even if succumbing sounded kind of nice.

His gaze locked onto hers, the brilliant color of those eyes seeming to intensify and almost glow.

She cleared her throat, at last withdrawing her hand from his. "When you stormed out of here, it seemed like you had a plan. What happened?"

"I can't do it."

"Do what?"

He squirmed in his chair, his mouth crimping. "Nothing."

She barred her arms over her chest. "You can't do that. If we're working together, we've got to be honest with each other. Agreed?"

"There are things I can't tell you, and things I won't tell you. Deal with it."

The flinty edge had returned to his voice. A defense mechanism, she decided. Act like a prick to keep anybody from asking uncomfortable questions.

"Cut the crap," she said, "I'm onto your game. We'll both have to share things we don't really want to share if we have any shot at stopping a massacre. If you know someone who can help—"

"No." He jolted forward, glaring into her eyes. "I can't go there. She—"

He clamped his lips together as if he'd slipped up.

"So, it's a woman," Kira said. "The person who might help but you won't go there."

"Can't go there." His features had gone hard again, his voice too. "I've screwed up enough for one day, for one lifetime, and I will not hurt another woman. Especially not this one."

The way he talked about the woman, the tone of his voice and the look on his face, suggested he had intense feelings for her. "Is she your girl-friend? Sister? Mother?"

"None of the above. She's married to my best friend."

"Are you in love with her?" Kira knew she shouldn't ask, and honestly, she didn't care about the answer. Why had she asked, then? The words sprang from her mouth before she could stop them.

One corner of Sean's mouth twisted upward. "No. She saved my life more than once. Grace and David—" He flopped back in his chair, hiss-ing a curse under his breath. The self-loathing on his face faded quickly, though, replaced by resignation. His shoulders slumped. "What the hell, huh? Might as well tell you about them since I blurted out their names. Grace and David gave me a home when I had nowhere to go, and they taught me how to control my powers and not be afraid of what I can do. I owe them everything."

Kira studied him for a moment as he lapsed into silence, seeming lost in his own thoughts, but she couldn't hold back her curiosity for long. They didn't have time to waste.

"Okay," she said, "they're obviously important to you. But why can't you ask Grace for help?"

He braced an elbow on the chair's arm, his hand raised, and rested his chin on his fisted fingers. His green eyes assessed her for a couple seconds before he spoke. "How much do you know about psychic abilities?"

"Not much. Just what I found on the internet." She shimmied backward until her back pressed against the bed. "Mostly conspiracy websites."

He rolled his eyes heavenward, shook his head once, and rolled his eyes back down to focus on her. "You know nothing, do you?"

She shrugged. "I'm telekinetic, I know that."

"Ever hear of the crossroads?"

Kira shook her head.

"Thought projection? Remote viewing?"

She shook her head again.

"Manifestation? The Golden Power?"

"No." She compressed her lips. "You can stop reciting the Dictionary of Psychic Stuff because I don't know about any of it."

He let out an irritated sigh. "Guess I'll have to explain everything to you, since you won't understand anything I say otherwise."

The condescending tone of his voice made her bristle. "Gee, I'm so sorry I didn't get my copy of the Psychic Powers Owner's Manual. Was there a club I should've joined? Freaks International, maybe?"

"We are not freaks." He shot forward, hands clamped on his knees, gaze nailed to hers and his irises glowing with a preternatural emerald fire. "None of us asked for these powers. The universe decided to play a sick joke on some people by stuffing crazy junk in our heads. You can call yourself a freak all you want, Bomb Girl, but don't ever call my family that."

She drew her head back, stunned by the vehemence of his outburst. Bomb Girl? He called her that when he was pissed at her—or maybe when he was scared. The rest of his outburst triggered more questions she probably shouldn't ask an unstable man, but she needed to know. After all, she had no choice but to hitch her fate to his.

"I didn't say anything about your family," Kira told him. "Do they have psychic powers too? I've wondered if these abilities have a genetic component, but my little brother doesn't have powers and neither do my parents."

The fire in his eyes dimmed a little, seeming to lessen along with his anger. His head drooped, leaving her to stare at his crown of dark hair. The roots looked lighter, slightly reddish.

"Grace and David," he said in a measured tone, "*are* my family. We may not be related by blood, but we've been through hell together. They are the only family I've got now."

"I'm sorry I used the word freaks. Didn't mean to insult your family." Kira clasped her hands on her lap. "I feel like a freak, and I guess that's what I meant."

His head tilted up, and those spooky eyes became riveted to her, but he said nothing.

She fidgeted, unsettled by the intensity of his gaze. "What happened to your birth family?"

"None of your business."

Bam. He'd slammed the book shut on that subject. Fine, she didn't really need to know, anyway. This guy was damaged goods, for sure, and she would not give in to her curiosity by pushing for answers that made no difference to her life.

She itched to know, sure, but she wouldn't ask.

"About those terms you mentioned," she said. "What do they mean?"

"You seriously have no idea about the crossroads?" He stared at her, his lips parted, for several seconds. Then he cocked his head. "When you use your powers, what do you see and feel?"

"I feel energy, kind of like electricity. Don't see anything."

He linked his hands, the intertwined fingers hanging loosely between his knees. "You aren't accessing the full potential of your powers. Not if you've never experienced the crossroads."

Kira bent forward a smidgen. "What is it?"

"A metaphysical place, sort of like another dimension of reality. The crossroads is a hub for psychic energy and for everything that is, was, or will be known." He leaned forward more, the force of his gaze almost mesmeric. "All the knowledge of the universe, all the psychic power in the universe, exists simultaneously in the crossroads. Once you access it, you'll realize the full magnitude of your abilities."

A tingle swept over her skin, lifting every tiny hair and raising goosebumps. She had trouble catching her breath, so caught up in the hypnotic effect of his deep voice and those burning eyes that she couldn't rip her focus away from him.

"What else?" she asked. "How do I access this crossroads?"

"The how we'll get to in a minute," he said. "First, you need to know a few things about being psychic. Most of us have more than one ability. In fact, having only one is pretty much unheard of. You've probably got more than telekinesis, abilities you haven't discovered yet. Most of us can do remote viewing, also known as traveling. It's when you can visualize anyplace you want by just thinking about it. You feel like you're there, like you're a ghost observing everything, and you can have referred feelings like your body is really there and you can really touch, smell, and hear the world around you."

Kira couldn't move, transfixed by his words and what they meant for her. She might have the ability to travel to other places in her mind. *Cool.*

"The next step up from traveling," Sean said, "is manifesting. That's when you actually create a duplicate body while you're traveling. Don't get excited about it, though, because only the strongest psychics can manage it. Manifesting is rare, but not as rare as the Golden Power."

"Golden Power?" The name alone shivered a thrill through her. It sounded exotic and potent.

"Yeah, it's the ultimate psychic ability. It, uh..." He fidgeted, his face pinched. "Gives the person a kind of omniscience. If you could tap into the Golden Power, you'd get access to everything in the crossroads—all the power, all the knowledge, everything."

Holy cow, to know everything...*Imagine the power.* She swallowed hard, suddenly needing to know the answer to one vital question. "I'm guessing there's a serious downside, right?"

"There is." He rose and moved around the table to the window, using two fingers to part the curtains an inch, his attention on the view outside. "Grace is the only person who's ever tapped into the Golden Power, as far as anybody knows. It almost destroyed her. She's determined never to use it again because she's afraid she would lose herself to it. The Golden Power is not a living thing, but it can seem like it is, that's what she says. It's energy, plain and simple. But the power is so intense it feels like a living, breathing, ravenous energy that craves a conduit."

He let the curtains flutter shut.

Kira thought for a moment, then asked, "Did you plan on asking Grace to use the Golden Power to help us?"

Sean winced and hunched his shoulders. "Yeah. For about three minutes, I thought it was a good idea. Her husband is in a coma, and I was ready to push her to tap into a power she fears more than anything else in the world."

The crazy impulse to comfort him rocked Kira, and she wrapped her arms around herself. This man had kidnapped her, but she was beginning to understand why. He kept up a facade of arrogant disinterest, occasionally broken by his anger. Yet underneath the facade, she sensed a vulnerability that seemed to relate to the things he didn't want to talk about—his family and his powers.

"You were desperate," she said. "I did a horrible thing out of desperation, and people got hurt. You stopped yourself before you asked Grace to do anything that might've hurt her."

He turned his head toward her slowly, his expression unreadable. "Are you trying to make me feel better?"

The hard tone he'd spoken with most of the time had softened a little, his voice expressing a faint surprise at the idea she might've wanted to commiserate with him.

"I'm just pointing out," she said, "we have things in common."

He strode toward her, dropping into a crouch to glare into her eyes. "Don't feel sorry for me, Bomb Girl. I don't need your pity."

"Pardon me for acting like a human being. Wouldn't kill you to give it a try."

"It might, actually." He surged to his full height, towering over her. "Time to teach you how to access the crossroads."

CHAPTER SIX

SEAN STARED DOWN AT KIRA, HIS FINGERS CURLING INTO HIS palms. What the hell was he doing? Offering to teach her about psychic abilities. Offering to help her find the terrorists who'd kidnapped her brother. Sure, both things dovetailed with what he wanted—revenge—but he didn't need this annoying person tagging along on his quest for justice.

Revenge. Justice. Which did he want? Vengeance had sounded awfully good right after the explosion, right after he'd seen David lying in a hospital bed comatose and Grace distraught over his condition. But would punishing the perpetrators make him feel better? Already, he'd abducted and tied up a girl.

His gaze flitted down to her wrists where red marks circled them.

Yeah, he'd done great so far. He'd hurt another woman, and he hadn't gotten one frigging inch closer to the real villains.

Kira huffed. "We don't have time for you to teach me anything. In less than three hours, either I set off a bomb or my brother dies. Either way, someone will get hurt."

She was right. And he had no idea what to do about it.

Her rosy lips tightened into a loose pucker, and her gaze sharpened on him. "Well, genius? What's your plan?"

"*My* plan?" He slanted toward her, looming over her in a way he hoped would intimidate her into not harassing him anymore. Yeah, sure, that had worked out great so far. "How about you come up with a clever way out of this mess you made?"

"I'm not Bruce Willis. I can't *Die Hard* my way out of this."

Sean canted his head, considering the strange girl in front of him. "You like action movies. Well, that figures, doesn't it? I mean, you blew up a building."

Kira flinched, and suddenly, he wished he hadn't reminded her of what she'd done. Again. Why did he keep feeling guilty about pointing out her actions? Studying her sapphire-blue eyes, he knew why he'd done it. He could still feel her emotions, just a little, and it messed with his head.

Why couldn't he block her out completely?

"Tell me about your powers," she said, her tone cool and calm, the opposite of her tempestuous emotions and the pain in her eyes.

"My powers?" Yeah, he was trying to avoid talking about this because then he'd have to explain that he was blocking his abilities. That would lead to needing to explain why. "I've got nothing that can help us."

She met his gaze head-on, her eyes simmering with a hint of the preternatural glow indicative of a psychic accessing her powers. He doubted she realized she was doing it since she seemed to know zip about psychic stuff.

"No evasions," she said. "If we're in this together, then we need to be honest with each other. What are your powers?"

Of course she was right. Of course she'd have to point that out to him. And of course he had no choice but to fess up.

He knew he should step away from her, but his body had become rooted to this spot. He couldn't make himself look away from her eyes, either. "Healing, mostly."

"You can heal injuries?" She shook her head. "Why haven't you fixed your best friend?"

The question sounded more confused than accusatory.

"I can't," he said. "I tried, but his injuries are too serious and I could kill myself trying to do it. Grace wouldn't let me, anyway. She says I need to conserve my energy in case I need it soon."

"Suppose that makes sense. I got tapped out setting off the bomb and trying to shake you off my tail." Kira folded her arms over her breasts, the fingers of one hand tapping on her arm. "You said it's rare for someone to have only one power. What else have you got?"

He fisted his hands, loosened them, fisted them again. "Empathy."

The annoying girl stared blankly at him for a second, then burst into laughter. "That's hilarious."

"In what way?" he said between his clenched teeth.

She reined in her amusement, though her lips stayed curved in a knowing smile. "You repress your emotions more than anyone I've ever met, and you're an empath. It's hilarious."

"You said that already." He leaned in closer, baring his teeth as he spoke. "It's not funny. You have no goddamn idea why I repress my feelings and throttle my powers."

Aw, jeez. Why had he said that? This woman pushed all his buttons like a wild toddler pounding her fists on the control panel of a nuclear missile silo.

Her eyes widened little by little as if understanding were dawning in her mind. Her mouth formed a little O. "That explains so much."

"No, it really doesn't." It probably did, but no way was he discussing any of this with her. "My powers can't help us. End of story."

"I don't think so." She watched him with that canny glint in her eyes that made him feel like she could expose all his secrets if she wanted to do it. "What else can you do?"

"Remote viewing, that's it."

"Have you tried to do anything else? Like maybe that thought-projection thing, or manifesting, or…whatever."

"Only Grace and David can manifest." Sean shoved his hands in his pockets, rocking back on his heels. "I've never tried thought projection. What I've got is bad enough."

"Bad?" She angled her head again, watching him with that disquieting interest like she could see straight into his soul. "Why would you call your powers bad?"

"Enough," he hissed. "Interrogation over. Neither one of us has the power to track down these bad guys."

"Maybe we could combine our powers. Is that possible?"

He froze, everything inside him going ice-cold. "Grace and David merged their powers, but she's an incredibly powerful psychic. Their emotional bond helped fuel the merging too because they're crazy in love." He waved a hand from himself to Kira and back again. "We don't even like each other."

Kira bit down on her lower lip. "Okay, no merging. If you can remote view a distant place, couldn't you track down a specific person that way?"

"I'm not that strong."

"Try. Please."

Sean grumbled because no way did he want to try this. It would require him to lower the shields he'd built up to contain his powers. Threads of ice slithered in his gut. Unleash his powers? *Bad, bad, bad idea.*

A memory exploded in his mind. Bree screaming. Beating him with her fists. Kicking and clawing and struggling to get away from him.

He'd sworn never to use his powers again, but if he didn't do it now…people would die.

"Fine," he said gruffly. "I'll try. But you have to go in the bathroom and shut the door."

"Is this a tornado drill?" she asked with a wry note in her voice.

"No, and it's not a joke either." Maybe the walls between them would prevent him from accidentally hurting Kira. It was the only thing he could think of to protect her. "Just do it, okay?"

She studied him for a moment, then nodded and trotted into the bathroom.

Once the door shut and the latch clicked into place, he began.

He closed his eyes, exhaling a slow, deep breath and letting it relax his muscles. He sank into his mind, floating within a black abyss, warm and free and untethered from his body. A force, like the gravity of a black hole, pulled him closer and closer to an unseen portal.

Whoosh.

He rocketed through a dark tunnel. Its confines squeezed him, but he couldn't turn back now. The crossroads had latched onto him, dragging him through the tunnel at breakneck speed and spitting him out into a field of glittering stars. Energy flowed into him, tingled through his astral body, reinvigorated him with its pure, untainted power. He had the odd sensation of inhaling a cleansing breath, though he had no physical body here.

Find the kid, he reminded himself.

A chill rippled through his psyche. How would he find Kira's brother? He had no idea what the kid looked like. Gah, he'd screwed up again.

Maybe not. He knew the kid's name. If he focused on the name, Caleb Magnusson, maybe that would be enough to guide him.

Sean concentrated all his will and intention on the name, repeating it in his mind over and over until the sounds no longer resembled words.

One star twinkled brighter than the rest. Was it the point that might lead him to Caleb?

More power, he needed more power.

A warning shiver racked his astral form. He brushed it aside and opened his mind to the power he knew lived in this place. The crossroads concealed it, but if he sought it with all his willpower, maybe he could tap into the ultimate source of psychic energy.

Something nudged him. Something cold and hard and inhuman.

Back away. Leave here now before it consumes you.

He couldn't. So many lives at stake…

The power reached for him, its fingers greasy and talon-sharp.

Sean launched back through the tunnel and the void, slamming into his body with a force that sent him staggering two steps backward. He stumbled into the table. It lifted up and thumped back onto the carpet.

The bathroom door swung open.

Kira raced out, heading straight for him. She stopped at the foot of the bed, her eyes large and her face pale. "What happened? Are you all right?"

"Yeah." Sean scrubbed a trembling hand over his face. "Bumped the table, that's all."

She shook her head slowly. "That's not what I mean. I felt something. It was dark and oily and…nothing I want to feel again."

He blinked rapidly. She couldn't have sensed the power he'd almost tapped into back in the crossroads. Could she?

"Was that the Golden Power?" she asked, her voice hushed.

"Not sure. Maybe." He leaned his butt against the table, his body weaker than it should've been considering the amount of energy he'd absorbed in the crossroads. "I'm not strong enough to access the Golden Power, though. It must've been something else."

"Or maybe you have more power than you realize."

"Doubtful." He gripped the table's edge and glared at the carpeting. "I couldn't find your brother."

Because he hadn't unleashed his powers, not all the way. He couldn't do it, so he'd failed. If he told Kira that, she'd push him to try harder and he couldn't do that either. Not after Bree.

Kira squared her shoulders. "Then we need a new plan."

"No problem, I've got one. Let's go to the cops."

She rolled her eyes. "We've been through this. The cops can't help us."

He glanced at the clock on the bedside table. "We don't have much time, anyway. There's only one thing we can do."

"And what's that?"

"Get all those people out of the movie theater." Sean held up a hand when she opened her mouth—to gripe, no doubt. "Listen, okay? We need to convince the people in the theater to get out, which means we have to give them a reason to think they're in danger."

"If we warn those people, Caleb will die."

"That's why we won't warn them. We'll give them a reason to leave on their own." He stepped closer to take her upper arms in his hands, and he tried really hard not to notice the warmth of her skin under his palms or the luminous blue of her eyes when they focused on him. "We start a fight."

Kira snorted. "You and I are going to start a brawl? That's a horrible idea."

"No, not like that. We use thought projection to convince somebody else to start a brawl."

She squinted at him. "And you can do this? You said you'd never tried thought projection."

"I haven't, but yeah, I should be able to do it."

"That's so comforting." She screwed up her mouth. "We don't need a brawl. Leave it to a guy to come up with a plan that revolves around fist fights."

He huffed out a breath and threw his hands up. "What do you suggest we do?"

"If you can make people believe whatever you want, then just make them all think they need to use the restroom."

"That's the dumbest idea I've ever heard."

Kira tapped her finger on his chest to emphasize each word. "No fist fight."

"Convincing everyone to take a bathroom break might not save them," he said. "What if the bathroom's right next to the theater? Or maybe the bomb's big enough to damage the whole building. We need everyone to go outside."

"Okay, so we could make them think the fire alarm went off. Or actually make it go off."

He made a frustrated noise, throwing up his hands and letting them fall slack again. "How do we do that? Can you affect electronics?"

She hunched her shoulders. "Don't know. I can make sparks, though. It's part of my telekinesis—I think."

"I really hope you're not suggesting we start a fire to get people away from the bomb."

"Do you have a better idea?" Before he could answer, she said, "No, you don't."

No, he didn't. But her idea still stank.

He couldn't think of anything better.

"Fine, have it your way," Sean grumbled. He grabbed his leather jacket and shrugged into it. "We go to the theater and convince everyone to take a piss at the same time."

"Then what? There's a bomb, we have no idea where it is, and they expect me to trigger it."

"For Christ's sake, this was your idea."

She wrapped her arms around herself. "I know, but I was thinking about evacuating the crowd, not what to do after that."

Awesome. Half of a half-assed plan, that's what they had.

With no other options, he added his own lame contribution to this lame idea.

"Once the people are safely out, we find the bomb and somehow neutralize it." He raised a hand to silence the protest he knew would come out of her mouth. "Don't ask me how. Not yet."

She rubbed her arms, goosebumps visible on her skin.

He took off his jacket and held it out for her to shrug into it. "You look cold."

She eyed the jacket like it might bite her but then accepted it. "Thank you."

Kira trailed him out the door and to the car. As he steered the vehicle out onto the highway, he considered the craziness level of this plan. High, for sure. But they had no choice. If he couldn't thought project those people into leaving the theater…if they couldn't find the bomb…

Everyone would die.

—

KIRA AND SEAN STOOD AT THE BACK OF THE THEATER, IN THE SHADows, while an action movie played on the grainy screen. The screeching tires and gunfire blaring from the speakers embedded in the walls grated on her nerves, but she knew Sean was right. They had no options except this insane one.

They had forty-two minutes left.

She looked at Sean and mouthed, "It's time."

He nodded, his expression grim, his lips flattened into a slash. His entire body had gone rigid, his shoulders bunched and a muscle ticking in his jaw. His green eyes had begun to glow faintly, but she had the oddest sensation of fear emanating from him. She wasn't empathic like he claimed to be. She couldn't detect his emotions in a psychic way, but maybe their shared pain and fear gave her insight of the normal kind. He didn't want to use his powers, for reasons he wouldn't share, reasons that made him anxious almost to the point of panic.

And yet he'd volunteered to do this. To save lives.

She folded her hand around his fisted one, gently pushing against his coiled fingers until he opened them in claw-like fashion. She slipped her fingers between his to grip his hand. He didn't move for a moment. Then his fingers loosened, though the rest of him remained stiff, and he clasped her hand in return.

He didn't look at her.

A few hours ago, she'd labeled him a creep and a kidnapper, thought of him as a cold-hearted criminal. Now, she was holding his hand, relying on him to save the lives of over a hundred innocent men, women, and children.

Yeah, her life had veered into Crazy Land.

Sean pulled in a deep breath and exhaled slowly. The tension eased a bit, making his shoulders slacken and his jaw muscle cease pulsing, though he kept his teeth gritted. He rolled his eyes to glance at her, gave a sharp nod, and returned his focus to the moviegoers.

It was time.

Kira clinched his hand tight, willing this to work, praying for it to work. With every fiber of her being, every shred of power she might have, she prayed.

Energy tingled through her palm, spreading out into her fingers and up her wrist into her arm. It coursed outward into her body, a stream of psychic power originating from their joined hands.

Holy heaven. Were they sharing their powers? Sean said that couldn't happen without an emotional connection, but maybe he didn't know everything.

Whatever it was, she didn't care as long as it helped them save lives.

Sean's eyes flared with green fire.

A chill shivered down her spine, raising the hairs all over her body.

In the middle of the theater, a man jumped to his feet, his head swinging left and right as he searched for something or someone.

Power tingled hotter and harder through her body, and her knees quivered.

Stay standing. Don't fall down. Stay standing.

While she locked her knees, the man in the audience thrust an arm out to jab his finger toward the man in the row behind him.

"You!" He shouted loud enough to be heard above the din from the movie. "You kicked my chair."

The other man leaped up and bellowed, "Sit down and shut up, you blockhead. The rest of us want to enjoy the movie."

The first man seized the shirt of the second man, hauling him over the seats, and pulled one fist back to wallop the guy.

What on earth was going on here? Sean had said he'd make people want to go to the bathroom, not start attacking each other. She glanced at him, but he'd squeezed his eyes shut, his mouth crimped, his whole face pinched.

She inched closer to him. "What are you doing? They're supposed to need a pee break, not start a riot."

"I'm trying to do that. Something's wrong, though." He squinted his face harder, his teeth gritted. "Can't make them stop this and do what I want. It's—can't—not working."

More power. More tingling. Her locked knees wobbled, her heart raced.

A woman screamed. Fists flew. And chaos erupted within the darkened theater.

"Dammit," Sean growled.

Other men joined the fight while more women screamed and shouted. A tough-looking woman charged into the fray to punch a wiry man. Children wailed.

The rest of the crowd stampeded.

Kira lost the capacity for breath, her heart pounding so hard and fast she could scarcely think.

Sean dragged her backward against the wall, against his body, her back to his front with his arms latched around her midsection.

People ran. They screamed. They shouted. The original fight seemed to have broken up, but now everyone barreled toward the exits. Bright light lanced the darkness when someone kicked open an emergency exit.

Footfalls pounded, drowning out the noises from the movie.

Kira squeezed her eyes shut, grateful for the security of Sean's arms encircling her. Somehow, she knew nothing would happen to her as long as he was there.

And yeah, she recognized the insanity of feeling safe with her kidnapper.

Former kidnapper.

Silence fell with such abruptness she thought she'd gone deaf. But then, she noticed the gunfire from the movie and the ragged huffing of Sean's breaths. They fluttered her hair as his chest heaved with labored inhalations. His hands, clamped over her belly, trembled the tiniest bit.

They stood there like that for a long moment before he released her, stepped back, and spoke.

"Your turn," he said. "Find the device."

"Did anyone get hurt in the panic?"

"Not that I could tell. I reached out with my empathic power a little bit but couldn't detect anyone suffering." He speared her with a sharp look. "Find the bomb. Before anybody decides to come back in here."

"What happened to our peaceful plan for a mass bathroom break?"

"Later. The bomb, now."

"I don't know how to find it."

He grasped her shoulders and bent his head to level their gazes. "Did you know exactly where the cafe bomb was?"

She shook her head.

"Right." He tightened his hold on her a smidgen. "You could set off a bomb in another room when you had no idea where it was. You can find this one, I know you can. Do what you did before, except instead of triggering the bomb, see its location."

His expression of faith in her abilities made her throat go thick. Since the day her powers had first emerged, nobody had trusted her with them. But this man did. Sean did.

Of course, he might've been saying whatever to make her try.

With his hands on her shoulders, anchoring her, she let his eyes transfix her with their shimmering emerald glow. She reached out with her powers, seeking the bomb, picturing a box with glass bottles inside it. A red trail formed in the air, but she knew this was no physical manifestation. The trail existed in her mind's eye. She'd never witnessed this phenomenon before, and yet she understood its purpose. The trail led to the bomb.

She sensed her mind detaching from her body, and she floated along the path delineated by the red trail. It drew her down the aisle between the theater seats, straight to the small stage that hosted the big screen on which the movie still played. The trail swerved right, around the edge of the stage, and then veered left.

It pierced a metal door.

Kira dived through the door to track the red path inside.

The trail dead-ended at a stack of metal shelves.

On the second shelf, a metal box sat in plain sight.

This looked like a storage room, filled with bags of popcorn kernels, containers of oil, and cannisters of soda syrup. The terrorists must've been certain no one would enter this room before the bomb detonated.

A chill skittered down her spine. They must've placed the bomb here moments before she and Sean arrived.

She zoomed back to her body. "It's in the storage room. Follow me."

They rushed down the aisle. She blew the storage-room door open with a telekinetic burst. They hesitated in front of the box on the shelf, exchanging glances, neither of them sure what to do now. She didn't need telepathy to realize he was as confused and scared as she was.

"We have to open it," he said. "I'll do it."

"Are you sure that's a good idea?"

"No." He felt along the seam where the lid met the box. "Can't find a latch or anything."

"Maybe they didn't bother with locking it up. I mean, they didn't bother hiding it."

"Good point." Gingerly, he lifted the lid with the tips of his fingers—and froze. "Oh hell."

She leaned in to peek inside the box.

Two thick glass vials lay nestled on a block of gray foam. Each vial held clear liquid. A thin red wire emerged from beneath the foam and snaked up to split in two, one end touching each of the vials, held in place with some kind of clear glue. A black rectangle with a shiny surface lay below the vials atop the foam.

"Something's not right," Sean said. "The first bomb had no evidence of a triggering mechanism, but this one has wires."

"Maybe—"

The black rectangle came to life. Green numbers counted down on the little screen. *Ten, nine, eight—*

"Run!" Sean hollered.

Seven, six, five—

He seized her hand, half dragging her out of the storage room. They bolted through the theater, up the sloping aisle toward the doors while green numbers flashed in her mind.

Four, three, two—

They burst through the swinging doors into the lobby.

A boom thundered inside the theater, shaking the walls and floor, and a cloud of dust and debris plumed out the open doors.

54

CHAPTER SEVEN

S EAN DIVED FOR THE FLOOR AND LANDED ON TOP OF KIRA FOR THE second time in twelve hours. Chunks of who-knew-what spattered his backside. He waited until the onslaught ended, until the rumbling subsided and the dust had cleared. Then he jumped up, hoisting her up with him.

Her eyes were big and glossy. Dirt crusted her hair.

Sean brushed the locks from her face. "You okay?"

His ears still rang, but he heard her say, "Not hurt."

"Good." He should've pushed her away, but a weird sensation in his chest made him hold still with her soft little body pressed against him. They could've both died, but he was more worried about whether his stunt had driven everyone out of the theater.

He should've checked before they fiddled with the bomb. He should've come up with a different plan. And what had gone wrong with his thought projection? He'd meant to make everyone leave in an orderly fashion, not start a freaking riot.

Another mistake. He couldn't seem to stop screwing up these days.

Kira peered around his shoulder at the dark and destroyed theater. In a halting voice, she asked, "Did everyone get out?"

"I think so." He prayed they had. Grace could've used her powers to check for any people hiding in the theater, but he hadn't even been able to track down Kira's brother. "I know my original idea was a brawl, but I swear I was trying to make people go to the restroom. Something got messed up. I couldn't control what was happening. Tried to send out a calming wave, but it was too late."

Jeez, that sounded idiotic. But he had tried to calm things down. Didn't work, naturally. He seemed incapable of doing anything lately except making things worse.

Kira pulled in a shaky breath, squared her shoulders, and looked up at him. "They all got out. I trust my intuition, and it's telling me we saved everyone."

"Thought you were telekinetic and nothing else."

"I've always had good intuition. Never thought of it as a psychic thing until now, until you explained that stuff to me." She glanced around as if only just realizing she was in his arms. Her brows crinkled. "Um…Why are you hugging me?"

Good question. He'd meant to support her until she regained her equilibrium, but she felt so nice against him he couldn't seem to make himself release her. Though he'd never been a big hugger, he'd liked to hold his girlfriends. But ever since Bree, he hadn't wanted anyone to touch him. His powers might've gone rogue again and gotten someone hurt.

Like they had a few minutes ago. Please let everyone be okay.

A chill rattled him down to his bones. What if he hurt Kira next time?

Clearing his throat, he backed away from her. "Sorry."

She puckered her lips, then took a deep breath and blew it out. "You're very confusing."

"I can live with that." He reached for her hand, intending to guide her out of the building, but then changed his mind and waved for her to follow him. "Let's get out of here before the cops show up. They'll have questions we can't answer."

As they pushed through the swinging glass doors and exited into the night, the cool air felt brittle on his skin. The parking-lot lights painted the scene in shades of sickly yellow. They hurried to the car, and just as they settled into their seats with Sean behind the wheel, Kira's phone rang.

She jerked, her hand flying to her chest.

"Better answer," he said.

Kira took a breath and exhaled it slowly, her lips forming a small O. Then she tugged the phone out of her purse and held it to her ear. Before she could speak, the caller started talking. Sean could hear the voice, tinny and indistinct.

"Okay," she said, and punched a button on the phone. "He's listening."

She must've meant him, Sean figured. But how could the bad guys know he was with her?

Psychic powers, numbskull.

That creepily altered voice emerged from the speaker, the words clipped with a funky cadence. "You betrayed us, Kira, and there must be consequences."

"The bomb went off," she said. "I did what you wanted."

"No, you evacuated the premises and searched for the device. We triggered it." A pause. "This was your mission, but you brought Sean Vandenbrook into it. We are not pleased."

Despite what the guy said—or the woman, he had no idea based on the distorted voice—it sounded like the person was kind of pleased with the situation.

Sean leaned over the center console. "Don't blame Kira. This was my fault. I made her take me along."

"Yes, we're aware of that," the voice said, with an oddly familiar tone that raised goosebumps on Sean's arms. Silence followed as seconds elapsed. "We've decided this is acceptable after all. Two of you will accomplish the next task faster. However, we know you chased the patrons out of the theater before the explosion. Therefore, we must exact punishment."

"No!" Kira shouted, jerking forward, her fingers clenching the phone. "Please don't hurt Caleb."

"Oh, he will remain unharmed—for now. Since Sean took it upon himself to become involved, the punishment will be his."

"Do whatever you want to me," Sean said. "I can take it."

"You misunderstand. We punish not you, but one you love."

His gut twisted, the pain visceral and real. "You bastard—"

"We will be in touch later with your next assignment."

The words "call ended" flashed on the phone's screen.

Sean yanked the key in the ignition, wrenched the gear shift lever into reverse, and floored the accelerator. The tires squealed as he swerved the car backward and to the left, then burned rubber out of the parking lot and onto the highway.

Peripherally, he saw Kira gripping the armrest and the center console. Her eyes had gone wide again.

"Who will they hurt?" she asked.

"Since they like hurting kids," he said, grinding the words out between his teeth, "I'm betting they'll try for Grace and David's daughter, Abby."

"Oh God."

"I'm not giving them the chance to hurt her."

The speedometer read seventy. He floored the gas pedal again, and the car shot forward, pinning them to their seats. Eighty, ninety. They flew over the asphalt.

He prayed they would get there in time. If they didn't...

Sean clamped his hands tighter around the wheel, his jaw throbbing from the pain of gritting his teeth. If they hurt Abby, he'd unleash his powers all the way this time. He'd hunt them down and show the scumbags the real meaning of pain.

TEN MINUTES LATER, THEY PULLED INTO THE DRIVEWAY OF A NONDEscript house in the suburbs. Kira peeled her hands off the armrest and center console, at last taking a good, deep breath. She guessed this drive would've taken twice as long, or longer, at normal speeds. Sean had driven like a genuine bat out of hell, like they were being pursued by flaming demons.

The fact his eyes had glowed softly during the whole trip only reinforced that imagery.

She'd never seen anyone so grimly determined, someone burning with an anger she couldn't comprehend. What had happened to him? She got the distinct impression he'd suffered way more than she could imagine.

As Sean shut off the engine, a porch light popped on. The interior of the house remained dark.

They climbed out of the car. Kira stopped at the front bumper, unsure of whether she should accompany Sean into the house. This was his family, not hers.

He cupped her elbow on his way toward the porch, urging her to follow. At the front door, they halted.

"Maybe I should wait in the car," she said.

"No." He swung his attention to her, and though the glow had subsided, the way his gaze bored into hers made her uneasy. "We stick together. Okay?"

She nodded.

A locking mechanism released with a click, and the door opened a couple feet. A bald man with a face etched with wrinkles peered out at them, at first seeming suspicious, but then he looked at Sean and relief flooded over him. A weary smile tugged at his mouth.

"Sean," the man said on a gusty sigh. "Thank goodness you're all right. I heard the news report a few minutes ago on the radio. Another explosion."

"Yeah," Sean said, "we were there. That's why we're here. Can we come in, Edward?"

The man blinked as if surprised. "Oh. Yes, of course."

He swung the door open wider, and Sean exerted slight pressure on Kira's elbow to lead her inside.

The house wasn't completely dark, she now saw. Blackout curtains shielded the windows. A low-wattage lamp situated on a table at the end of a sofa cast its warm, muted light into the room.

Edward, the bald man, glanced from Sean to Kira. He hiked up one eyebrow.

"Oh, uh…" Sean waved a hand toward her. "This is Kira Magnusson. She's helping me look for the scumbags who were responsible for both explosions."

She squelched the surprise that surged inside her. Mere hours ago, Sean had called her Bomb Girl and a terrorist. Now, he told this kindly looking man she was helping him hunt for the culprits.

Yep, her life had totally veered into Crazy Land.

"This is Edward McLean," Sean told her. "He's Grace's grandfather."

Kira offered her hand to the older man. "Nice to meet you, Mr. McLean."

He took her hand, sandwiching it between both of his. "Call me Edward. I'm glad to see Sean with a girl since he's been avoiding other people for two months."

She threw Sean a sidelong look. Months? Avoiding people? This guy kept a secret, for sure, but she hadn't thought he kept it from the people he said he loved.

He must've guessed what she was thinking, because his gaze slid away from hers and he scratched his neck.

"Where's Abby?" Sean asked.

"Sleeping in her room."

"Gotta check on her." Sean started for the hallway, but Edward grasped his arm. Sean's expression turned almost panicked. "Please, I have to check."

"I just looked in on her a minute ago. She's fine." Edward tugged Sean's arm until the younger man gave in and faced him again. "What's going on?"

Sean's expression hardened into steel. "Something bad."

———

SEAN CRACKED THE BEDROOM DOOR OPEN JUST ENOUGH TO PEEK in at the small body tucked under the covers. In the twilight within, Abby was a shadowy lump in the bed, though he could make out enough to tell she was sleeping. Safe. For now.

He shut the door gently and headed back to the living room. He'd checked on Abby twice in the past five minutes, but he still didn't feel secure about her safety.

Edward had switched on a second lamp and sat in the armchair across the coffee table from the sofa. Kira perched on the sofa's edge, hands clamped together over her lap, spine straight.

Sean settled onto the sofa a few feet from her and slouched back into the cushions. His body ached like he'd gone on an exercise binge, and a deep weariness penetrated him to the core. His mouth split open on a yawn that was loud and inappropriate.

Edward leaned back in his chair, one elbow on the puffy arm, his raised hand braced under his chin. "You've checked on Abby twice. I know you're worried about her, but no one will get into this house without our knowing. It has a state-of-the-art security system."

Sean drummed his fingers on his thigh. "We're dealing with nutjobs who use psychics to commit terrorist acts. Can't be sure any security system will be enough. Maybe you should call Grace again."

"Grace and David are fine."

His fingers drummed faster, harder. Sean couldn't stop them, couldn't stop his thoughts from whirling and colliding, couldn't make his stomach settle down either. *We punish not you*, the disembodied voice on the phone had said, *but one you love.* If not Grace, David, or Abby, then who? He didn't care about anyone but them and Edward.

A shiver sidled down his spine, raising the hairs all over his body. Could these bad guys, whoever they were, somehow hurt Edward? Losing her grandfather would destroy Grace. And Edward had become a kind of substitute grandfather to Sean, a replacement for the lunatic who had been his actual grandfather. Maybe Sean did love Edward, kind of. Being a guy, he would never say it out loud because guys didn't do that kind of thing.

The psycho on the phone couldn't have meant...

Sean shot upright, hands gripping his knees. "Edward, how do you feel?"

The older man smiled with the sort of calmness only a mature person with seven decades of life under his belt could pull off. "I'm fine. Your terrorists must have changed their minds, or else they were simply trying to unsettle you."

"Yeah, they've done a bang-up job of that."

"Terrorists want to incite fear, Sean. You can't believe everything they say."

"I know, but—" Sean rubbed his jaw, realizing he'd been gritting his teeth hard enough to trigger pain. "They said they'd punish me by hurting someone I, uh, care about."

A small smile tightened Edward's mouth. "Glad to know you care, but they can't get to me here."

"Psychically, they could."

Edward sighed. "If they have psychic powers themselves, or have others with them who do, why would they need you and Kira to perform their evil deeds for them? Why would they need a physical means to detonate the bomb in the theater?"

Sean shook his head, unable to come up with an answer.

Kira cleared her throat. "Um, what if they needed my specific powers? Maybe none of them have telekinesis, and they can't set off the bombs on their own."

"It's possible," Edward said. He tapped a finger on his chin as if considering the idea. "I suppose—"

He jerked. His eyes bulged, his mouth fell open, and he slapped a hand on his chest.

Sean's heart thudded, but he couldn't move. "What's wrong?"

The older man clutched at his chest, his fingers twisting in his shirt. He gasped.

"Edward!" Sean launched off the sofa and bolted for the armchair. On his knees beside Edward, he grasped the other man's wrist to feel his pulse. Fast. Thready. "Kira, call nine-one-one."

She fumbled with her phone. It tumbled to the floor.

While she cursed and snagged the phone, Edward lurched up and forward, half out of the chair.

"No," Sean said, grasping Edward's shoulders in his own shaking hands. "Sit down, don't try to move."

Edward collapsed to the floor.

Sean was paralyzed, in body and mind, unable to move or think.

Legs and arms bent at odd angles, Edward lay motionless on the carpet. His eyes were open and lifeless.

No, no, no. Not lifeless. Sean's heart pounded so hard and fast he could barely breathe. *Not losing anyone else, not now, not ever.*

A harsh noise erupted from Kira's phone, the sound of a busy signal.

She made a choked sound. "I can't get through to nine-one-one. System must be overloaded."

Gulping against the parched tightness of his throat, Sean scrambled closer to Edward. No sign of breathing. He felt for a pulse in Edward's wrist and his throat. Nothing. Panic ripped through Sean, freezing his muscles and his brain, freezing the blood in his veins.

Kira waddled toward him on her knees. She clamped a hand on his arm. "Can't you heal him?"

Her voice trembled, her hand too.

Wake up, he commanded himself. Wake up and fix this.

Sean carefully rolled Edward onto his back. He laid his palms on the man's chest, closed his eyes, and focused on the power. His mind soared out of his body toward the crossroads.

And slammed into a barrier.

He sucked in a heaving breath, knocked off kilter by the psychic momentum of his ejection from the crossroads. What was going on? He knew how to get there, how to access the energy contained in the metaphysical plane.

"I can't," he gasped. "I can't get to the crossroads."

Kira seized one of his hands, pressing her palm to his. "Let me help, like you helped me in the theater."

Could it work? He had to try.

Sean clasped her hand tighter, his other palm flat on Edward's chest over his heart. Eyes closed, Sean willed the power to come. He couldn't get to the crossroads, wouldn't attempt it after the last time when he'd been ejected. Instead, he took them both up the tunnel, almost to the crossroads, close enough the power inherent in that place sought them out like a magnet seeking metal. Energy poured into them, warm and tingling, energizing their powers like nothing he'd experienced before. In the theater, their joined hands had amplified their powers somehow, but without them traveling out of their bodies. Bound to each other as they floated in the ethereal tunnel, he let the energy stream into him until the flow dwindled into nothing.

He hummed with power.

As they flew back into their bodies, Sean opened his eyes and concentrated on the sight of his hand plastered to Edward's chest. He willed the energy crackling within him and Kira to flow into Edward, to repair the damage and restore vitality. The hairs on Sean's arm raised visibly as if an electrical current stirred them.

His hand. He stared at it, not blinking, not breathing. Must've been an optical illusion or something, but he swore—

"Your hand is glowing," Kira said, breathless, her large eyes glued to the sight.

And yeah, his hand was glowing. A faint white light emerged from his palm, seeping out around the edges. Power pulsated through their joined hands, through his body, down his other arm into his glowing hand.

Edward's chest heaved with a hoarse inhalation.

The energy fizzled out. Sean's hand no longer glowed. Frozen in place, his hand around Kira's and his palm on Edward's chest, Sean waited for...more.

Edward's breathing normalized. His eyelids fluttered open.

He glanced down at Sean's hand on his chest and then eyed Sean and Kira with curiosity. "What's going on here?"

"You died," Sean blurted out, seeming to have lost control over his brain-to-mouth filter. "I mean, it seemed like you did. Your heart stopped, and you weren't breathing, and I—we—"

Sean glanced helplessly at Kira.

Her lips curved into a sweet smile, aimed first at him, and then at Edward. "Sean healed you."

Edward sat up, as spry as ever, and patted Sean's arm. "Thank you."

"You're, uh, welcome," Sean mumbled. "You feel okay?"

Stretching, Edward drew in a long, deep breath. His lips formed a satisfied smile. "I feel excellent."

"Good," Sean said, because he couldn't think of anything else to say. He'd healed Edward with Kira's help. They'd saved someone's life together. Though the energy that had powered up his healing ability had faded, a tingling still energized every cell in Sean's body. He felt awake, alive, and…aware.

Abruptly, he noticed Kira's hand still latched onto his. The softness of her palm. The heat of her skin. The way her thumb traced circles on his flesh.

Her gaze swiveled to him, her blue eyes shimmering, almost glowing with residual energy.

Right there in front of Edward, without a thought for anything except the need that surged up inside him, Sean took hold of Kira's face and crushed his mouth to hers.

CHAPTER EIGHT

For a stunned moment, Kira was paralyzed by the feel of Sean's lips on hers. She gazed at his face so near to hers, gazed into his smoldering green eyes, while her pulse raced and a warmth blossomed in her chest. It spread outward on a tingling wave of sensation. Her body softened, her eyes drifted closed. His lips, warm and firm against hers, began to move over her skin, sweeping back and forth as his tongue teased the seam of her mouth.

She melted against him, against his firm chest, his big hands still bracketing her face.

When he withdrew his lips for a second, her lips parted like they had a mind of their own. He tunneled his fingers into her hair, pressing his mouth to hers once more, and slipped his tongue between her lips. Slick. Hot. Agile. He explored her mouth with leisurely sweeps of his tongue, his fingers massaging her scalp, his breaths tickling her skin.

Edward cleared his throat deliberately.

Kira and Sean froze at the same instant, their lips fused.

Sean ripped his mouth away from hers and jerked his hands away too, flinging them wide like he'd just realized he was touching a radioactive object.

"I don't mean to interrupt," Edward said, "but we do have urgent matters to discuss."

Jaw slack, face blank, Sean stared at Kira for a long moment before he pulled in a big breath and retreated into his hard facade, teeth gritted. He jumped to his feet. "Better check on Abby again."

He sprinted down the hall.

Edward eyed Kira with something akin to humor tinged with curiosity.

His attention made her squirm. She scrambled to her feet and offered him her hands. "Let me help you up."

"I'm old, not infirm." He rose without her assistance, brushing his clothes off with his hands. "But I appreciate the offer, dear. How long have you and Sean been dating?"

"Dating?" Her brain blanked, leaving her to flounder through an answer on her own. "We just met earlier tonight. Yesterday, I mean. Last night. What time is it?"

Edward smiled a touch. "Two-thirty?"

Where had the hours gone? Sucked into the void of desperation and panic, that's where.

She tried not to let Edward's keen gaze unsettle her, but it did anyway. The man wanted to know more about how she and Sean had met, she could tell that much. He didn't need to hear about how Sean kidnapped her and the strange truce they'd reached, not to mention their idiotic scheme to chase everyone out of the movie theater. If Sean wanted to share all that information with Edward, she wouldn't stop him. But she would not reveal it without his permission.

He'd *kissed* her.

The thought burst into her mind, setting off a replay of the sizzling heat she'd experienced when he took her mouth. Not only had she let him kiss her, she'd responded in kind. She'd liked it.

Stockholm syndrome, for sure.

Didn't matter right now. She had no option except to keep trusting Sean and keep working with him. No more power sharing, though. Absolutely none.

Sean tromped back into the living room. "Abby's fine."

Edward nodded, then settled down in the armchair again. "We should call Grace."

"I'll do it," Sean said, digging his phone out of his jeans pocket.

"Don't tell her what happened to me. Say you're checking in again, nothing more."

Sean nodded and dialed a number.

While he retreated to a far corner of the room, Kira perched on the sofa, her hands clamped over its front edge.

Edward observed her with even more interest than before, rubbing his chin with his thumb and forefinger. "You and Sean seem closer than two strangers who met earlier tonight."

She shrugged. "Things aren't always how they look. Besides, we've been through a lot together in the past few hours."

The forced intimacy of shared trauma made them seem closer than they were. That had to be the answer. Like Sean had said earlier, they didn't even like each other.

But lord, did he know how to kiss.

"Grace and David are okay," Sean said, approaching the sofa to take a seat on it a few feet from Kira. "He's still in a coma, but his condition is stable. Unchanged. Those bastards didn't get to Grace or David."

Edward flattened his lips, his attention diverting to the corner. "Sean, why do you talk as if the terrorists had something to do with my heart attack?"

"They must have." Sean leaned forward and braced his elbows on his knees. "They said someone I care about would be punished and then you almost died."

"It could've been a coincidence."

Sean huffed. "You had a complete physical two months ago, and your heart was fine."

Edward's expression turned pained, and his shoulders slumped.

"You don't want to believe it," Sean said, his tone gentler than Kira would've thought he was capable of sounding. "It's too scary, I get that. But somebody must've gotten to you. Did you run into anyone strange at the hospital? Maybe you got poisoned or something."

"Poisoned?" Edward rubbed his forehead. "I was in a public place, a hospital, for most of the day. I ran into dozens of strangers. But I've been here at home for more than eight hours, and I felt fine until moments ago. Poison seems unlikely."

"Yeah, it does," Sean said, scowling down at the carpet. "It had to be a psychic assault, but I've never heard of anybody having the power to kill remotely."

Kira wriggled in place, biting down on her lip before deciding to speak. "Sean, if you could heal Edward's heart, then why couldn't someone else make it stop beating? I'm sure you don't know everything there is to know about psychic powers."

Sean rotated his eyes to nail her with a hard look. "Never said I know everything. But if these terrorists have got people who can kill remotely, why would they need you and me to set off bombs for them?"

"Maybe the heart-stopping psychic can't affect multiple people at once."

He nailed his gaze to hers, his eyes faintly luminescent, his mouth tight.

She refused to break eye contact and give him the satisfaction of knowing he'd unnerved her, even though he had. The intensity of his gaze, the steely expression on his face, they reminded her of when he'd dragged her into his car. A chill raced over her skin at the memory. He'd been nicer since then, but she still didn't know whether trusting him was a good idea.

Especially when he glared at her like that.

But it was a defense mechanism. She'd recognized that hours ago. If he would talk to her, really talk to her, she might understand his motivations and his actions.

Sure, he'd rip open all his old wounds and show them to her anytime now.

"Maybe," she said, forcing her tone to remain level, "they don't need us to do these things. Maybe they have some reason to want us involved, to use us as scapegoats once they do whatever it is they're trying to accomplish."

"Scapegoats?" Edward said, scratching his chin. "I suppose that could be."

He sounded unconvinced, despite his assertion.

"Bull," Sean said. "There's something else going on here. Don't know what it is, but this is not about needing somebody to take the blame."

Kira raised her brows. "How do you know?"

He swerved his gaze away from her. "I feel it. Intuition."

"Okay," she said slowly. "Considering this is all about psychic abilities, I guess I have to accept your intuition as evidence. If these bad guys don't want us as patsies, what do you think they want?"

He shrugged.

Edward cleared his throat. "The only way you'll find out is by tracking down these terrorists. The two of you are the only ones who've had contact with them. Find these criminals. Stop them. I know you can do it."

"How?" Sean asked. "How do you know?"

"I may not have powers, but I do have a functioning brain, Sean. I know the facts of this case, and I know you." Edward glanced at Kira. "And this young lady seems as stubborn, determined, and intelligent as you are. I'd say you're a perfect match—as psychic detectives."

The twinkle in his eyes and the slight upward tick of his lips suggested he thought of them as a perfect match in other ways too.

And the idea made Kira's skin itch.

Yes, she found Sean attractive—and sexy, in an alpha-male sort of way that made her want to deck him—but she did not believe in soul mates or whatever Edward thought they might be.

"Go," Edward said. "Find these villains."

"What about you and Abby?" Sean asked. "And Grace and David too. We can't leave all of you alone. What if somebody tries to kill one of you again? I won't be here to heal you."

"Make them believe you're doing what they want, and we will be fine."

"You don't know that."

Edward blustered out a breath and slapped his hands on his thighs. "Go, Sean. Don't make me throw you out the door."

Sean tensed as if he wanted to complain, but Kira laid a hand on his arm.

"Let's go," she said. "He's right. Our best hope is to play along and keep trying to hunt down these bad guys."

He rubbed his nape. "I know."

Dragging in a breath, he surged to his feet.

Kira pushed up off the sofa too.

As Sean passed Edward's chair, he paused to gaze down at the older man. "Be careful."

"You too."

Kira trailed Sean out of the house.

———

OUTSIDE, THE SUN PEEKED OVER THE HORIZON, PAINTING THE SKY in shades of gold and pink. In the false twilight within the motel room, slumped in a chair by the window, Sean watched Kira sleeping on the bed. She lay on her side with one hand tucked under the pillow, her face slack and her eyes darting the way they did when someone dreamed. He hoped she was having nice dreams, but he kind of doubted it after the hell they'd been through last night.

He'd slept for a few hours, fitfully.

Yawning, he scrubbed a hand over his eyes. No way could he hope for more sleep, not now, not anytime soon.

A sigh whispered out of Kira between her parted lips.

Sean studied her sleeping form, noting her eyes had stopped fidgeting and her lips had curled into the barest of smiles. For a little while last night, while she slept, he'd considered the possibility she might've done something to Edward to cause his heart attack. Kira had been alone with Edward while Sean checked on Abby. She could've slipped him a poison or, hell, used her powers to try to kill him. If she could set off bombs with her telekinetic abilities, then maybe she could use them to squeeze Edward's heart until it seized up.

But Sean couldn't make himself believe it.

Yesterday, when he'd found Kira at the ravaged cafe, he would've believed her capable of any depraved act. Now...His stupid intuition kept niggling at him, encouraging him to trust her for reasons he couldn't understand.

Empathic abilities, moron. You've got 'em, remember?

He'd blocked his powers, shut them up in the deepest vault of his mind, but how could he be sure the seal hadn't cracked? When she wept over her brother, Sean had sworn he experienced her emotions, her pain, her fear. Maybe he couldn't contain his powers behind a mental shield as thoroughly as he'd thought. Maybe something of her got through the barrier.

She hadn't hurt Edward. Sean knew it on a visceral level, and he didn't have time to explore the reasons why.

His phone vibrated in his pocket. He'd set it to vibrate instead of ringing, so the noise wouldn't wake up Kira if someone called. He dug the phone out of his pocket, trotted into the bathroom, and shut the door while he muttered hello.

"Sean, I was concerned for you."

He bristled at the sound of Gabriel Amador's voice, but tried to keep his irritation out of his tone. Yeah, he always had great luck with that. "What do you want?"

"I heard of another bombing on the news this morning, and I was worried since you did leave to search for the culprits of the first attack." Amador paused, then added, "Where are you?"

"What do you want?" Sean repeated with more emphasis this time.

"Have you spoken to Grace this morning?"

"No. Why? Is something wrong with her or David?"

Amador said nothing for several seconds, the silence reverberating through Sean's soul and making his pulse quicken. If something had happened, Edward or Grace would've called Sean. Unless the terrorists had gotten to both of them.

"I'm afraid," Amador said, speaking slowly and with a grim tone that implied bad news ahead, "your mission of revenge is causing Grace distress. You are, after all, only a boy and ill-equipped for the task."

The way Amador had drawn out his answer, the way he'd started with "I'm afraid," it had triggered a stark panic that overtook Sean for the briefest moment that seemed like an eternity. Sean had the weirdest feeling the guy had done it on purpose to make him worry. To cause him stress. To hurt him. And the jibe about him being "only a boy" and "ill-equipped" struck him as weird too. Annoying, for sure, but weird. Even Amador wasn't normally that rude. Had the guy wanted to tick him off?

Sean had never liked Amador, but he'd never done anything to the guy. He couldn't imagine why Amador would want to hurt him or tick him off. He must've misread the man.

If Sean turned on his empathic ability, he might know for sure.

Too dangerous.

"Was that it?" Sean said. "Or did you have something else to say? I'm kinda busy."

"I will let you go now, with a bit of advice. Give up on finding the parties responsible for these attacks, Sean. Allow the authorities to handle this."

Amador hung up.

Sean stared at his own reflection in the bathroom mirror. He'd developed reddish stubble and reddish roots showed close to his scalp. Hints of the past. Reminders of his bloodline. Acid burned in his gut, but a coldness slithered in his chest.

He searched the bathroom for a razor but couldn't find one. This was a cheap motel, not the Hilton. The only amenities were a tiny bar of soap and plastic cups on the counter. He scratched his head, suddenly itchy on the outside and the inside. *Got to get rid of the red.* But he couldn't.

With his hands on the counter, he bowed his head. No way to erase the past.

After a moment, he shambled out of the bathroom and slumped into the chair again.

Kira stirred, made a little moany sighing noise, and rolled onto her back. Her lids fluttered open, and she focused her lustrous blue eyes on him.

"Good morning," he said.

"Morning." She pushed into a sitting position, wriggling backward to lean against the headboard. "Not sure it'll be a good one, though."

Sean crossed one ankle over his other knee. "Might as well start off optimistic."

Her brows shot up. "You're feeling optimistic? Mr. Gloom and Doom?"

"I have my moments." He folded his hands over his belly. "Sleep okay?"

"Well enough." She stretched and yawned. "What about you?"

"Good as I ever do these days."

She squinted at him, biting down on her lower lip. "You don't look rested. There are dark circles under your eyes."

He hissed out a sigh. "Forget about my sleep habits. We've got more important things to worry about. Like teaching you how to access the cross-roads."

"Can we get some breakfast first?"

Sean's stomach grumbled at the mention of food. He couldn't remember the last time he'd eaten, and Kira probably hadn't grabbed a snack either. Leaving her while she slept so he could get some food hadn't seemed like a good idea.

Thinking about it had made him...uneasy.

"Now that you're up," he said, thrusting his body up and out of the chair, "I'll run over to the burger joint across the street. I saw they do breakfast too. Got any preferences?"

"Food. That's my preference."

She smiled, her lips sealed, her eyes sparkling in the muted lighting.

His chest tightened, his groin too. She looked so beautiful and innocent with her sleep-tousled hair and her rumpled clothes.

Sean coughed into his fist. "I'll be back as quick as I can."

Kira slid off the bed and stretched again, her breasts rising with her arms. "Think I'll freshen up."

He stared at her shapely ass while she sashayed into the bathroom. When she shut the door, he headed out.

Maybe he liked her ass and her breasts, and maybe he didn't think she was a cold-blooded killer, but he did not like her or have…feelings for her. No way.

As he strode across the street toward the burger joint, he tried to ignore the images that flickered in his mind. Kira sleeping. Kira smiling. Kira stretching her lithe body.

Not feeling a damn thing.

CHAPTER NINE

TWENTY MINUTES LATER, THEY'D POLISHED OFF THEIR BREAKFAST OF biscuits loaded with eggs, cheese, and bacon. He'd eaten three, while Kira managed one and a half. Sean had finished off the half she left, then swigged milk from a tiny carton. Kira had daintily drunk her milk throughout the meal, but only after complaining he'd bought low fat instead of whole milk.

"I thought women ate low fat all the time," he'd said. "Every girl I dated would've shrieked at me if I bought whole milk. Besides, the restaurant didn't have any."

"Maybe other girls are constantly dieting," Kira had told him, "but not me. I believe in eating what I want, not what's in fashion. I am not obsessed with having the perfect figure."

He'd eyed her up and down, admiring her curvy body. "You don't need to diet. Your figure is just fine."

She'd looked shocked for a second but then went back to consuming her meal like she hadn't eaten in weeks.

Now, she swallowed the last of her milk and plunked the empty carton on the table. She sat across from him, her legs tucked under her cross-legged style. Her hair was wet, since she'd showered while he got the food, but her clothes were still rumpled.

"We should go to your place," he said, "and get you fresh clothes."

"Later." She folded her hands on the tabletop. "First, I want to know more about you."

"Why?" Despite his casual posture, with one arm draped over the table and his legs stretched out with his ankles crossed, he felt tension rippling through his body, tightening every muscle.

"Because we're in this together," she said, "and I need to know who I'm dealing with."

He rapped his knuckles on the table. "I've got powers, you've got powers, we're both being blackmailed by anonymous psychos. Nothing else to know."

She sat back and barred her arms over her chest. "You're reining in your powers, aren't you? If that's the case, I need to know why. Your pent-up powers might bite us both in the ass."

"What makes you think I'm reining in my powers?" He was, big time, but he'd never told her that.

She made a derisive noise. "Please. I'm not stupid. You say you're an empath, but you act like you haven't experienced a genuine emotion in your entire life."

"I've got feelings." The statement came out harsher than he'd meant it to, almost a growl. He did not want to talk about this. Ever.

"Working together means trusting each other, which means understanding each other." She dropped her hands to her lap, and her expression softened. "I need to know, Sean. What happened to you? What happened to your real family?"

"Grace and David are my real family." Sean fidgeted in his chair. His stomach churned with acid that burned into his chest. His jaw ached, and he tried to stop gritting his teeth but couldn't make himself relax.

"I didn't mean to offend you," Kira said, her voice so gentle he felt like a bastard for snapping at her. "I'm sorry, Sean. But you have to realize I need to know what's going on with you. Like it or not, we are stuck with each other for the time being."

"Yeah, I know." He closed his fist around the empty milk carton and crushed it. "What makes you think anything happened to me?"

Delay. Denial. He'd go for any D-word that might keep him from having to talk about things he'd vowed never to talk about again.

"Things you've said," she told him. "You decided I was guilty because, in your words, innocent people pray for help and fight to get away until they're bloody and beaten. They scream for help until their throats are raw and they can't breathe. Those were your exact words."

He let go of the milk carton, giving it a little shove that sent it skittering across the table. "Let me guess. You've got a photographic memory."

"No, but the words of my kidnapper seemed important to remember."

Sean winced and snatched up the milk carton. Kidnapper. Yeah, that was him.

Kira angled her head, studying him with a keenness that made his skin crawl. "Edward said you've been avoiding other people for months. And you're sensitive about your powers, don't like to talk about them, much less use them. I had to go in the bathroom while you tried to access that crossroads thingy."

He pitched the crushed milk carton into the trash can behind Kira's chair. It flew past her head, and she cringed away from the projectile.

She shook her head. "Throwing things at me won't make me stop asking questions. Who made you scream for help until you couldn't breathe?"

Memories. They assailed his mind like nightmares, except these had been real moments in his life. Real terror. Real agony. Never talk about this again, he'd vowed. But Kira was too stubborn to let him get away with holding back, and she was right, they were stuck with each other. Dependent on each other, in a way. She needed to know, but he didn't know if he could speak the words. Relive the pain.

"It's okay," she said, her voice soft and full of compassion. "I won't tell anyone what you tell me. It'll be our secret, I promise."

Last night, she'd promised not to run away if he untied her—but she'd run anyway. So much had changed since then. He didn't want to trust her, but he had the weirdest feeling he could trust her. She'd suffered too, at the hands of these scumbag terrorists.

Sean braced his elbows on the table and cradled his forehead in his palms. "I don't remember my dad. My mom was all I ever had, and she died in a car wreck when I was fifteen. Her name was Sophie, which means wisdom, and it suited her. We had moved to California the year before because my mom got a job there. I was walking home from school one day when I saw her car come around the corner from the other direction, two blocks away. She was driving so fast the tires squealed. She kept going faster and faster. I stood there like my feet had gotten buried in concrete, watching, somehow knowing what was about to happen. She lost control and slammed into a utility pole. Died instantly."

"Oh, Sean." Kira stretched her hands across the table like she might touch him, only to pull them away. "I'm so sorry."

"Yeah, everybody was sorry." He couldn't meet Kira's gaze, instead focusing on the scratched tabletop. "I came into my powers when I was fifteen. My mom, she was amazing. She didn't get scared of my powers, she didn't freak out when I healed the old guy who lived next door to us. I freaked, but she told me I was special, and I should be proud of what I could do. Somehow, she found out about a research project in California at a place called ALI. They wanted to study psychic phenomena. My mom thought maybe they could help me cope with my powers. Edward McLean ran Project Outreach back then, and he gave my mom a job so we could afford to move."

Though he avoided her gaze, he sensed Kira's attention on him. It affected him like physical contact, like she'd laid her soft hands on him.

"Something happened at ALI, didn't it?" she asked.

"It was great at first. I met David and Grace there, and I got more comfortable with my healing power." He shifted in his seat, suddenly uncomfortable. "A year after we moved to California, my mom died. I was a mess, but David and Grace helped me through it. I moved into a suite at ALI since I had nowhere else to go. Six months earlier, a company called Digital Prognostics had bought ALI, but I didn't realize things were changing. I hadn't spent much time in the facility at that point. I mostly talked to Edward and Grace, plus her parents who were scientists like Edward. We would meet at the house where my mom and I lived. After Mom died, things got way worse."

Nausea swelled in his gut, his gorge surging high in his throat as he recalled those months after the accident. Edward and Grace's parents, Christine and Mark Powell, hadn't realized what was going on at first. Most of ALI's scientists were let go and replaced with people handpicked by Digital Prognostics, but the Powells and Edward were kept on as managers who had little involvement with the psychics living at the facility. The new scientists hid their increasingly invasive techniques from their supposed bosses, Grace's family. They realized the truth only when Karl Tesler came on board two months later, and everything went to hell in the most literal way.

Sean explained all of this to Kira in a voice devoid of emotion despite the pain and fear swirling inside him. He stopped short of delving into the torture, and Kira noticed his reticence.

"You can tell me what happened to you there," she said. "Please."

He palpated the partially healed cuts on his arm one by one, a reminder of the latest tragedy, the one that left David in a coma. His chest grew heavy, weighed down by memories of yesterday and other days much further in the past.

"Grace's parents died two months after that," he said. "Another car accident. This one was caused by Jackson Tennant, and it was not an accident at all. They'd discovered what the lead scientist, Tesler, and his buddies were up to and vowed to stop them. JT made sure they never could."

"JT?"

"That's what Jackson Tennant liked to be called."

"Do you think, um…" Kira squinted her face, clearly loath to ask her question.

"Spit it out."

She bit her upper lip. "Do you think JT or someone else at ALI might've caused your mom's accident?"

"I saw it happen. She lost control."

"How did JT cause the accident that killed Grace's parents?"

Sean scratched at one of his cuts. "He took a serum he'd concocted that brought out latent powers in people who didn't have them otherwise. It could also enhance existing powers, but he didn't have any without the serum. He traveled to the Powells, in the psychic sense, and used telekinesis to flip their car end over end."

"Well, if he could do that..."

Maybe he or someone in his cadre might've caused the accident that took Sean's mom away from him. The revelation rushed through him on a tide of tingling cold. If someone had killed his mom—

"No," he snarled. "It was an accident."

Kira raised her palms. "Okay, take it easy. I was just thinking out loud."

"Keep your thoughts to yourself." He scrubbed both palms over his face. "I'm sorry. I don't like to talk about the accident."

"I get that, I do." She hesitated before saying, "You haven't told me what Tesler and his cohorts did to you."

He had to tell her. She needed to know because everything that went down at ALI influenced him to this day. "When Tesler and Xavier Waldron took control of ALI, they stopped pretending it was a benevolent research facility. They turned Project Outreach into a nightmare. Torture was their favorite tool, and later, drugs came into the picture. I was—" Sean gulped but couldn't dislodge the scratchy, sharp rock in his throat. Maybe saying it out loud would be cathartic, but he doubted it. "They cut me. Burned me. Beat me. Whatever it took to make me do whatever they wanted. I remember the drugs more than the torture, though. It was like fire scorching my veins, melting my brain, and I'd convulse until my body throbbed with a kind of agony I can't describe."

He felt Kira's attention on him, sensed her compassion even through his mental shields. Staring down at the tabletop, at the scrapes in the fake-wood vinyl surface, gave him something to focus on besides the memories. Not that it helped much. He followed the jagged line of the deepest scratch. It reminded him of lightning.

"Oh God," Kira said. "That's—I can't even imagine what that was like for you."

No one could imagine it. No one who hadn't lived through it.

"I screamed," he said, "until my throat was scorched raw and I couldn't talk anymore. I cried until my eyes were swollen shut. I fought the restraints on the chair they strapped me to until my wrists were bloody." He lowered his hands, forcing himself to meet Kira's wide-eyed gaze. "But that wasn't the worst part. Torture seemed like a walk in the park compared to finding out the truth about my family."

She kept watching him, her big eyes locked onto his.

He sank down in his chair. "Karl Tesler was my grandfather."

CHAPTER TEN

"HE WAS WHAT?" KIRA ASKED, HER VOICE A BREATHLESS WHISPER. SHE couldn't believe what Sean had said, figured she must've misheard him. Her heart ached for him, for everything he'd been through, and she'd begun to understand why he behaved the way he had yesterday when they first met. She wasn't excusing him for kidnapping her, but his past gave her an idea of why he'd snapped.

Any victim of torture would suffer from PTSD. A man tortured by his own grandfather…She couldn't comprehend the damage that would do to a person's psyche.

"Karl Tesler," Sean said, sounding weary and angry at the same time, "was my grandfather. My mother's father. I knew she'd run away from home after her mom killed herself, but I had no idea her father had any involvement in psychic research. After Grace and David got hold of ALI's files, I found out some other stuff too. Like that my mom had known dear old Gramps wanted to experiment on me. He'd known I might have powers because my grandmother had them. My mom never did. She took me to ALI because she believed Christine and Mark Powell would keep me safe, and they helped her hide from her father, giving her a house owned by ALI and a job too. Tesler tracked her down right before she died. JT told him where we were. He knew because he owned ALI by that point. I don't know what my mom and Tesler talked about. All I know is she died a week later."

"And your father?"

"Told you, I never knew him. Never knew his name or anything. Mom never liked to talk about him."

"God, Sean. What you went through…" She had no words adequate to describe it or to express her sympathy. He probably wouldn't like sympathy, anyway. "Is this the reason you're afraid to use your powers? Because of being tortured?"

"No, that's why I don't trust people. Except for Grace and David and Edward." He squirmed in his chair, his face pinching. "I've been blocking my powers for two months. It's because—because something happened."

Kira studied his face, the bleakness in his eyes, and another statement he'd made came back to her. "You said once you would never hurt another woman. What did you mean by that?"

"Nothing."

"Sean—"

"Not talking about it. Understand?"

"I get that you don't want to," she said, "but you have to. Stuck together, remember? Anything that affects your powers and your psyche might get us both in trouble if you keep holding it all in. You need to tell me, please."

Sean levered his body out of the chair and wandered to the window, lifting the edge of the curtain away from the wall to peek outside. After a moment, he shambled to the bed and flumped onto it, feet on the floor, slumped forward to stare at the carpeting. "There was a girl. Bree Johnson. We'd been dating for three months and, uh, sleeping together. I decided to tell her about my powers, and she seemed cool with it. At first."

Kira didn't move, still cross-legged in her chair, afraid if she budged at all or said anything he might stop talking. Whatever he was about to say, she sensed it would be important.

He ran a hand over his face, but with his head downcast, she couldn't make out his expression. When he spoke, his voice was a monotone.

"One night," Sean said, "she told me she wanted to experience my powers. Said I shouldn't hold them back while we made love, she wanted to feel it. I warned her I'd never had empathic sex before, and I didn't know what might happen. She swore she could handle it, practically begged me to show her what I can do. We got naked and started kissing in bed. Things were progressing, and then..."

His shoulders bunched. He grasped his forehead in both hands but didn't speak.

Reluctantly, Kira pushed a little. "What, Sean? What happened with Bree?"

Forehead still in his hands, he continued in that unsettling monotone as if keeping a tight rein on his emotions deadened his voice. "At first, she liked it. The exchange of our emotions and sensations, it was intense, but she liked it. Suddenly, she got agitated. I thought she was getting, uh, more excited. Then she started pounding on my chest, shouting at me to stop. I did, but she was still freaked. Kept thrashing and screaming that she didn't want this and somehow I'd made her do it, but she didn't want it. I didn't get what she meant until she screamed I was raping her. I would never force a girl to—" His voice cracked, his hands trembled. "She jumped up and started grabbing her clothes to pull them on, but she was shaking so bad she kept dropping things. I tried to help her, but she just kept hitting me. I said I'm sorry, I didn't mean to hurt her, and besides, she'd wanted to feel my powers, hadn't she? I begged her to calm down and talk about this. She swore at me, punched me in the face, and told me—she said—"

He thrust his shaking hands into his hair, his head bowed so far it ducked between his knees.

Kira couldn't stop herself. She flew out of the chair to crouch before him, her hands on his knees. "Sean, what are you saying? What did she think you did to her?"

He sucked in a deep breath, and as it blustered out of him, he responded in that monotone voice. "Bree said after the way I'd just violated her mind she had no idea if she'd ever really liked me in the first place. Maybe I'd made her believe she did. After she left, I realized I couldn't swear I hadn't done what she said. I didn't mean to do it, but I might've accidentally used my empathic powers to force-feed her my feelings. I wanted her from the moment I saw her. I thought she liked me, but what if she never really had?"

"No, Sean, you wouldn't do that. Not even by accident."

"You don't know that, not for sure." He lifted his head, his gaze flinty, his upper lip twitching. "My grandfather was a monster. Maybe I am too."

Her throat had gone thick. She had no clue what to say to his revelations, but she could not believe he'd been able to influence a girl strongly enough to make her have sex with him when she didn't want to, when she didn't even like him. The girl had panicked when she experienced his empathic power. Most people would. Kira doubted Sean had told Bree about his horrific past, and so the girl hadn't realized she needed to be careful with him. She'd wounded him more deeply than ever.

Without any conscious intent, Kira took Sean's face in her hands. "Maybe you projected some of your feelings into her mind, but I don't believe you made her feel all of that. She must've liked you, must've been attracted to you. She panicked when she realized your powers are real. Hearing you tell her about them is different from feeling their direct effect. She wasn't strong enough to deal with it. Probably thought, subconsciously, psychic abilities couldn't be real."

"No. This was my fault."

She tugged his face down until their noses grazed each other. "Sean, you can't keep torturing yourself over something that was an accident."

"You don't know what you're talking about." He pushed her hands away. "Don't know what it's like to have the power to influence people's minds and not be able to control it."

"I don't know about that, you're right." She sat back on her heels. "But I know how it feels to have a power inside you that you can't control and don't understand."

He broke eye contact, rubbing his palms on his thighs.

She studied him for a moment, then said, "This is why you're repressing your powers. It's why you're afraid to go into the crossroads. You think you'll hurt someone else without meaning to."

Though he said nothing, he winced the tiniest bit.

"You can't live like this, Sean." She moved onto the bed beside him. "You have to forgive yourself."

"Can't. I'm a monster." He held up a hand to stay her response. "No point telling me I'm not. I kidnapped you, remember? I'm one screwed-up asshole."

"Yeah, you are," she said in a softly teasing tone. "But I'm beginning to understand why. You've been through hell for a lot of years, and that's bound to screw with your head."

He grunted, but his hard expression had relented somewhat.

"Thank you for telling me all of that," she said. "It couldn't have been easy, but I'm glad you shared this with me."

Although his head stayed aimed straight ahead, he rolled his eyes sideways to look at her. "How can you not want to run after what I just told you?"

"I'm not afraid of you."

He stared at her for several seconds, unmoving, unblinking. Then he squared his shoulders and aimed his bright green eyes at her. "You should be."

⁓

FOR THE REST OF THE MORNING, THEY DID MEANINGLESS THINGS THAT got them nowhere. Sean let Kira drive them to her house—her parents' house, she'd insisted on calling it—only because he had no idea where it was. After she'd changed into fresh clothes and packed an overnight bag, they headed to his apartment so he could do the same. After that, they returned to the motel. At Kira's urging, Sean tried again to get into the crossroads, but it didn't work any better this time. He was, according to her, too pent up with angst and self-loathing to make good use of his powers. He'd become useless.

Why had he told Kira about his mom? His grandfather?

I did love her once. The words slithered through his mind, an echo of a recurring dream he could never quite remember. Strapped to a chair, he recalled that part. A chair like an evil version of what dentists had in their offices. Red, raw wounds on his arms. Pain. Crying. *She loved you,* a voice would say. And then, *I did love her once.*

A nightmare, nothing more. It didn't mean a thing.

Kira offered to tell him her secrets since she'd encouraged him to spill all of his to her. Sean had told her to wait. His confessions had left him raw inside, emotionally spent. He needed a chance to regroup before she told him everything about her. Maybe he was a little afraid of what she'd say. She'd mentioned the bad guys hurt her to prove they could and would hurt her brother, though she hadn't given details. He couldn't bear to hear about it right now, not until the old wounds he'd just ripped open scabbed over again.

Selfish? Yeah, probably. He couldn't help that.

Back at the motel, he tried to teach her how to access the crossroads, but after an hour of instruction, she'd flopped onto her back on the bed and announced, "Your instruction technique bites."

"Sorry, I didn't sign up for the Psychic Teaching Skills class at college." He'd dropped onto the chair by the window. "Grace would be a lot better at this."

"Maybe your repression is affecting your ability to teach me about this stuff."

He'd slapped his palm down on the table, making it quake, and hissed, "Stop calling me repressed and pent up."

And of course, she'd rolled her eyes. "You really need to get laid."

Even now, forty-five minutes later after a silent lunch of burgers and fries, Sean still remembered the exact shade of pink her cheeks had turned when she realized what she'd blurted out. The color reminded him of the hydrangeas his mother had grown in their backyard when he was a kid. The flowers, normally white, took on a pale pink blush when the soil conditions were right. Kira's cheeks had looked like that, creamy underneath the faint blush of salmon pink.

He'd been a gentleman for once and not made a big deal about what she'd said, biting back a retort about whether she subconsciously wanted to help him out in the laying department.

Even if he wanted to, he couldn't touch her. Couldn't let her touch him. The risk of hurting her was too high. And still, he couldn't stop thinking about her curvy figure and those sweet little lips.

Perched on the edge of the bed, Sean slanted forward to rest his elbows on his thighs, hands draped over his knees. Six feet away, Kira sat ramrod straight in a chair by the window. With the thick drapes shut, the yellowish glow of the bedside lamp spilled across her features, accentuating her high cheekbones and her blue eyes, turned a deep shade of sapphire by the muted light. She stared at her purse where it slumped on the bedside table, her expression filled with morose longing.

She carried a pack of cigarettes in her purse, he knew. Because he'd rifled through her purse yesterday while she glared at him like daggers might shoot out of her eyes to stab him. When she'd been his hostage. When he'd been acting like a gigantic dick. *When did you stop being one?* his stupid brain asked. He told it to shut up.

Kira absently rubbed her wrists, and he caught sight of the faint red marks around them. He winced. He'd cinched the zip ties too tight yesterday. *Damn.* At least he'd untied her—eventually.

He shouldn't care. He didn't care. More to the point, he *couldn't* care anymore, since he'd locked down his empathic powers and his emotions. Besides, this girl had tried to blow his surrogate family to smithereens. He pinched the bridge of his nose between his fingers, squeezing his eyes shut. Trouble was, he believed Kira when she said she had no idea the device was an explosive, not just a smoke bomb. Her look of sheer horror right after the bomb went off...

Dammit. He did not care. Feeling for other people brought nothing but misery.

Whatever they'd shared earlier when he'd blabbed about his past, that didn't mean anything. Why had he told her all of that? Things he'd never told anyone. Okay, fine, he trusted her not to blow his head off with a gun or a bomb. But he would never trust himself with a woman. Never again. *Never.*

While he watched Kira, she watched her purse, bit her lower lip, and tapped her toes on the ancient carpeting. She heaved in a breath, and her shapely breasts lifted ever so slightly. Sean shifted his weight, his pants too tight all of a sudden.

Kira wound a lock of her raven hair around her middle finger, twirling it round and round while worrying her lip.

His body ached in ways he'd never experienced before. This woman stirred his desire. So what? He could want her without...feeling for her.

She let out a long, wistful sigh, her gaze fixed on her purse.

He stifled a chuckle. "Jonesing for a smoke?"

"What?" She whipped her head toward him. "Oh. No. I quit six months ago."

"You're staring at your purse like you want to rip it apart with your teeth to get to the cigarettes."

With a snort, she twisted her mouth into a half frown.

Sean leaned back, braced with his hands on the mattress, and gave her his best suggestive smile. "Go on, suck that smoke. I don't mind."

Kira rolled her eyes. "Is everything about sex with you?"

"I was talking about smokes. Maybe you're the one with sex on the brain."

She huffed, sprang to her feet, and marched to her purse to yank open the zipper. Her dainty fingers dug inside the bag until she snagged something, her face lighting up with satisfaction as she extricated the foil-wrapped object and held it up for him to see. For a blood-scorching second, he thought it was a condom. But no. She held up a candy, sheathed in red-and-gold foil.

"This is what I wanted," she told him, chin lifted. "Whenever I resist the craving for a cigarette, I let myself have one chocolate."

As she licked her rosy lips, gaze locked on the candy, she slowly peeled the foil wrapping open, exposing the dark, decadent square of chocolate nestled inside it. With her thumb and forefinger, she plucked up the treat and slid it between her moist lips. They puckered slightly when she drew on the confection, and a little moan of pleasure escaped her.

A bolt of hot lust shot through Sean. The breath caught in his throat. He jerked forward, his attention riveted to her lips, to the way they worked in rhythmic motions as she devoured the chocolate, her eyes almost closed. He cracked open the vault door in his psyche, admitting a taste of her emotions inside him. Warm. Satiated.

Her lids fluttered open. Her eyes had gone glossy, lit by a fire within. A thread of heated desire unfurled from her, through him, snaking deep inside to tease his body and his...heart.

Sean slammed the vault door shut. *Do. Not. Care.*

But he could want. Take. Savor. He pushed up off the bed and sauntered to her. She darted her tongue out to swipe away a smear of chocolate with one languid stroke. He imagined pressing his mouth to her throat, dragging his lips down, down, down until he nuzzled his face between her breasts.

He snatched the foil wrapper from her fingers. "I can think of better ways to satisfy a craving."

CHAPTER ELEVEN

ATISFY A CRAVING?" KIRA STRUGGLED TO KEEP HER TONE EVEN, TO not expose the fact she'd gone warm and liquid in the most intimate places. How could she want Sean? He was a jerk most of the time. So what if she'd learned the reasons why. So what if he'd revealed his vulnerable side enough to make her feel oddly protective of him. He was still a jerk.

A hot one with smoldering green eyes and a body that made her want to climb all over him.

Kira ripped the candy wrapper from his fingers. "I don't need to know your ideas, and I definitely do not need to satisfy anything. I'm fine, thanks."

Never in this lifetime or whatever came after would she ever tell him she hadn't been craving a smoke. She'd been craving him.

The chocolate hadn't helped. Its rich, dark flavor reminded her of him, of their kiss last night and the way he had tasted—like sin.

He leaned in, his voice deep and sensuous. "I think you need a hit right now, but not from a cigarette."

The candy wrapper fell from her fingers, fluttering to the carpet. Her pulse accelerated, and her skin tingled.

Sean skimmed his thumb over her lips. "I'm not the only one who needs to get laid."

Breath. Hard to catch. Hard to hold in her lungs. It emerged as little panting exhalations. He was so close, too close, his firm body within an inch of hers.

He slid his hand up her cheek, diving his fingers into her hair to cradle her nape.

She angled her head back into his hand, her lips parting without her permission.

"You smell good," he rumbled, his mouth a hair's breadth from hers. "Taste good too, the way I remember it. Need to taste you again to be sure." He brushed his lips over her mouth. "Bet you'll taste like chocolate now. Sweet, with a dark undercurrent."

No breath. No thoughts. A need burgeoned inside her, searing and intoxicating.

He pressed his lips to hers tenderly.

She sagged against the dresser, her knees buckling under the weight of this lust for him.

He flicked his tongue out to tease her mouth, and she moaned low in her throat. His hand in her hair gripped her a smidgen tighter, those big fingers encompassing her nape.

Those hands. On her body. She wanted it like she'd never wanted anything, not even a cigarette.

"Sweet," he murmured against her lips.

And then he took her mouth, mashing his lips to hers while he thrust his tongue inside. She met his lashes with her own, savoring the flavor of him, the taste she couldn't quite describe, the way it erased her inhibitions and liquefied her entire body. Only the dresser and his hand on her neck held her up—until he slipped his other arm around her waist to hug her to him. She gasped into his mouth at the feel of the hard bulge in his pants.

He jerked away from her as if an electric shock had jolted him. His eyes flared wide for a split second, then narrowed to slits while his mouth compressed into a line.

She folded her arms over her chest, doing her damnedest to pretend that kiss hadn't left her breathless and confused. When she could speak in a normal voice without risk of stammering or panting, she said, "Don't glare at me. You started it."

"I know." His features relaxed a bit so he no longer seemed pissed, but he fisted his hands and veered his gaze away from her. "Shouldn't've done that."

"Because you think you don't want to be touched, right?" She just stifled a derisive snort. "That's a load of crap. You're afraid, I get it. After what happened with that girl, I can't imagine how awful that must feel. But it's clear you do want to be touched."

He gritted his teeth, slinging a sideways glare at her. "Not by you."

A spike of…something jammed into her chest. Resentment? Disappointment? She wasn't sure, but she knew one thing for certain. Hoping for any kind of intimacy with this man was a setup for disaster. Maybe he was too damaged for her, or anyone, to fix him.

Trying to save a person who didn't want saving would be the dumbest idea ever.

She stuffed her hands in her jeans pockets. Sean didn't like being this way, that much was clear. Maybe he did need someone to…What? Smack him upside the head and throttle some sense into him? She doubted anything less would make an impact.

Not saving him. Not going there.

Her cell phone rang, muffled by her purse.

She jumped, and Sean whipped his head around to nail her purse with a hard glare like the bag had committed a heinous crime. Kira tore open the zipper and dug out her phone, answering it on the fifth ring. One more ring and it would've gone to voicemail.

Before she could say hello, an all-too-familiar altered voice resonated in her ear.

"Your next assignment," the voice said, "will require travel. Go to Great Falls, Montana. Once you've arrived, we will call again with more instructions. You have three hours before we will call again, and you had better be in Great Falls by then."

"Is this another explosive device?"

"Think bigger, child. Think much bigger."

Click. The call ended.

Sean raised one brow. "What is it this time?"

"Not sure." She dropped the phone into her purse. "We have to get to Great Falls, Montana. They say they'll know when we arrive and call with more instructions. We have three hours to get there."

He cursed under his breath. "Another bomb?"

"They said to think bigger." She rubbed her chest, right over her breastbone, but the slithery feeling inside wouldn't abate. "I have a really bad feeling about this."

Sean gave a derisive huff. "Worse than when they ordered you to set off two bombs?"

"Yes. Much worse."

His expression crumbled into a kind of shock she recognized all too well from glimpsing her own face in the mirror. Every time the terrorists called with a new mission, she wore that look. She felt it in her soul. The horror of being at the mercy of lunatics bent on terrorizing the world for incomprehensible reasons.

She looked at Sean. "How do you think they'll know when we get to Montana?"

"Could be tracking our phones, or tracking us psychically."

"They can do that?"

He shrugged. "If they've got a powerful psychic on their side."

Great. Villains who commanded powerful psychics. How could she and Sean defend against that kind of spying?

"Three hours isn't much time," Sean said. He lodged one hand on his hip and scratched his head with the other. "We can't drive there fast enough, and we can't rely on commercial air travel. Topeka doesn't have any flights, I'm sure, and Kansas City is fifty miles away. Plus, I doubt they'd have a direct flight to Great Falls."

"What do you suggest we do?"

"Borrow a private jet."

THEY FOUND AMADOR AT THE HOSPITAL, IN THE WAITING ROOM, SEATed beside Grace on a cheapo couch. He held her hand with a familiarity that bristled Sean's nerves, but he said nothing because Grace's husband was in a frigging coma. She needed support, and Sean hadn't been here to give it.

But he had an idea of how to fix things.

Grace glanced up at Sean when he and Kira walked into the waiting room. Her smile was bittersweet, and her eyes were red.

"Hey," Sean said, parking his butt on the squat table in front of her. "How are you doing?"

She lifted one shoulder in a weak shrug. "I can't help him. It stinks."

The resentment in her tone told him it way more than stank. The way her voice cracked a little told him she was fighting to stay calm and think positive.

Sean took hold of her free hand, the one not suffocated in Amador's palm. "I've got an idea about that. I want to heal David."

"No," she said slowly, biting her lip and shaking her head once, "We've been through this already. I can't let you try. Your powers have been off for a while now, and besides, healing David might drain you to the point of sickness. I won't let that happen."

The decisive edge in her voice told him the old Grace was still in there. The stubborn woman who'd traveled thousands of miles to rescue her soul mate, braving murderous bad guys and the harsh desert to get to him.

"Listen, Grace," Sean began.

Amador cut him off. "Grace has made her decision. Respect it."

Oh, Sean really wanted to deck the bastard. So what if the guy had no friends or family of his own anymore? Sean had sympathized for about six months before Amador's glom-on-iness started to grate. Even Roland Wickham, Amador's right-hand man, had gotten sick of it and taken off two years ago. Amador claimed Wickham left without notice, leaving only a note to explain he was homesick for England. *Yeah, right.* Wickham had no doubt gotten weary of holding his boss's scattered wits together with his bare hands. Like anybody could manage that for long. Amador was nutty, batty, and loony all rolled up in one big ball of crackers.

Instead of decking Amador, Sean wrested Grace's hand from the other man's hold and clasped both her hands in his. Focusing on Grace—and only on Grace, despite Amador's irritated noise and the way he glowered at Sean—he said, "I've got help now."

He nodded toward Kira, who'd hung back near the doorway.

Grace glanced a Kira, then swiveled her gaze back to Sean. "I don't understand. Who is she?"

Oh crap. He'd forgotten to introduce them.

"This is Kira Magnusson," Sean told Grace. "She's a friend. The terrorists kidnapped her brother and—" Telling Grace about Kira's Bomb-Girl activities didn't seem wise right now. "And they're blackmailing her into doing what they want. We're still not sure what they really want, ultimately, but they're determined to cause trouble and hurt people. Anyway, Kira's helping me look for them."

"Okay," Grace said, sounding confused.

"The point is," Sean said, "Kira gave me a psychic assist earlier, and I think together we can get David fixed up."

Kira gave him a confused look this time, which he noticed peripherally.

Sean grasped Grace's hands more firmly and looked straight into her eyes. "Let us try. Please."

Grace gnawed on her bottom lip for a moment, the sheen of burgeoning tears in her eyes. "Okay. But if you kill yourself doing this, I'll hunt you down in the crossroads and whup your hide."

"I know." He almost smiled at her vow of retribution. Releasing her hands, he squeezed her shoulder. "It'll work."

Grace left to find a nurse and ask about taking two friends into David's room in the ICU.

Kira sidled up to Sean and muttered, "What are you doing?"

"Saving a life."

"What if we can't?"

He'd asked himself the same question, but he refused to consider failure as a possible outcome. Negative thinking had interfered with his powers before, but he couldn't allow it to interfere today, not with David's life on the line. "If we can bring Edward back from the dead, we can heal David's injuries."

"I don't think it's the same thing. Edward must not have been really dead, not yet. His heart stopped, but he didn't have wounds." She laid a hand on Sean's upper arm. "David's injuries might be too severe."

"You don't know that," Sean snapped, realizing he sounded like a jerk but not caring. He would not leave David in a coma if he had even the remotest shot at fixing his best friend. "I'll do it by myself if you're scared to help."

"I am scared, but not for myself." She squeezed his arm gently. "Grace said this could kill you. And you aren't exactly operating on all thrusters with your powers, are you?"

"Don't worry about me," he said, his voice harsh like it belonged to somebody else.

Kira withdrew her hand, her lips cinched into a tight expression. "Have it your way."

She hadn't said whether she'd help him this time.

The three of them—Sean, Kira, and Amador—waited in awkward silence for Grace to return. Amador kept giving Sean weird looks, like the guy knew something or thought he knew something about Sean but wouldn't say so. Screw Amador. They had bigger problems than one nutty guy who wanted to get in Grace's pants even while her husband lay in a coma. Sean would've loved to punch Amador for the way he'd glommed onto Grace, clearly determined to take advantage of David's absence and Grace's weakness to make a play for her. Amador needed a good beat-down.

The guy had always had a thing for Grace.

But she was devoted to David, and that pissed off Amador.

Sean knew this, despite Amador doing a bang-up job of concealing his irritation. Maybe no one else would've noticed, but Sean did. Before he'd locked up his empathic abilities, he'd sensed Amador's true feelings—and it had given him a serious case of the creeps.

Could Amador have something to do with the terrorists?

No, that was crazy. Sure, Amador was crazy, but conspiring with terrorists...

Kira poked his arm and murmured, "What's wrong? You've got that storm-cloud look on your face again."

"What?" Sean glanced down at her, noticing the slight upward curve of her lips and the sparkle in her eyes. "Not in the mood for jokes."

"I wasn't making a joke." She stretched her lips into a closed-mouth smile. "Teasing you, sure. But not joking."

"Why are you teasing me about the fact you think I look mean or whatever?"

"Decided you need more teasing to loosen you up."

He stared at her for a moment, baffled by her inappropriate humor and charmed by it at the same time. She wasn't afraid of him. Even when he'd held her hostage, she hadn't acted terrified of him. She'd razzed him then too.

"You do seem upset," Kira told him, with no humor.

Sean took hold of her arm and guided her to the farthest corner of the waiting room. He bent his head closer to hers and said, "It's Amador. Something about him is…off." Sean sighed. "More than usual."

"I don't understand. He seems genuinely concerned."

"You don't know Gabriel Amador like I do." Sean glanced at the other man, who was watching them with an oddly calculating expression. Amador noticed Sean watching him and reverted to a bland expression. Sean turned back to Kira. "I'll explain later, but trust me, Amador is not someone you want to put your trust in."

"Grace seems to trust him."

"She's got blinders on where he's concerned. Never could figure out why. Maybe she feels sorry for him." At Kira's questioning look, Sean added, "Explain later. Okay?"

She nodded.

Grace walked into the waiting room, waving for Sean and Kira to follow.

Amador got up as if he intended to go with them.

"Stay here," Sean said, meaning to sound sharp this time.

The jackass looked to Grace, clearly hoping for permission from her, but she just shrugged. "This is a delicate operation. Sean's right, you should stay here."

Something flashed on Amador's face, but it passed too swiftly for Sean to identify it. The guy sat down.

Grace led Sean and Kira through double doors that swung open for them automatically and down a corridor to the ICU. They entered David's room where he lay on the bed as motionless as a corpse. Only the faint rise and fall of his chest suggested he was alive.

Sean's chest tightened with a pang behind his ribs.

David was pale, hooked up to multiple machines. Though breathing on his own, he languished in a limbo Sean couldn't comprehend. Would he hear them if they spoke? Would he understand what they were about to do? Or did he exist somewhere beyond his body, beyond this room? The crossroads, maybe?

Sean spoke to Grace. "You said he's in there, you can feel him. Did you go to the crossroads?"

Grace shook her head. "I can feel him through our innate connection. I tried to access the crossroads, but I'm too weak to get there."

Weak with grief and pain and fear and exhaustion.

Sean clasped her hand. "We're not losing him."

Grace squeezed his hand, then let go and clamped her hands under her arms. She backed up to the wall across from the foot of the bed.

Sean approached the side of the bed and gestured for Kira to come up beside him. When she did, he slipped his hand into her palm, his fingers laced with hers. As one, they closed their fingers around each other. A current zinged through him from their joined hands.

"You ready?" he asked.

She nodded. "Let's do this."

He spread his free hand on David's chest.

Energy flowed through him, through his palm, into David's body.

Nothing happened. He sensed the energy seeping into David, but it couldn't gain enough momentum to regenerate the cells, fizzling out before it reached the most damaged parts of him.

"Dammit," Sean hissed, even as he struggled to pull in more power, to no avail.

"What is it?" Kira asked in a rough whisper.

"It's not enough. David's injuries are too severe." Sean flung his hands up to cover his face, scrubbing as if he might clear his mind that way. Healing someone whose heart had stopped due to psychic manipulation was one thing, but repairing damage caused by a very real, very physical explosion proved something else altogether. And it didn't help he'd been suppressing his powers.

My fault. The thought burst in his mind. If David didn't recover, if he died, it would be Sean's fault. He held the power to fix this but couldn't make it happen because he'd repressed his gifts. Kira was right. He was repressed.

"What can we do?" Kira asked.

"Need more power," Sean said. "We have to get into the crossroads."

CHAPTER TWELVE

HE ZEROED IN ON KIRA'S EYES, WILLING HER SHOCK AND CONFUSION to melt away. How could he expect her not to be stunned? He'd suggested doing the one thing he'd failed at yesterday and earlier today—accessing the crossroads to gather more psychic energy. He'd failed at teaching Kira to do it too. They had to try, though, because he would not run off to Montana while David lay comatose in a hospital, his spirit and his body withering away.

David had saved his life, literally and metaphorically. Sean owed him everything.

No backing out. Despite the cold knots cinching tight in his gut and the cold tension stiffening his body, he would make this happen. He would heal David. He had to.

His gaze flicked to Grace, where she hunched in the corner of the room, her haunted eyes locked on her husband's inert body.

Teeth gritted, Sean focused on David. He would fix this—for David, for Grace, and for Abby. Sean would heal David even if he had to drain every iota of energy in his body and his mind.

Even if it killed him.

"How do we do that?" Kira whispered. "I can't get there, and you said you couldn't either."

"I'm repressed, remember?" He twisted his lips in a sardonic smile. "But this is what we've got to do. Fear can be a great motivator."

"Then abject terror must be the key to accomplishing the impossible."

"Not impossible. We can do this if we both believe we can."

Her eyebrows rose a smidgen, and her lips kinked up at the corners. "You're expressing optimism? Wow, that's twice in one day."

"Don't get used to it." He clamped his hand around hers. "Follow my lead."

Kira nodded.

Sean closed his eyes—then cracked one eye open to peek at her, just to make sure she'd closed her eyes. She had, so he shut his own again. He drew in a slow, deep breath and released it gradually, willing his muscles to unwind. For Kira's benefit, he murmured, "Relax."

Her hand, enclosed in his, loosened the tiniest bit, and he sensed her relaxing into the moment, into the connection their joined hands provided. A modest current of power coursed between them, through their palms. They needed more.

Release the vault.

A frisson of anxiety slithered through him, but he'd made a vow, and he never reneged on a promise to the ones he loved. He took another deep breath and exhaled in a rush this time, shedding the anxiety like a wet dog shaking water off its body. Some of the fear lingered, until a sweet pulse of Kira-flavored energy flowed into him, triggering a memory of their kiss earlier, of her soft lips and the enticing if all-too-brief taste of her he'd enjoyed. Buoyed by the memory and the sensation of a sliver of her inside him, he let go of the fear.

The chain that had fettered his psyche crumbled away.

He soared out of his body with Kira tethered to him, flying through the dark tunnel toward a destination beyond the comprehension of the average human. They burst out into a field of stars peppered across an inky blackness. The sensation of chilled air on his skin was a phantom, he knew, his mind's way of making sense of his surroundings. Nothing physical existed here. And yet, he felt his hand around Kira's and her presence beside him. Phantoms, but he'd take them.

The stars glittered all around them, white pinpoints in the darkness.

He'd done it. He'd gotten them into the crossroads.

Something nipped at him, seeking, testing, an unseen force hungry for power.

No, not again. The same force had pushed him out last time, but he would not let it happen again. Drawing on the energy trickling into him from Kira, he shoved the hungry force away.

Free. Unfettered.

More than his astral body had broken free. For the first time in two months, he'd unleashed his powers.

And more than psychic energy pulsed down the link with Kira. He experienced her emotions, just the surface ones but enough to send a thrill racing through him. He'd really done it. He was liberated.

God, it felt good.

No time to revel in the freedom. He let his mind go blank as he floated with Kira amid the field of stars. He threw open the gates of his psyche, letting the energy inherent in the crossroads pour into him and into Kira through the connection of their hands. A sliver of fear sliced through her, he sensed it, but she let it go with a rush of heady exhilaration.

She'd never been to the crossroads before. Of course she'd be excited.

But her enthusiasm swirled through him laced with another kind of excitement. Desire. He struggled to ignore it because getting turned on wouldn't help them right now. The connection they'd forged to get this far mimicked genuine intimacy in many ways, but it wasn't intimacy. It was shared power. Shared lust. Nothing more.

When he'd absorbed enough energy, he shut off the spigot. Too much power was bad, Grace had warned him once upon a time. He trusted her assessment. Invigorated by the energy, he whisked Kira through the void of the tunnel.

He slammed back into his body with a sharp grunt.

Kira's gasp told him she'd returned too.

The power surged through them both, hot and urgent, desperate to serve a purpose.

Sean slapped his palm on David's chest. Sean's hand glowed around the edges as if the light emanated from his palm. He funneled everything he had into the act of healing, visualizing tissues and cells, commanding them to regenerate with a level of power he'd never achieved before. It scorched in his veins, ripped through his mind, sizzled on his skin even as goosebumps erupted up and down his body.

David's chest heaved once.

More energy. More. Targeting damaged cells. Rebuilding and reshaping the molecules.

Sean couldn't breathe, couldn't move, wouldn't stop the energy from performing its task. Never had he wielded so much power. Maybe the intensity of it should've unsettled him, but Kira's warm and calming aura centered him, steadied him, kept him sane.

The moment he sensed the last shred of damage had repaired itself, he yanked his hand away from David. Sean was breathing hard, his heart racing, his body alive with power. He glanced at Kira, and her eyes nearly undid him. Her pupils blown, she locked her gaze on him with her irises burning like rings of blue fire. Her lips had turned a darker pink, and a beautiful blush tinted her cheeks.

Desire. Hot. Hard. Unstoppable.

He battled against the urge to drag Kira into his arms and kiss her again like he had after healing Edward. The impulse raged stronger than before, thanks to the massive amount of energy they'd both ingested. He needed to devour her mouth, to run his hands all over her body, to meld with her in a very physical way. But he couldn't do that here in the ICU with Grace huddled in the corner and David lying unconscious on the bed.

David.

Sean ripped his hand away from Kira's, severing their link. He bent over the bed, scrutinizing David's face, searching for a sign of…anything.

David's eyes darted behind his lids. His chest rose and fell on deepening breaths. The pallor of his cheeks had given way to the faint pinkness of life.

He was alive, yes. But would he wake up?

A groan resonated in David's chest. His eyelids fluttered.

Sean stepped back, waving for Grace to come.

Just as she hurried to the bedside, David's eyes opened. He blinked rapidly, then focused his clear blue eyes on his wife—and smiled.

"Hi," he said, his voice a little hoarse.

Grace burst into tears of joy. Her trembling lips formed a lopsided smile. "Hi."

David lifted his head off the pillow, glancing around with a furrowed brow. "Why is everybody staring at me like I just came back from the dead?"

His wife flung her arms around him and kissed him—on the mouth, on the cheek, on the forehead, on the nose, anywhere she could.

Sean lodged his hands in his pants pockets. "You kinda did come back from the dead, man. You were in a coma."

David looked down at his body, the parts he could see with his wife plastered to him kissing his ear and his cheek. He raised one arm to gaze at the IV attached to it, his expression curious. Next, he took in the medical equipment around him, and the heart rate monitor measuring the beats.

Grace tore herself away from him long enough to perch her behind on the bed and seize his hands, kissing each of his knuckles in turn. Her tears had dwindled, but she still seemed vulnerable like she couldn't quite believe David was awake. She brushed her fingers over his cheek. "How do you feel?"

"Fine." He shrugged. "Like I never almost died and fell into a coma."

She kissed him full on the mouth, with tongue and everything.

Kira averted her gaze, her mouth warped with a mostly suppressed smile.

Sean looked away too, giving Grace and David a modicum of privacy. After a minute, though, he had to interrupt. Clearing his throat, he said, "Kira and I have to go."

"Kira?" David said, and he glanced at Sean's companion.

"It's a long story," Sean said. "Grace can explain. We're trying to find the bastards who made the bomb that—" *Almost killed you.* Sean's throat tightened. "The bomb at the cafe, and another one in a movie theater."

Kira waved to David. "I'm Kira Magnusson, by the way."

"Nice to meet you," David said cautiously, his confusion evident on his face. "Seems like I missed a lot."

Grace cupped his face with her palm. "I'll explain it, honey. But yeah, you missed a lot."

She gazed into his eyes, hers full of love.

Sean coughed. "I'll call you guys later, but we have to go now. Be careful. Those creeps are still out there and still want to do more havoc-wreaking."

"We'll watch our backs," David said. "You be careful too, Sean. You can't keep healing everybody without exacting a toll."

"I know." Sean rested a hand on Kira's back, guiding her toward the door. "See you guys later."

They'd see each other again if he and Kira stopped the bad guys. Otherwise…

He couldn't think about that right now.

In the waiting room, Amador was pacing with his hands linked behind his back. When he spotted Sean and Kira, he stopped moving, his expression expectant.

"David's awake," Sean said. "He's all fixed up."

Sean swore disappointment flashed across Amador's face, but he couldn't be sure. Maybe his dislike of the man made him see things that weren't there.

"I need a favor," Sean said, resisting the urge to grind his teeth. He hated asking Amador for anything, but they had to get to their destination fast. "We need to borrow your jet."

THE JET TOUCHED DOWN AT THE GREAT FALLS INTERNATIONAL AIRport thirty minutes shy of the deadline laid down by the terrorists. Kira would've loved to admire the scenery, since she'd never visited Montana before, but they weren't tourists. They were marionettes for madmen.

When Sean had asked to borrow Gabriel Amador's jet, the man had agreed without hesitation. On the plane, Sean had expressed his surprise.

"First, he tells me not to get involved," Sean had said, scratching behind his ear, "and later he tells me I'm not equipped to handle the mission. Then, he gives us his jet without any bitching or insults. I'll never understand that guy."

"Maybe you should stop trying," Kira had told him.

Sean had only grunted.

Gabriel Amador had wanted to come with them—insisted on it, actually—but Sean talked him out of the idea by reminding him Grace would still need support. She could tell Sean hated encouraging Amador to hang around Grace, but it seemed like the only tactic that would convince the man not to tag along on this mission.

The puppet master pulling their strings wouldn't like that one bit.

Sean rented them a car using a credit card Amador had given him. The card had no limit. She'd noted the way Sean's mouth tightened when Amador gave him the credit card, but he'd accepted because they had no choice. Kira didn't have any money, and Sean seemed not to either. Thanks to Amador's financial assistance, they secured a car and a motel room.

They had just walked into the room when the phone on the bedside table rang.

Both of them froze, their gazes snapping to each other.

Sean moved to grab the phone.

Kira stayed his hand with her own. "I should answer."

He nodded and sat down on the bed.

Neither of them wondered how their enemy had gotten the phone number here. No point in wondering since the villains seemed to have vast resources at their disposal.

She picked up the phone. "We're here."

"We know," the eerily calm, distorted voice said. "You are in place for your next mission. We realize this one is more complex and will require more time to accomplish, so we're granting you eighteen hours to rest and recharge your powers. We need you both at full strength."

Complex? She clutched her belly with her free hand, exchanging tense looks with Sean. Though he couldn't hear the phone conversation, he must've sensed her mounting unease. A complex mission that required eighteen hours of psychic recharging beforehand? This sounded so much worse than the two explosive devices they'd forced her to detonate.

"I want to talk to my brother," she said. Maybe it was partly a delaying tactic since she dreaded hearing the details of what they would make her and Sean do next. Mostly, though, she needed to hear Caleb's voice to know he was all right.

"We will grant your request," the voice said.

A scuffling sound followed and then Caleb spoke through the phone, his voice not altered like the kidnapper's was. "Kiki?"

She choked back a sob of relief. "Yes, baby, it's me. Are you okay?"

"Yeah, I'm okay." He sounded tired and a little depressed, but otherwise normal. "I want to go home."

"I know. Soon, I promise."

More scuffling. The unknown voice returned, distorted as usual. "That's enough."

At least she knew Caleb was still alive. How long could she keep promising him they'd be reunited soon? She had no clue if she was lying about that since she had no clue what these madmen might do next.

"Your instructions," the voice said, "will be delivered later. After you have rested and are ready for the mission. Do not attempt to thwart our plans or locate us, or your brother will be punished."

Click. The call disconnected.

Kira slapped the phone back into its cradle, biting down on her bottom lip hard.

Sean leaped up, grasping her upper arms. "What did they say to you?"

"We're supposed to rest and recharge our powers for eighteen hours, then they'll call back with instructions for our next mission." She chewed her lip. "If we try to stop their plans or find them, they'll hurt Caleb."

Kira fought the tears burning in her eyes, refusing to let them roll down her cheeks, blinking furiously to keep them at bay.

"Your brother?" Sean asked.

"He's okay." She forced herself to stop gnawing her lip, squared her shoulders, and lifted her chin. "We have to find them. Stop them. They'll hurt Caleb anyway, I'm sure of it. They'll probably kill all of us once we've done all their insane missions for them."

"No more missions." Sean's voice was gruff, but his grip on her had eased. "We've got eighteen hours to hunt them down."

She considered the terrorist's words for a moment. "Isn't it odd they gave us eighteen hours with nothing to do? They must figure we'll try to find them since they told us not to. It doesn't make sense."

"None of it makes sense. We're dealing with whackjobs."

"I know, but even crazed terrorists have an agenda."

"Yeah, terrorizing lots of people. That's the agenda." Sean frisked his hands up and down her arms. "We'll find Caleb and rescue him."

"How?"

Sean guided her to the bed, and they both sat down. The mattress creaked. The room smelled of stale cigarettes and mold, but she couldn't complain about the accommodations. People on the run didn't have the luxury of…luxury.

"I'm all Caleb has," she said. "He's sure I'll come for him. But I can't risk more lives just to save my baby brother."

Sean studied her for a long moment, his expression unreadable. "Where are your parents?"

Kira blinked at him. "What?"

"Your parents. What happened to them? Your brother's been kidnapped, but nobody called the cops about it. Nobody calls you, either. You said your parents are gone, but they're not dead."

"They're alive as far as I know." She focused on her hands, which had begun to wring themselves on her lap. "I haven't seen or heard from them in sixteen months. They took off for Uganda on a humanitarian mission. They'd never been very civic-minded before, but they needed any excuse to get as far away from home as possible. As far away from me and Caleb as possible."

"Why?"

She clamped her hands together to still their wringing. "My powers emerged when I was seventeen. My parents adjusted to the reality of psychic abilities pretty well, I thought, better than I did. I was twenty when they abandoned me and Caleb, leaving nothing but a crappy little note as explanation. The day before, everything seemed fine. I still don't understand what happened. They just…left while we were asleep."

"Jesus. I'm sorry."

The tone of his voice made her look up at him. He sounded genuinely sickened by the idea of parents forsaking their children, and his expression matched his voice. He seemed stunned, like he couldn't quite comprehend how anyone could do such a thing.

"What was your mom like?" she asked. "You said she was okay with you having powers."

"She was. I mean, she worried about me, but she never made me feel like a freak." He gazed at the window, shielded by curtains, his gaze going distant. "Mom was awesome."

"You really never met your dad?"

With a groaning sigh, he aimed a warped smile at her. "No, I never met my dad. Don't even know his name or what he looked like. Mom never wanted to talk about him, so I figured he wasn't a nice guy. Whenever I asked about my dad, she'd change the subject. I didn't push."

Kira turned toward him slightly. She couldn't imagine not knowing who her parents were. They might've turned into jerks, but at least she knew where she'd come from. "Didn't you ever want to know about your dad?"

"Sure, but I gave that up after I met my sweet old granddad." Sean laughed without humor, the sound harsh and tinged with anger. "When my gramps turned out to be a psycho scientist bent on torturing me and digging the powers out of my head, I figured I was better off not opening any more cans of family worms. One slimy, spineless bastard in the family tree was enough."

"I can't imagine finding out you're related to someone as awful as that." She watched his face, though he'd gone stoic again, retreating behind a mask to escape the horrors of his past. *Can't blame him.* "You said before that Tesler was related to your mom, right?"

"He was my mom's father. She never talked about him, and I kind of thought he was dead. Mom probably hoped he was." Sean's expression darkened. "Now he's six feet under with the maggots, where he belongs."

She studied his eyes, their green irises shimmering in the light from the bedside lamp. After learning about his family, she understood why he preferred to put on an ironclad facade and lock up his emotions—and his powers. He'd shown her glimpses of the man beneath that facade, a complex person composed partly of a teenage boy who'd lost everything and suffered more than anyone should, and partly of the adult who struggled to move on while coping with the fact he'd inadvertently tormented someone. The girl, Bree, had torn open old wounds that had never quite healed.

Kira settled her hand over his where he'd crooked his fingers into his thigh. "You worry you're like your grandfather, don't you?"

He ground his teeth, a muscle popping in his jaw. "Karl Tesler was insane."

"You are nothing like him."

Sean grunted. "You've known me for less than two days. And I kidnapped you."

"I understand why now." She slipped her fingers under his palm, clasping his cold hand. "And I forgive you."

He stopped blinking, and his features went slack. "You can't."

"After everything you've been through," she said, sidling a little closer, "you've earned a few mistakes. Besides, your best friend had just been seriously injured in an explosion I caused. We've both made big mistakes. It's time to forgive ourselves and move forward."

"You were protecting your brother. I was—"

"Protecting your family." She raised her other hand to his cheek, his skin cool against her palm. "You are not a bad man."

Their gazes had become locked, and she couldn't have looked away if she'd wanted to. The connection between them, it was more than psychic powers or traumatic experiences. They shared a pain no one else could understand. The pain of doing terrible things in the name of sparing the ones they loved, sparing the world.

She skimmed her thumb across his lips. "We do these things so no one else has to, but that doesn't mean we have to punish ourselves. We deserve happiness too."

His breathing had grown labored. She fought to catch her breath too, entranced by the green of his eyes and the way his skin seemed to be warming under her touch. Dragging her fingers down his jaw, she realized he *was* getting warmer. A matching warmth blossomed inside her, spreading out into her entire body, settling low in her belly as a delicious pressure. Her hand floated down to his chest, her fingers exploring the muscles concealed under his shirt.

"You don't want this," he said, his voice a rough whisper. "Not with me."

"Don't wreck the moment, Romeo." She gave him a playful smile. "I'm trying to seduce you."

Sean choked on a breath. "We can't. My powers—"

"Everything will be fine. Trust me."

"You can't know—"

Kira took his face in her hands and scraped her lips over his. With their mouths in contact, she murmured, "Shut up."

His lips curled into a sexy smile. "Yes, ma'am."

Both his hands landed on her back, gliding up to cover her shoulder blades.

She sagged into him, one hand trapped between their chests, the other resting on his thigh. She squeezed his leg, relishing the firmness of his thick, powerful thigh.

He plowed both hands into her hair, caging her head. "No turning back now."

"Don't want to turn back."

A sound, half growl and half groan, reverberated in his chest and tickled the stiff peaks of her nipples, crushed to his body. She gasped, her mouth falling open.

He devoured her mouth in the deepest kiss she'd ever experienced.

No turning back.

CHAPTER THIRTEEN

WHEN KIRA HAD OPENED HER MOUTH, SEAN HADN'T BEEN ABLE to stop himself from taking advantage. He'd plunged inside with abandon, savoring the sweet flavor of her, loving the way she responded with the same reckless passion that had taken hold of him. Their tongues tangled and separated, teased and glided over each other. No kiss had ever been this good.

They shouldn't be doing this, no way, but he couldn't break away from her. Touching him, getting close to him when they had clothes on, those things endangered her enough. But doing this...In a few minutes, they'd be naked on this bed together. He knew it. The last time he'd had sex, he'd tormented an innocent woman. Not on purpose, but that didn't matter. His powers had hurt her. Bree had thought she understood what she was getting into with him, with his powers, but she'd known nothing.

Kira was different. She'd experienced his powers. More than that, she'd shared them in a way more intimate than sex. They'd forged a psychic bond.

She shoved her hands under his shirt, whisking her soft, warm palms up his chest to push his shirt up over his head. They tore their mouths apart, both gasping for breath. He tossed his shirt aside, not giving a damn where it landed. They ripped each other's clothes off, alternately kissing and groping, sometimes both at the same time, until they wound up naked and sprawled across the bed at a diagonal on top of the bedspread.

He pushed up on straight arms to gaze down at the woman underneath him. Kira was gorgeous. With her pink cheeks, swollen lips, and soft eyes, she looked like an angel with a naughty streak. She'd wanted to seduce him, and holy smokes, she'd done it. He let his gaze travel down her body so he could admire her perfect breasts and the taut nipples jutting up from them, her wide hips and the gentle curve of her waist.

"You're perfect," he whispered, his tone expressing the awe that swept through him when he drank in the sight of her nude body. She was perfect. And despite knowing what he'd done to Bree, she wanted to be with him. Here. Now.

She lighted her palms on his chest and skated them up to his shoulders. "I want you. Please."

God, he wanted her too. But his powers…

As if she'd heard his thoughts, Kira cupped his face and said, "I've felt your powers before. I can handle it."

Maybe she could read his mind. They were both psychics after all.

He pressed his lips to hers, then kissed a trail down her throat and between her breasts. He paused there to draw one nipple into his mouth, suckling and flicking his tongue over the stiff peak.

She gasped and tunneled the fingers of one hand into his hair.

The scent of her arousal teased his senses. He dragged his lips down her belly, circling his tongue inside her navel, and kept going down, down, down until the hairs at the juncture of her thighs tickled his chin.

A soft moan whispered out of her as she lifted her hips.

He slid his hands between her legs, one palm on the inside of each thigh, and eased her open for him. When he caught sight of her flesh, glistening and pink, his breaths grew ragged. *Perfect.*

"Sean," she moaned, clutching at his head. "Yes, please."

Taste her. He couldn't resist the urge. Without a thought for what might happen, he gave in to the desire for her. His mouth descended on her sweet, soft flesh, and with every throaty moan from her, his exploration grew fiercer. She tasted like heaven, like everything good in the universe, like…salvation. His salvation. He tormented her nub while she thrashed under him, kept tormenting her until her breaths came quick and sharp, then he thrust a finger inside her wet sheath. Then another finger. And another. She bucked and cried out, riding his fingers to the rhythm set by his mouth on her nub.

Her body went rigid.

A hoarse cry burst out of her as her back flattened into the mattress, her fingers dug into the covers, and her body pulsated around his fingers.

She went limp, panting, her cheeks ruddy.

He raised his head. The sight of her, so soft and willing, made his chest ache. He wanted her, yeah, but he wanted more than to get off. He wanted to share everything with her.

But his powers…A cold pit congealed in his gut. His every muscle seemed to transmute into brittle steel. He couldn't do this.

She pushed up on her elbows, gazing at him with complete understanding. "It's okay. If you're not ready for this, we can stop." Her luscious mouth curled into a sexy smile. "But I'm really hoping we don't."

"I don't want to hurt you."

"You won't." She stretched out one hand to caress his cheek. "I trust you."

He swallowed against the tightness in his throat, his mouth suddenly parched. "What if I can't control it?"

She went silent for a moment, her fingertips dancing along his jaw. "Do it on purpose. Open up your empathic powers. Try it before you get too caught up in things to think about controlling yourself."

"I don't—Are you sure you want me to do that?"

"Yes, I'm sure."

He stared at her, unable to comprehend that she wanted him to invade her psyche, to steal her emotions and inject his own into her. Bree had wailed and beat him, screamed he was a rapist, kicked and clawed and—

"I'm not her," Kira said. "Psychic stuff doesn't scare me. You don't scare me. Give it a try and see how it goes."

His chest seemed to have a weight bearing down on it even though he hovered above her on hands and knees. He couldn't pull in a full breath. She wanted this. She wanted him, powers and all.

"Okay," he said shakily. "But you have to promise to tell me if anything I do makes you uncomfortable."

"I promise." She painted a cross over her heart with one slender finger.

Sean summoned all his willpower to haul in a long, slow breath and release it bit by bit. He shut his eyes for a second, then forced himself to keep breathing in a regular rhythm. *Slow and easy. Just keep breathing.* He could do this without hurting Kira. She trusted him.

He opened the vault door a crack.

Warmth stole inside him from her, the supple and sultry heat of desire. This was the surface, though, and he needed to go deeper to know for sure she could handle it. Handle him.

He pushed the door open farther.

Emotions poured into him, so many he couldn't sort them out. Sympathy. Affection. Fear for the future, tempered by excitement about the present, this moment, here with him. He let his eyes drift shut, floating on the tide of sensations from her.

"All the way," she murmured. "Let go, Sean."

He shoved the door wide open.

Kira. Warm and strong, like a summer breeze, full of life and power. Sizzling currents of electric energy danced in the metaphysical space between them, borne from the psychic powerhouse contained within her. Everything about her turned him on, from her psychic abilities to her sarcasm and especially the way she understood him so thoroughly after two days like she'd been meant to be his and he was meant to be hers. Never before had he believed in fate, but this woman made him believe.

She whimpered.

His eyes shot open. He gaped at her, terrified she was suffering because of his emotions, forced into her in a torrent.

Eyes half closed, she worshiped him with her gaze, soft and heated. Her breasts rose and fell on heavy breaths. A rosy flush dusted her creamy skin. She slid her tongue out to moisten her lips, their pink color having turned a dusky shade of rose.

Not terrified. Aroused.

A pulse of lust ripped through him.

She whimpered again, her neck arching, her mouth falling open.

That sound, it had nothing to do with pain. It was all pleasure.

"I can feel it," she murmured, her voice throatier than he'd ever heard it. "I can feel you. What you want. What you need." She gasped, her back bowing. "I need it too."

He hadn't even touched her, and she seemed about to come.

But he had touched her. With his mind. With his emotions.

Her desire pulsated through him, hot and liquid, irresistible.

She spread her thighs, bending her knees just a little.

An invitation.

How many times had he fantasized about a woman wanting him this way? A heady rush swept through him until cold reality crashed down around him.

Sean dropped his head. "I don't have a condom."

Kira placed one finger under his chin and urged him to look up at her. "I'm on the pill. We can skip the condom this one time. And honestly, if you don't do something right now I'm going to lose my mind."

"Can't have that," he said with a smirk, though underneath the humor he experienced a pang of something else. Something way more intimate. It felt like tenderness.

She latched one leg around his hip, tugging lightly, all but begging him to take her.

And at that moment, every last shred of the fear vaporized.

He plunged into her fast and hard, driving deep inside her hot, slick sheath. He plowed in and out, lost to the sensation of her flesh around him and the drugging scent of her desire, the little noises she made that drove him wild, the vision of her breasts jostling with every inward stroke. She locked both legs around him, offering up her body for the taking. And he took her. With swift, strong thrusts that had her moaning and clutching at his shoulders. He pushed deeper, as deep as he could possibly go, desperate to meld with her in every way while their powers surged inside them, between them, an indescribable ebb and flow. He could no longer distinguish his powers from hers, his needs from hers, and that thought should've unnerved him. Instead, it amped up his lust until the world telescoped down to the two of them on this bed, bodies entwined, powers entwined, and he couldn't hold back anymore. He pounded into her with a relentless need, bouncing her body off the mattress with every wild thrust.

The bed creaked and thumped on the floor. Their bodies slapped together. The sounds they made filled the room, mingling until he couldn't tell which cries were hers and which were his. They had joined completely, as one in their pleasure and their powers.

Energy coursed through him. Tingling, electric energy.

She dug her nails into his shoulders, squeezing her eyes shut as her mouth opened wide on a cry of pure ecstasy. Her body clenched around him, wave after wave of her pleasure, and he lost it. He spilled himself inside her until he couldn't give any more, his shouts echoing in the room.

He collapsed onto the bed beside her, tugging her close, tucked under his arm. Their bodies were slicked with sweat, and the scent of sex permeated the room.

"Wow," she said between panting breaths. "That was…"

She shook her head as if she couldn't find a word to describe it.

"Yeah," he said, not even trying to describe the experience. "It was."

"I wish we could stay like this forever, cocooned in our own little world." She draped an arm over his chest, snuggling into him. "But we can't."

"No, we can't." He kissed the top of her head, inhaling the perfume of her shampoo mixed with the smell of sweat. "We have to find the terrorists."

"How?"

"In the crossroads."

***

KIRA DREW FIGURE-EIGHTS ON SEAN'S CHEST WITH HER INDEX FINger, loving the feel of his muscles and his smooth skin. This body had just taken her to the heights of pleasure, delivering more satisfaction than she'd ever known in her life. She wanted him to make love to her again, not remind her of the looming threat of unknown terrorist acts and the fact the world's fate rested in their hands.

Make love? She didn't love him. Not yet, anyway.

She gave herself a mental eye roll. Sure, that was the part of her thoughts she ought to ponder deeply right now. Sex. Not whatever horrible things the bad guys would make them do next.

He nuzzled her hair.

A pang ached in her chest, and she couldn't prevent herself from saying, "I like you, Sean."

With his face in her hair, his chuckle was somewhat muffled. "I like you too, Kira."

"Don't laugh. Yesterday, you said we don't like each other. So, I thought I should make it clear." She pressed her lips to his chest, then dragged them to his collarbone, peeking up at him through her lashes. "I like you now."

"Message received." Humor glinted in his eyes and twitched his lips, making him seem younger, not burdened by guilt and fear. "I've decided I'll put up with you."

She slapped his chest. "You can't take back saying you like me."

"Not taking it back." His expression turned serious, putting an end to their playful exchange. "I don't get what these terrorists want. They instigated two explosions and didn't take responsibility for them. Now, they want us to wait around for a day. It doesn't make sense."

"I told you that earlier." She kept a hand on his chest, unwilling to give up the physical connection yet. "What if they're not terrorists? What if they have some other purpose besides scaring everybody?"

He threaded his fingers through her hair, teasing her scalp. "Like what?"

"I don't know." She chewed on the inside of her cheek. "Maybe it's got more to do with us. Our powers."

"Your powers, you mean. They had no idea I'd be at the cafe."

"Are you sure?"

He combed her hair with his fingers. "Right after it happened, I thought maybe the attack was aimed at me and David. Doesn't make sense, though. Nobody could've known we'd be there. David showed up at my apartment that day and practically abducted me to that restaurant. His version of an intervention. He picked the cafe because he drove past it on his way to my place. None of it was planned."

"But we're dealing with psychics. One of them must've caused Edward's heart attack." She sat up, propped on one elbow. "Maybe they've got somebody who can see the future or track people like GPS."

"Maybe. The only way to find out is to find them—in the crossroads."

"Together? You and me?"

"No, I thought I'd get a dog to go with me." He tucked his hands under his head. "Yeah, with you. Unless it's too scary."

"The crossroads doesn't scare me. Lunatics with murky plans do." She shoved a hand through her hair, and her breasts jiggled, attracting Sean's attention. Though his lustful gaze triggered a new ache between her thighs, she told him, "We better get a move on if we're going to hunt down these crazies."

For the first time since they'd met, he hit her with a genuine smile. "I'd rather lie here and admire your tits, the way they wiggle when you move your arms, but you're right. We have to do this."

They got up and got dressed without saying a word to each other.

Sean patted her butt through her jeans. "Shame to cover up this body."

"Ticking clock, remember?"

"Yeah, thanks for the reminder. I almost forgot."

The sardonic tone in his voice assured her he hadn't forgotten anything.

She sat down on the bed, her feet on the floor, and Sean settled onto the mattress beside her. The lamplight caught his hair in a different way, highlighting the paler roots. She couldn't resist whisking her fingers through his hair to feel its sleekness against her skin, the way she had when he'd ducked his head between her legs earlier. But then those roots caught her attention again, and thoughts of being naked with him gave way to a question.

"Do you dye your hair?" she asked, spreading her fingers to expose the lighter roots. "Is your hair actually red?"

He flinched away from her touch. "Yeah, it's red. So what?"

"Why did you change the color?"

"Brown suits me better." He leaned in to graze his lips over her cheek. "The color of dirt, and you know how I like to get dirty."

Despite his sultry tone, she sensed the tension in him. He didn't want to talk about his hair color for some reason, but her intuition told her this topic was important.

She captured his face in her hands, spearing him with her gaze. "Why change your hair color?"

He scowled, but only for a moment before he sighed with a resignation that slackened his features. "My grandfather had red hair the same color as mine."

"This would be the grandfather who, um…"

Sean's lip curled. "The sweet old guy who tortured me for months and months. Yeah, I inherited my hair color from him. My mom had strawberry-blonde hair, but I inherited the full-on flame red from dear old Gramps."

That explained so much, more than she could comprehend right now.

He combed his fingers through her hair, so tenderly she couldn't help sighing with contentment.

"You said the kidnappers hurt you," he said. "But you've never seen them. What did they do?"

"Tossed a cannister of poison gas into my house. My parents' house, I mean. The cannister shattered a window and landed five feet from me, already spewing gas." She tried to stay relaxed, to let his touch keep her from tensing up at the memory, but it didn't work. "It burned my eyes, my throat, my lungs. I thought I was going to die, slowly suffocating from the gas. I'd been on the phone with the kidnappers, and somehow, I managed to hold on to the phone even while I was balled up on the floor choking and gasping. The same voice I always hear told me if I wanted to live I should swallow the pill hidden in the box under the table with the palm tree lamp on it. I belly-crawled to the table and found a plastic box. I took the pill inside it. Turned out it was the antidote to the gas. They said that was the kindest death they might give my brother if I don't follow their instructions."

Sean's hand in her hair went still. "Christ, Kira…"

"I don't want to dwell on it. They made their point, end of story."

He resumed brushing her hair with his fingers. "I admire your tenacity."

"Not tenacity. I have no choice but to keep going. For Caleb."

Sean fell silent for a moment, then asked, "What went down right before your parents took off? Anything unusual?"

This was turnabout. She'd quizzed him about his family, so he got to ask her similar questions. As much as she hated talking about it, she owed him reciprocation.

She rested her cheek on his shoulder, needing his warmth to banish the chill growing inside her. "There was something. A week earlier, I got into an argument with my parents about a boy I was dating. They'd seen him getting very cozy with another girl, but I didn't want to believe it. I got so upset I sent the barbecue grill flying across the backyard. Things escalated from there."

"Escalated?"

The way Sean kept stroking her hair helped her stay calm even while she related painful events she'd never confided to anyone before. "I confronted my boyfriend. He admitted to, in his words, getting it on with girls who knew how to make a guy feel good. He said there was nothing wrong with screwing around because one girl couldn't satisfy a real man like him. He needed lots of hotties to take care of his needs."

Sean's body tensed, and he pulled his hand away. "That guy sounds like a real prick."

"Dylan was," she admitted. "I got very upset again listening to him explain about his 'needs.' This time, I sent *him* flying—across the quad on campus. Other people saw it, but they started cheering because they thought it was a stunt for one of those TV prank shows. Dylan realized I'd done it. He was really shaken up, almost freaked out, and he screamed that he wished he'd never touched a freak like me."

"That dirtbag needed a beat-down," Sean said, his voice deceptively soft and calm, though tainted with a sliver of cold anger. "What happened with your parents?"

"Dylan called to tell them what a freak their daughter is." She cuddled closer to Sean, grateful for his warmth and tenderness as the memories chilled her. "They told me he's a jerk and I'm better off without him. Honestly, they seemed okay about it. Three days later, they vanished. Took off in the middle of the night and left a note on the refrigerator. The note said they needed to get away for a while to think about things, so they'd signed up to do humanitarian work in Uganda. Caleb never even got to say goodbye to them. When I told him they'd left, he didn't cry. Just hugged me so hard for so long I thought I'd pass out from lack of oxygen."

"That's all your parents said?" He wrapped his arms around her, tucking her head under his chin. "I can't understand how anybody could do that to their own kids."

"Not everyone is as accepting as your mom," Kira said. "My parents never believed in the paranormal until I came into my powers. Maybe the Dylan incident was too much for them, the proverbial last straw. The note they left said, 'Don't hate us, we never wanted this.' That was sixteen months ago. I had to drop out of college to get a job and take care of Caleb. Every day I pray social services won't come knocking on my door. Maybe I should've reported my parents abandoned us, but I was terrified they'd take Caleb away from me. What an awesome parent I turned out to be. My brother got kidnapped by lunatics."

"Stop blaming yourself." He turned their bodies so they faced each other, his hands bracing her upper arms. "You did the best you could. And there was nothing you could've done to protect your brother from these people. They've got resources and power you couldn't fight."

Tears slid down her cheeks. "What good is telekinesis if I can't use it to save my brother?"

He swiped her tears away with his thumbs. "You couldn't stop them from taking Caleb, but you're not powerless now. You and I can find them. We will find them. We'll shut down their big plans for terrorizing the world and rescue your brother."

"You're awfully sure we can do this."

"I'm dead sure." He kissed her softly. "It's time we paid another little visit to the crossroads."

CHAPTER FOURTEEN

S EAN AND KIRA LAY ON THE BED, ON THEIR BACKS WITH THEIR clothes on, eyes closed. He took hold of her hand, twining their fingers. Unease trickled through him, but he focused on her, on the connection between them and on what they needed to do.

"This is our anchor," he said, squeezing her hand and talking like he knew what the hell he was doing. He'd never gone into the crossroads with anyone except Kira, and he'd never had any luck tracking someone this way. Neither of them had. "Don't let go no matter what happens."

"Don't let go of your hand? Or don't let go psychically?"

"Uh…" Why did she have to ask questions he didn't know the answers to? Made him feel like a moron, though he knew she didn't mean it as an insult. She genuinely wanted to know, so he told her the truth. "I'm not sure. Both, I guess. Don't break the connection, that's the important thing."

"Okay. Got it." A hint of humor colored her voice when she added, "Probably."

"We're real superheroes, aren't we? Two psychics who've got no clue what the hell we're doing."

"You know more than I do about this stuff." She bumped her shoulder into his. "I'll follow your lead."

He grumbled. "Hope I don't lead you into a big honking mess."

"Sean, you really need to start trusting yourself."

"That's a tall order." Keeping his eyes closed, he lifted her hand to kiss it. "But I trust you."

"And I trust you, so by extension, you trust yourself."

He snorted a laugh. "That's some impressive whacked-out logic."

"Thank you."

Sean lowered their linked hands to the bed again and took a deep breath. "Time to do this. Focus on Caleb. You have a connection with him, so tap into that."

"I will."

He led the way, soaring up through the dark and desolate tunnel holding on to her in the physical and metaphysical sense. The real world receded like an image in a rearview mirror while they barreled closer and closer to their destination. They popped out into the crossroads. Black emptiness, glittering with the whitest stars imaginable. A blanket of pristine, flawless points of starlight. Hovering there, unable to speak to Kira because they had no vocal cords or spinal cords or any physical form, he did his damnedest to send her a pulse of encouragement. He sensed her bearing down on a single thought, a single destination, a single human being among billions.

Caleb.

Though he had no ears to hear it, he perceived her thought. A beacon in the abyss.

Nothing happened.

Sean concentrated on her, firing one idea straight into her mind. *Try harder.*

Her irritation came through loud and clear. She tried again, and this time, he sensed the call resonating through the crossroads.

A star flared bigger, brighter. It pulsated and shimmered, calling to them.

Their astral selves couldn't resist the call. They rocketed toward the star so fast the rest of the stars blurred into elongated shapes, and the speed of their travel ripped them through the tunnel out into a blinding brightness.

Before Sean had time for his astral eyes to adjust, sharp talons of psychic energy scrabbled for a hold in his mind. Seeking, digging, demanding. Someone in the vicinity had detected an intrusion but couldn't yet zero in on the source of the breach or its nature. He slammed his mental shields down hard—around Kira and himself. How he expanded the shields for her, he had no clue. He'd wanted to cover her, and the shield obliged.

He'd given up trying to understand this stuff a long time ago. When it came to psychic abilities, a person could understand only so much. The universe seemed content to keep the rest a secret.

Beside him, now an astral body invisible to everyone except Sean, Kira cast him a surprised glance.

Yeah, he was kind of shocked this had worked too.

They stood inside a windowless room with concrete walls and carpeted floors that, he felt sure, concealed more concrete. The ceiling was barrel shaped, the side walls curving up to it while the ends of the long, narrow room had flat walls. Everything was painted gray. Furniture of the utilitarian and totally uncomfortable variety littered the space, from metal chairs and tables to laminate cupboards and cardboard boxes. At the far end of the room, a wall partitioned off a smaller space beyond. The wall reached the ceiling but left gaps at either side like ceiling-height doorways without doors.

Up against the island wall, on the other side of a low table, a little boy huddled on a puffy couch that seemed out of place in the Spartan room. The kid had his knees drawn up to his chest, arms folded over them, and his face buried against his arms. His dark hair matched Kira's.

"Caleb," she breathed as if she couldn't believe they'd found him.

When she moved in the boy's direction, Sean stayed her with a hand on her arm. "He can't see you. And we came here for answers, not a reunion."

Her lips puckered, and her eyes narrowed.

"I'm a big, mean jerk," he said. "I know. But we need to scour this place for clues, and I have no idea how long we can hold on to this remote-viewing session. Besides, even if we could let Caleb see us, he might accidentally let on we're here. He's a kid, not a grown-up used to repressing his feelings." Sean twisted his mouth into a rueful smile. "Not like me, you know."

Kira gave him an empathetic smile that made his chest hurt.

On the couch, Caleb lifted his head and sighed. No tear tracks stained his cheeks, his color was good, and he seemed more bored than terrified. The kid dropped his feet so they dangled over the couch's edge and stretched his arm out to snatch a thin paperback book from the table. A pencil was stuck between the book's pages. Sitting back, Caleb flipped the book open to the page marked by the pencil.

The book's cover said, "Crossword Puzzles for Kids."

Caleb concentrated on the page, his fingers wrapped around the pencil.

Kira gazed at her brother with a melancholy expression, squashing her lips between her teeth. Her hand seemed to float up without her consciously realizing it like she wanted to touch her brother from afar. She glanced at her hand, her eyes flew wide for a heartbeat, and she lowered her hand as she faced Sean.

"He's okay," Sean told her. "Caleb's doing crossword puzzles, so I don't think he's in danger at the moment."

"You're right," she said, casting one last glance at her brother. "Let's dig through this place."

They explored the room from one end to the other, combing through everything they could see without needing to touch it. To interact with the environment would've required manifesting, and Sean had never done that on his own. Grace had helped him do it once or twice, but he'd never managed it without the assistance of her incredible powers.

None of the cupboards contained anything more illuminating than cans of beans and packages of ramen noodles. The cardboard boxes held paper plates and plastic cups along with plastic cutlery.

Kira gestured toward the area behind the island wall. Sean headed in that direction. They discovered a ten-foot-wide space with metal file cabinets lined up down the center.

Sean cursed under his breath when he discovered the file cabinets were locked.

Kira pointed a finger at the key lock. "I could pop that for you."

"No." He couldn't help staring at the cabinet like it was a bratwurst slathered with cheese. Not being able to access the files inside made the cabinet seem like the best food he couldn't have.

"Why not?" she asked. "One little flick and—"

"Don't." He tempered his tone with a lot of effort and explained, "Unless you can break into this thing without breaking the lock, we can't risk it. Can't have our enemies figuring out we paid them a visit."

"Oh." She folded her finger into her palm. "You're right."

Even if they manifested, they couldn't breach the cabinets without leaving behind evidence of their burgling.

Kira's mouth slid into a sly smile. "What if we poke our heads inside?"

"Poke our—huh?"

She nodded toward the file cabinet. "Poke our heads inside there. Take a peek. We don't have physical bodies right now, so why can't we just—" She mimed shoving her head into the cabinet. "You know."

He stared at her, totally bewildered. This girl had the weirdest brain of anyone he'd ever met. Damn if it wasn't the hottest thing ever.

"I've never tried that," he said. "Not sure if it's possible."

She tapped her lips together several times, making a faint popping sound. Then she hiked up her shoulders and let them fall again. "I'll give it a go."

"Kira, come on, this is nuts."

Flashing him a devilish smile, she thrust her head into the metal cabinet.

She went right through the barrier—which was no barrier at all to an astral-projecting, remote-viewing, badass psychic.

Despite the fact he had no physical body here, his dick ached with a burgeoning hunger for the bizarre, brilliant, and beautiful woman who had her head stuck inside a file cabinet.

Kira pulled her hands into the cabinet too.

He couldn't stop his lip from curling. It was too weird. He couldn't do that.

Oh what the hell.

Sean dived his head into the file cabinet at the opposite end from where Kira hunched with her head and arms inside it.

The interior was lighted.

He blinked slowly, sure he must've been hallucinating. *Nope.* A tiny ball of gently flickering fire hovered between their heads, bathing the interior in a soft light reminiscent of candlelight.

A hushed exclamation rushed out of him. "What the hell?"

Kira jumped, and her head disappeared above the cabinet for a second before she ducked inside again, aiming a half scowl, half smile at him. "You scared me."

"Sorry." He pointed at the tiny fireball. "What on earth is that?"

"A light," she said, like he'd asked what that thing was attached to her neck. "I couldn't see these papers in the dark."

"You made a light?" he said, not even trying to disguise his shock. When she nodded, he asked, "How'd you do that?"

"Kinetic energy." The unspoken *duh* in her voice matched her expression. "It's my thing, you know. You've seen me create sparks. I manipulated the kinetic energy of the air molecules to make them vibrate and—" She made a growling-grunting noise. "Really, I don't know how to explain it. I just do it. End of story."

Scientific explanations never took the paranormal into account. How could any psychic explain the use of their powers?

"Never mind," Sean said. "I couldn't give you a detailed explanation of how my powers work either."

Kira resumed rifling through the hanging file folders in the cabinet. The pink tip of her tongue poked out between her teeth. She looked so adorably focused on her task that he wanted to kiss her, but he couldn't have done it even if he'd tried. No bodies, no smooching.

Later, he'd kiss her good.

She looked up at him. "Why don't you search another cabinet instead of watching me?"

Busted. "Uh, yeah. Good idea, except I don't have a little fireball for a flashlight."

Giving him an exasperated look, she rasped her index finger across the pad of her thumb. A spark ignited, swelling into a ball of fire. It clung to her fingertip. She stretched out her astral finger, offering the fireball to him.

"What am I supposed to do with that?" he asked.

"Take it." She lunged her finger closer to him.

He raised one finger near hers, gingerly accepting the fireball when she tipped her finger to roll the ball onto the tip of his finger. No heat. No burn. He turned his finger left and right, admiring the tiny light. "Not sure how I can be holding this when I don't have a body."

Kira smiled. "It's magic."

Well, he supposed psychic stuff was magic, in a way.

Sean retreated from the cabinet, found another, and dived inside. With his miniature flame poised in the air, he searched the files but uncovered nothing more informative than a bill for propane. Maybe they had a stove or a furnace powered by propane, but the fact was irrelevant. He moved to a different cabinet with no better results. Boring accounting ledgers there, and he'd never taken accounting classes so he couldn't decipher the ledgers. He doubted they contained the solution to the mystery of who was behind the kidnapping of Kira's brother and the bomb they'd made her detonate. None of the documents included an address for the bunker property.

After browsing a third cabinet, he gave up.

Kira was hunched inside the last cabinet in the row.

He strode to her and shoved his head inside the cabinet. "Got anything?"

"Zilch." Sighing, she abandoned the hanging files and pulled out of the metal box with Sean right behind her. "Guess it was too much to hope they'd leave their manifesto lying around for us to find. These files seem to be from decades ago. I think this place was a bunker for a survivalist group, and these are their records. I've seen enough receipts for freeze-dried meals to know I never want to live in a bunker. I'll let the apocalypse take me, thank you very much."

Her gaze wandered across the length of the room to her brother on the couch. He was engrossed in his puzzles. A crease tightened between her brows, right above her nose.

She worried for her brother, he knew. The kid was okay for now, but the ordeal wasn't over yet. Sean wanted to hold her but couldn't.

"Maybe there are other rooms," he said. "Hidden doors. Something."

Kira compressed her lips, her eyes glistening with the sheen of newborn tears. "Couldn't I talk to Caleb? Let him know we found him and—" She bit down on her bottom lip. "Tell him he's not alone."

"Even if you could, we can't risk it. We talked about this, remember? He's just a kid, he might slip up and tip them off to the fact we were here. We'd lose our advantage."

Though she nodded, the tears in her eyes multiplied, threatening to spill out and roll down her cheeks.

He reached for her, but his hands passed right through her astral body. To see her brother but not be able to speak to or touch him must've been a gut-wrenching torment. He knew a lot about gut-wrenching anguish, and he would never have wished it on her. She deserved better than this. Her brother deserved a normal childhood, safe and happy with his family.

But all this psychic baloney had ripped the kid's family to shreds.

Sean stalked to the wall, examining every inch of it for hidden panels. Kira joined him, exploring the walls in the opposite direction to cover more ground faster.

"Wait," she said. "Think I found something."

He hurried to her, squinting at the straight line she indicated with her finger. The line stretched up the wall, made a ninety-degree turn, continued for three feet, and shot down again at another ninety-degree juncture.

A door.

Unfortunately, it had no handle.

He shook his head at his own dumbness. Like they needed a handle.

Kira studied him with a quizzical expression. "Why do you look like you just found the secret door to El Dorado?"

He smirked and strolled right through the closed door.

When she didn't follow, he poked his head out to say, "Hurry up, slow poke."

She stepped through behind him, and they turned around to find themselves inside a gloomy room occupied by banks of electronic equipment with flashing lights and steady, glowing lights. The electronic hum of the equipment merged with the whispery hum of the ventilation system. In the center of the room, a table hunkered next to a chair that resembled the ones found in every dentist's office, except this chair featured leather straps and metal shackles.

They'd walked into Sean's worst nightmare.

"What is it?" Kira asked. "You're white as a sheet. What is this room?"

He gritted his teeth, fisting his astral hands so tight pain lanced through them, which must've meant he was clenching his actual hands just as tightly back in the motel room. The sting of his nails piercing his skin couldn't tear his attention away from the chair.

"This," he said in a hard tone he hardly recognized as his voice, "is an isolation room. It's where they torture psychics."

Chapter Fifteen

Kira gave the room a cursory inspection, moving only her eyes. Then she returned her attention to Sean. The hardening of his features and the coldness of his voice belied the pallor of his skin. This room had shaken him deeply, and she wondered if she wanted to know what had been done to him in a room like this one. He'd mentioned being cut, beaten, and burned. She wanted to know the details, but she didn't know if she could handle the information. Her heart might break.

It already ached for him, for the boy who'd been tortured by his own grandfather and for the man who feared hurting innocent people even by accident. His fears ran deep, she understood that, but she would not push him to share more than he had so far.

She moved her hand as if to touch him, but of course, she couldn't. A pain tightened the back of her throat. She longed to pull him into her arms and soothe away his angst. Unable to do that, she strived to make her voice soothing and comforting. "We can leave this room. Right now. We might not learn anything in here, anyway."

His lower lip quivered ever so slightly, but he clamped his lips together, squeezing them into a pale slash. "No. We have to look around. This room is important."

To him, for sure. She recognized that the moment they'd walked inside the isolation room.

"Okay," she said. "We'll look around."

He nodded gravely, his expression still granite-hard but his eyes haunted.

They roamed around the room examining the banks of equipment and the computer monitors recessed into them. The computers had been logged out with a password login visible on the screens. No chance of perusing their computers, then. *Damn.*

She spotted a sticky note half-hidden under a computer keyboard and leaned closer to examine it. Someone had scrawled an address on the slip of paper. Her intuition urged her to remember that address, and she'd learned to trust her instincts.

Kira reached the end of the equipment banks and spotted a well-camouflaged door there. Turning away from it, she faced Sean and froze.

He lingered in front of the chair, the one with leather straps and metal shackles—like one or the other wouldn't have been enough. What had these evil people done in this room to make psychics fight so wildly they needed two types of restraints on one chair?

A shiver rattled down her spine. She probably didn't want to know.

Had Sean been strapped into a chair like this one?

No, she didn't dare think about that.

Kira moved alongside the chair, a few feet from Sean, who kept staring at the contraption.

Sean raised a hand, hovering it over one arm of the chair, above the straps and shackles. His fingers trembled so faintly she might not have noticed if she hadn't already become intimately acquainted with his strong, steady hands.

"What is it?" she asked.

He curled his fingers into his palms. "Nothing. There's nothing here to help us."

"Let's go, then," she said. "Look for other rooms."

"Yeah." His voice was hushed and uneven. "I've had enough of this room."

The door she'd discovered a moment ago burst inward.

A group of men dressed in black uniforms stormed inside, two of the men hauling another person between them. They had their hands under their prisoner's arms. The prisoner's legs dragged along the floor, scraping across the concrete. The man's head drooped and lolled, his face concealed. The uniformed men seemed not to see Kira and Sean.

Remote viewing, remember?

Sean gestured for her to follow him toward the door to the room where Caleb was being held. They stopped a few feet from the door and observed the goings-on inside the isolation room.

The uniformed men—guards, she decided, based on their outfits and the guns strapped to their hips—hoisted their prisoner to his feet, spun him around, and shoved him into the chair. One guard strapped the man in with the leather restraints. The other guard joined his friends where they'd lined up along the equipment banks.

Four guards in total, Kira noted. Four men to transport and restrain one man?

The prisoner blinked slowly as if coming out of a trance or fighting off the effects of drugs. Streaks of gray tinged his light-brown hair, and faint wrinkles stretched out from the corners of his eyes when he squinted. Gray-tinged stubble roughened his cheeks. Dark circles discolored the skin beneath his eyes. His pale-blue irises were glassy.

The man twitched his arm, seemingly a weak attempt to shake off the restraints.

"Oh no, Nathan," the guard at his side said. "You're not getting away this time."

A slender woman strolled through the door the guards had left open to halt in front of the chair. Dressed in a pant suit and utilitarian flats, she surveyed the prisoner with her cool, detached gaze. Her blonde hair was cut short with a few locks curling over the tops of her ears. Her dark eyes gave away nothing.

She might've been beautiful if not for the icy hardness of her stare.

"Yet another escape attempt," the woman said, shaking her head. "Really, Nathan, you should've learned by now you won't get away. After all these years, how can you hold out hope? I'd be impressed if it weren't so pathetic."

The prisoner, Nathan, squeezed his eyes shut and opened them wide. The action didn't clear his gaze or, apparently, his mind.

"He's high as a kite," the guard said. "Might as well be talking to the wind."

"Give him the antidote," the woman said.

"You sure, Dr. Ferrell? You know how he gets when he's wide awake."

Dr. Ferrell shot a piercing glare at the guard. "Do as I say, Watkins. Now."

Watkins nodded, pulled an autoinjector out of his pocket, and stabbed it into the prisoner's arm.

Nathan roused swiftly, his eyes clearing and his demeanor turning attentive. He sat up straight and glanced around the room as if assessing it for the first time—or just now realizing where he was. Recognition made his jaw tighten and his gaze narrow on the blonde doctor.

"Welcome back," Ferrell said. "You were out a long time this go-round. I doubt you remember all the things you told us."

"I told you nothing," Nathan said, his voice sharp and rough and deep. "No matter what drugs you force-feed me, I will never betray my family."

"Your family?" Ferrell said with a mirthless little laugh. "Your wife is dead. And you will never see your child again."

Nathan fisted his hands, his arm muscles bulging from the intensity of his grip. "I got away once. I can do it again."

"You escaped once, briefly, a decade ago. And that was under the inauspicious supervision of Karl Tesler." Ferrell swept her gaze over the guards arrayed along the wall. "I have much better—or rather, much less moral—employees than Tesler did. Give up the fantasy, Nathan. You will never get away from me."

The prisoner lifted his chin and glowered at her.

"Defiance," she said in a mock-wistful tone. "It's charming, but it will do no good. I'm giving you one last chance to tell me what I want to know."

"Kill me. I don't care."

"You misunderstand." Ferrell sauntered up to the chair, stopping alongside it and resting her hands atop his arms. "I won't kill you. I'll kill more innocent people, and I'll keep killing them until you cooperate." She leaned in, her face inches from Nathan's, and snarled, "Give me the boy."

Nathan faced straight ahead.

"Have it your way." Ferrell raised one arm, flicked her wrist, and walked out of the room with the guards in tow. As she pulled the door shut, she said, "Enjoy solitary confinement."

The door chunked closed, indicating a powerful lock had engaged.

And then the lights went out.

Sean's voice murmured close to Kira. "Let's get out of here."

"We should help him escape."

"No. It's way too complicated, and we have a deadline. Remember?"

She turned and stepped through the darkness, through the wall, into the room where Caleb sat on the puffy sofa. He had a tablet computer in his hands now, his gaze riveted to the screen. Cartoon noises emerged from the tablet's speakers. Caleb smiled at whatever the characters on-screen were doing.

At least he wasn't suffering. She had to take solace in that.

I'll get you back, baby, whatever it takes.

What if "whatever" entailed detonating more bombs?

It wouldn't go that far. She and Sean would stop this madness before anyone else got hurt.

A wave of dizziness set her head to rocking and rolling.

"What is it?" Sean said, his voice tight with concern.

"Suddenly feel…weak."

"Power drain. We've been traveling too long. Time to get back to the motel."

Though her stomach churned at the thought of leaving Caleb alone here, she knew he was right.

Sean stepped in front of her, and together, they fled through the crossroads to slip back into their bodies. Kira stared numbly at the ceiling with its swirling pattern of plaster and dirty spots here and there. It took a minute for her brain to adjust to the change from remote-viewed world to real world. Her body felt heavy, her mouth cottony. She pushed up onto her elbows.

Beside her, Sean stretched and yawned. "Long excursion."

"What?" She sat up and studied him, surprised to find him looking so relaxed and almost refreshed. "I'm ready for a nap, and you look fresh as a daisy."

"I've had powers longer than you have. Traveling's kind of second nature."

"So, I'll get better at it? Stop feeling wiped out when I come back from—what did you call it?—an excursion."

He levered up into a sitting position, legs stretched out before him. "Yeah, you will."

Kira rubbed her arms, struck by a sudden chill. "Caleb's all alone with those people. That woman doctor, what if she's hurting Caleb the way she hurt that man, Nathan?"

Sean spread a hand on her back and caressed it in big, slow circles. "Relax, Caleb's okay. I took a little peek through my shields and felt it. He's scared, and he misses you, but nobody's hurt him."

"A peek? Through your shields? What are you talking about?"

"It's how I rein in my powers. I built a kind of mental shield to keep anybody's shit from getting into my brain or vice versa." He grimaced. "Empathic shit."

Oh, that explained a few things. "That's what I felt when we traveled. You somehow included me in your shields to keep the bad guys from sensing us."

"Yeah."

"Was it safe to take a peek? I mean, what if the psychics these terrorists are using noticed?"

"I doubt it." Sean slid off the bed and unfurled his body to full height. "It was a split second, and just a sliver of a crack in my shields."

Kira shimmied to the bed's edge, her legs dangling. "Do you think that Nathan man is the one helping them? Maybe he caused Edward's heart attack."

"Maybe." Sean rubbed his chin. "But I'm not sure that guy has powers."

"How can you tell?"

"Intuition." Sean shrugged. "Or maybe it's a wild guess. One can feel just like the other. The more important thing we learned is that Tesler was kidnapping people long before he and Jackson Tennant took over ALI. Ferrell said Tesler had been holding Nathan prisoner for at least a decade. Tesler didn't become chief mad scientist at ALI until six years ago."

"Thought Tesler only kidnapped psychics."

"So did I."

Kira gave him an exasperated look. "Doesn't that mean Nathan must have powers?"

"If I know anything about my sweet grandfather," Sean said, his gaze going flinty, "it's that he would do anything to anyone if it helped him achieve his goals. This Nathan guy has a kid. Maybe the kid has powers, and that's why Tesler took Nathan—to torture him into saying where his kid is. Ferrell seems to have picked up Tesler's research where he left off."

Kira shimmied farther forward, about to jump off the bed, but Sean held out his hands to her. When she clasped his hands, he hoisted her to her feet.

"That doesn't make sense," she said. "Ferrell talked about Nathan's son, but she also said Nathan had been a prisoner for more than a decade. Any child Nathan might've had would be a teenager, maybe even an adult, by now. How could Nathan know where his son is today when he's been a prisoner for all these years?"

"Maybe Tesler told him."

"Which makes no sense either. If Tesler knew where the kid is, why keep Nathan alive?"

Sean let out a frustrated sigh. "I don't know. I may be psychic, but I don't read minds. Gramps liked torturing people. Maybe he kept Nathan around for fun, or maybe he thought he could use the guy as leverage to get the kid to do whatever he wanted."

A chill of knowing shivered through Kira. "The way Ferrell and her gang are doing with Caleb. They took him as leverage."

"Exactly like that." Sean clasped his hands at his nape. "It's pretty obvious now we're dealing with the remnants of Tesler's research. We thought Jackson Tennant's death put an end to it, but Tesler survived him. Then we thought Tesler's death put an end to it, but somebody must've had a copy of his research. The sweet and huggable Dr. Ferrell must've gotten her mitts on it, or maybe Tesler shared his data with her. She might've been his protégé."

Too many unknowns. Too many questions they didn't know to ask.

"We know one thing we didn't know before," she said.

"Yeah, my grandfather's research is the monster that won't die, like Dracula in all those movies."

"No." Kira laid her hands on his chest, angling her head back to meet his gaze. "We know where they are."

He crimped his lips. "We know they're in a bunker, that's all."

"And we have their address." She patted his chest, smiling with what felt like a bit of smugness. She'd earned the right to crow a little. "I saw an address on the console over there. I'm sure it's the location of this property. So I memorized it."

CHAPTER SIXTEEN

HE COULD'VE KISSED HER. SERIOUSLY, HE COULD'VE DRAGGED HER into his arms and kissed her like she'd offered him the keys to Fort Knox. But he didn't. He could've hauled her down onto the bed and taken her in a frenzy like they were the last two people on the planet. But he didn't. Mostly because he'd lost the ability to move or speak.

Luckily, his voice came back after a few seconds of gaping at her. "You did what?"

"I memorized the address." She tapped her head with one finger.

"You're amazing," he said with an awestruck tone because she'd awed him at every turn. "I didn't even think of that. Didn't see any addresses, anyway."

She glided her hands up to his shoulders. "You were distracted by bad memories. That's why we're good together. I fill in when you're freaked out and vice versa."

Good together. Them. Him and her. Together.

Kira talked like they were a couple, two average people involved in a romance.

That's when it hit him like a bolt of lightning slamming into the top of his head, splitting him in two. He shouldn't be doing this with her—or anyone. He shouldn't have dragged her into his messed-up world. She didn't need him. Her powers were strong enough to get her where she needed to go to save her brother.

"I'm no good for you," he said, taking a step away from her though he wanted to pull her into his arms and never let go. "You've been amazing, and I need your help, but you get nothing from me. I'm so messed up I don't think I can ever get back to normal. Whatever 'normal' means."

"Of course you can." She moved toward him, but he held up a hand in warning. "Sean, stop it. We're in this together."

"You're strong all by yourself. Go save Caleb and that Nathan guy. I'd get in the way."

She shook her head, a small movement that conveyed more emotion than he cared to figure out. "I'm not going without you. Where is this coming from? We just had a big success with our joint excursion. Is this because of what we saw in the bunker? In the isolation room? I get that it brought up bad memories for you, but—"

"You know nothing." He suppressed a flinch at the frozen edge in his voice. "I kidnapped you, have you forgotten?"

"No, I haven't."

He expected to hear anger in her voice, but instead, she sounded…sympathetic.

Dammit, he could've handled anger. But caring was too much. Way too much.

"I am not a good person," he told her. "I kidnapped you. I tied you up. I'm not sure what I would've done to get information out of you. Don't you get it? I'm exactly like my grandfather, stopping at nothing to get what I want. I'm like that Ferrell bitch too. And like Gabriel Amador. That whackjob abducted a teenage girl and did God knows what to her until she caved and used her powers to torment Grace, all so Amador could get what he wanted. That's what I did to you."

Kira watched him, her eyes shimmering with unshed tears, but she made no move toward him. The look on her face, it bit into him like cold metal teeth.

"Don't you get it?" he hissed through clenched teeth, his body quivering from head to toe. "Once, I was Nathan. A prisoner. A test subject. I was tortured until I caved and told Tesler…I don't even know what I might've told him. And something inside me got broken, something that will never heal. I'm so fucked up I kidnapped you and vowed to myself I'd do whatever it took to find out the truth, even if that meant hurting you. I am my grandfather. I am Amador."

She said nothing, her gaze trained on him.

He jabbed a finger toward the motel-room door. "Get out of here. Go rescue your brother. But stay as far away from me as you possibly can. I will bring you down."

Blue eyes glistening, she shook her head.

With his finger still aimed at the door, he glared at her.

She exhaled a deep breath, wiped her eyes with the backs of her hands, and squared her shoulders. "No."

His jaw dropped. His arm fell to his side. "What? Were you not listening?"

"I heard everything you said." She marched up to him, her faced tilted up to his, her expression defiant. "But you are full of crap. I understand you've been through a horrific experience, and I can't imagine what that did to you. But I know you, Sean, and you are not a monster."

"You know me? We met yesterday."

"Doesn't matter. I know what kind of man you are." She captured his face in her soft, warm hands. "You never hurt me. When those zip ties scraped my wrists, you put padding under them. You let me go because you realized you'd made a mistake out of desperation and fear. I could've run, but I didn't. I chose to stay with you."

"Because you thought you needed my help. You don't."

"Yes I do." An intense certainty imbued her voice with a depth of emotion he hadn't heard from her before. She sounded resolute, like he never had been about anything. "Together, we're strong enough to stop these scumbags, and we have less than eighteen hours to do it. Now you want to abandon me? No way. You're sticking around, buster, whether you like it or not."

One corner of his mouth twitched in what felt like a smile trying to take hold but failing miserably. "Whether I like it or not? Are you planning to tie me up?"

Her sexy little mouth formed a sexy little smile. "Only if you want me to."

"Kira..." He tried to back away again, but her hands rooted him in place. "I was never this powerful before, only with you. That means the power boost is coming from you, which means you don't need me. You're as strong as Grace, maybe stronger."

"Baloney. I was never this strong before either." She hopped up onto the tips of her toes to level their gazes, and though he tried to look away, her sapphire eyes captured him. "We are powerful together."

He couldn't tear his focus away from her eyes. They'd begun to glow faintly with a lighter-blue fire, a sign she'd tapped into her powers. Though the scientists at ALI had assumed the paranormal fire in the eyes of psychics occurred only when they traveled, Sean had learned a long time ago that wasn't true. Anytime a psychic tapped into their powers, their eyes would glow, faintly if they used latent power, more strongly if they accessed the crossroads to engage their higher abilities. Kira seemed to open up her powers without thinking about it whenever she experienced strong emotions.

To experience her emotions right now...He battled the impulse to crack open his shields and let a piece of her inside. *Bad idea.* If he tasted her soul, he'd never want to stop.

"Do it," she whispered, "feel what I'm feeling. I want you to. Maybe then you'll understand why I'm not letting you run away."

He hiked up one brow. "If I do that, we'll wind up naked on that bed again."

She looped her arms around his neck, her luscious body plastered to him. "Maybe that's what you need right now. A quickie to temper your high-voltage stress."

"We can't. No time."

"That's why I said a quickie." She unhooked the button of his jeans and dragged the zipper down, then sneaked her hand inside. When he sucked in a choked gasp, she smirked. "This is therapy."

Maybe he should've said no, but his mind blanked the second her warm hand closed over his dick.

And he gave in.

KIRA GUIDED THE RENTAL CAR DOWN ROADS LEADING AWAY FROM the city and out into the wilds where fields of cultivated wheat gave way to grassy hills. They'd ditched their phones and bought a new, throwaway smartphone nobody could trace with any luck. Sean had left Amador's credit card at the motel, using what little cash he had to buy the new phone. He'd looked up the bunker's address on the "burner phone," as he'd called it, using an app to find their way.

Her suggestion for stress relief had worked like a charm, and he now smiled and joked with her, even sang along with the radio a few times. She had no illusions that she was so good in bed she'd cured him of his guilt and fear. Sex with him was hot and made more intimate by their psychic connection, but she knew sex with anybody would've relaxed him.

This guy had turned stressed-out into an Olympic sport. And he'd won the gold medal.

When he wasn't stressed, he could be so...nice.

Maybe his rough charm and sense of humor explained why she'd invited him to read her emotions. She couldn't think of a single valid reason for letting him do that because, although he'd refused to do it, she'd wanted him to do it more than she'd ever wanted anything. What would he find out if he took a peek? The possible answers should've frightened her, but she had never feared him or what he could do. Even when he'd held her hostage, she hadn't been afraid of him.

Sean brought out the phone and peered at its screen. "Got a signal. Three bars. That oughta work."

"Work for what?" she asked, easing the car around a curve in the bumpy dirt road.

"I need to call Grace and David."

"Shouldn't you leave them alone? They've been through a lot the past couple days."

"Yeah, but they've got a flash drive that used to belong to Jackson Tennant." Sean curled his hand around the phone, and she could sense a wisp of his anxiety rippling through the air between them. "I need to have Grace do a search for me in those files. To find out if Nathan what's-his-name is in the list of travelers involved in Project Outreach. Grace and David can sense when a person has powers, but I've never been very good at that. I don't think Nathan has powers, but this is the only way I know of to find out for sure if he's a psychic or just a normal guy being used as a pawn to get to his kid."

"What if he's not in the files?"

Sean shrugged. "Then we won't know for sure either way."

"Is it weird that I'm getting used to everything being a mystery?"

"You're a woman of mystery, for sure." He flashed her a mischievous smile. "And I like it."

Why did her tummy flutter whenever he smiled at her? What bothered her most was the pain in her chest she'd started to get when he looked at her that way. "Make your call, Casanova."

Sean dialed up his friends—his family, he'd called them—and played the audio through the car's stereo. When a man answered, he said, "David, I've got you on speaker with me and Kira. We—"

"Grace and Abby are gone," David said.

"What?" Sean bolted upright, his head bumping the car's roof.

Kira glanced at him, her pulse quickening, but he was staring out the windshield at nothing.

"Someone took them," David said, "They shot a cannister through the living-room window and gassed us. Some kind of knockout drug. When I woke up, Edward was here but Grace and Abby were gone."

Sean squeezed words out between his clenched teeth. "How long ago did this happen?"

"An hour. I tried to call you, but there was no answer."

"We switched phones." Sean squinted his entire face, squeezing his eyes shut for a second. "I'm sorry. This is my fault."

"It's their fault," David snarled. "The bastards who made those bombs. They did this, and you have to find them. Find Grace and Abby. Took me a while to charter a jet, but we're about to take off for Great Falls."

"Where the hell's Amador? He's got a jet."

"I don't know where he is. He's not answering his phone either."

Gabriel Amador was missing too? Something was up, for sure, Kira realized. Something bad.

"Can't you travel to Grace?" Sean asked. "Manifest and get her and Abby away from whoever took them."

"I can't." David hesitated. "My powers are gone."

Sean's eyes flared wide.

Kira pulled the car over to the side of the road.

"How is that possible?" Sean asked. "I've only ever seen it with an EM field."

"I would've felt that," David said. "Besides, I would've had to stay within the EM field for that to work. This isn't electromagnetic. I don't know what it is."

"We're going to find Grace and Abby," Sean said. "We're on our way to the bunker where these lunatics are holed up. Kira and I RV'd the place and saw her brother. I'm betting that's where they're taking Grace and Abby too."

Sean rattled off his new phone number and gave David an abridged recap of events today.

"I hate to ask this," Sean said, "but are you where you can plug into the flash drive?"

"Yes, I have it with me and I have a laptop. What do you need?"

"Search for a traveler called Nathan. Don't know his last name."

"Give me a minute."

The sound of fingers tapping keys ensued. After a moment, David said, "I'm not seeing anyone called Nathan." He fell silent for a moment, then said, "If these people have an isolation room…"

"No one's hurting them," Sean said, his dark tone saying more than his words could. "I'll make sure of it."

"I know you will," David said. "I'll call when I get to Great Falls. Be careful, Sean. Both of you be careful."

"We will." Sean disconnected the call. "Get us back on the road."

Kira steered the car back onto the dirt road, glancing at Sean while the vehicle rolled down a straight stretch. He stared out the side window, giving her a great view of the back of his head. The anxiety that had wafted out of him a few minutes ago had become a churning sea of tension between them. It swirled around her, cold and sharp, nicking her psyche. He believed he held everything inside his mental shields, and at first, she hadn't been able to perceive anything from him. She'd assumed it was because she had no empathic abilities. After learning about his shields, she'd assumed she couldn't sense anything from him because she wasn't an empath and he had barriers to protect himself.

Both times they'd made love, she felt him. The real Sean, the one he guarded closely, letting no one touch that part of him. Whether he'd meant to or not, he'd shared himself with her during their intimate encounters.

And now, she realized she could perceive his emotions—despite having no empathic powers before today. Maybe it wasn't empathic sensing. Maybe it was the intensity of their emotional bond carving out a channel between them for their powers to flow down. She had no idea, really, and asking Sean seemed like a bad idea right now. He was stressed again. And who could blame him? The villains had abducted the woman he clearly viewed as a mother figure. They'd taken her daughter too.

Sean faced forward, his expression grim. "We need to stop before we get any closer to the bunker. They might've already seen us coming, but we can't risk getting any closer. We'll RV from here."

"Is it safe to do that? What if they come grab us while we're out of our bodies?"

"Have to hope they don't."

She threw him a sidelong look. "A nice, vague answer. Totally helpful."

"Excuse me for not knowing everything. I doubt they can track us, anyway, with our burner phone."

They lapsed into silence as the car sped down the road. She decided to cut him some slack considering the circumstances. A vague answer would do for now.

"Pull over there," Sean finally said.

He pointed at a two-track road on the right. Weeds poked up between the twin trails etched by car tires.

Kira squinted at the road, slowing down as they approached it. A gate closed off the two-track with a sign on it that read "No Trespassing." She let the car roll to a stop alongside the overgrown road. "This is a driveway, not a road. Somebody might live down there."

"I'll find out." He whipped out his phone again and tapped items on the screen.

"How are you going to find out?" she asked, helpless to keep the skepticism out of her voice.

"RV." He used his thumb and forefinger to zoom in on something on his phone's screen, then tapped once. "I pulled up a satellite image of the property. Not great resolution, but good enough to get me there."

"What if the owner went to the grocery store? You might think the place is unoccupied when—"

He relaxed into his seat, his gaze going distant.

The jerk had gone on an excursion in the middle of their conversation.

Kira huffed, barring her arms over her chest and glaring out the windshield since she couldn't glare at him. Not with any effect, at least. He was out of his body, traveling through the metaphysical plane. She wanted to follow him just so she could punch him for bailing on their conversation and making a decision without asking how she felt about it.

She glanced at his vacant body. *No more sex for you, mister, no matter how uptight you get.*

In the passenger seat, Sean's body jerked. He gurgled like someone being strangled.

Her heart raced, and adrenaline spiked through her. What if the bad guys used another psychic to get to Sean in the crossroads? Was that even possible? She reached for him, about to shake the heck out of him until he came back to her, but then he went motionless.

She held motionless too, her torso twisted toward him, her hands clamped over the center console. *Please be okay, please.*

His chest heaved with a sudden, deep inhalation. He blinked rapidly, cleared his throat, and sat up straighter. "The place isn't in use. The furniture's covered with sheets and there's no electricity. The windows are covered up with shutters. It's the perfect place to hide while we RV the bunker."

She eyed him up and down, her body still twisted to face him. "Are you okay? Your body seemed to be in distress for a minute there."

"I'm peachy." He gave her a placid smile. "Everything's fine. Chill, Kira."

Chill? Peachy? She'd never heard him talk that way except in sarcasm. Granted, she'd known him for little more than a day, but she felt like she knew him pretty well. For now, she'd have to let it go.

"We have less than fourteen hours," she said, easing the car into the driveway, forced to stop at the closed gate. "What if we can't stop them in time? What if they order us to murder everyone in Great Falls or they'll kill our families?"

"Deal with that if it happens."

"Aren't you worried they'll kill us and get somebody else to do their bidding? And what about Grace and Abby? And David's lack of powers?"

He shrugged one shoulder. "One thing at a time. We can't worry about everything at once or we'll never get anything done."

Suddenly he was pragmatic. *Terrific.*

Kira waved at the gate and the conspicuous padlock holding it shut. "What about that?"

He rolled his eyes at her. "You're telekinetic, baby. Bust that thing open."

Baby. The word tripped her up for a minute while she struggled to decipher the meaning of those two syllables. Was he being sarcastic? Or was he really calling her by a pet name?

She rolled down the window, thrust her arm out, and flicked her fingers toward the padlock. It burst open, flying off its chain to plunk onto the ground.

"Good job," Sean said, hitting her with a sly smile. "Now let's go whup these dirtbags."

His abrupt switch to enthusiastic optimism left her with a gnawing, burning-acid sensation in her stomach.

"Take it easy," he said. "We've got this, baby."

Her tummy fluttered every time he called her "baby." Why did he say it? Didn't matter.

The odds were high they wouldn't survive to see tomorrow.

Chapter Seventeen

THE TIRES CRUNCHED OVER ROCKS IN THE TWO-TRACK DRIVEWAY as the car raced closer and closer to the cabin Sean knew was hidden among the trees. They would find the bunker and stop the bad guys. He knew this too, with a certainty that should've disturbed him, but he didn't care if it was irrational. He recognized the truth. He felt it in his soul.

Kira kept giving him funny looks. She didn't understand his newfound optimism.

He didn't either, but he was going with it. When he'd flown through the crossroads to remote view this property, something had rushed through him. Oh, not just anything, no. Power, warm and viscous and seductive, had flowed through his psyche and tingled down his metaphysical nerves, enlivening him, filling up his psychic energy reserves, depleted by everything he'd done today. The power had beckoned him to linger in the crossroads, to consume more and more and more fuel. Talon-like shards of energy had dug into him, pulling him back while he fought to keep moving, all the while tempted to slide back into the unknown force that craved him as much as he craved it.

Breaking away from it had taken a split second that yawned like an eternity.

In the crossroads, time seemed to have little relevance. It was a metaphysical plane, not the real world.

Twice before, he'd experienced something like that. Talons. Power. A massive source of energy reaching out for him. The first time, he'd almost given in and tapped into it to find Kira's brother—except he'd realized at the last second he might lose himself to that power. It hungered. Grace had warned him, but he'd never really thought he'd be desperate enough to consider ignoring her warnings.

But the second time the power had touched him, seeking him with its greasy talons, he'd assumed it was nothing but another psychic sensing his and Kira's intrusion into the bunker. Now, he had to wonder.

No, he didn't need to wonder about anything. He knew. The ultimate source of psychic power had tried to ensnare him again.

The Golden Power had tasted him, and it hungered for more.

His shields wouldn't keep it out forever. They'd almost crumbled when he traveled moments ago. *Be careful,* David had said. Sean had thought David meant don't get killed. But maybe he'd also meant it as a warning against giving in to the Golden Power. Sean hadn't told David about his previous encounters with it, but his friend knew enough about the Golden Power to worry as much as Grace did.

The driveway opened out into a small clearing with a log cabin situated at its center. Shutters concealed the windows.

"Park behind the house," he said. "Under the trees."

Kira obeyed without even making a snide remark about his bossiness. Unhooking her seatbelt, she asked, "What now?"

"We can either go inside or stay on the porch. Doesn't matter to me where we do this."

"On the porch." She pushed her door open. "Rather not invade someone's home."

Sean grinned. "If the owners show up and get mad, I'll just make them forget they ever saw us."

With one foot out the door, she paused to fix her unblinking gaze on him. "That's not funny. Manipulating people's minds for our convenience? I can't believe you'd even joke about that."

He was kind of surprised too, but he didn't see what was wrong with it. The owners would never know anything had happened.

Kira's mouth fell open. "You still think it's a good idea, don't you?"

Oh shit. He did. The Golden Power had infected him.

She climbed out of the car and slammed the driver's door.

Numbly, Sean clambered out of his side and jogged to catch up to Kira. She was stalking toward the covered porch and stomping up the wooden steps. He sped up and snagged her arm as she turned left to head for a wooden swing suspended from the porch ceiling at the far end.

She aimed her bleak gaze at him.

A shiver sidled up his spine, rousing every fine hair on his body.

"I'm sorry," he said, releasing her arm. "I think, uh, something's happening to me. Something not good."

"Whatever it is, it started when you traveled to check out this place."

"Yeah." He shoved a hand into his hair, dragging it down to his nape. "I think maybe the Golden Power got inside me. A little bit."

"Inside you?" She leaned back a touch like she wanted to back away but wasn't sure he'd let her. "The way you described this Golden Power, it sounds like pure evil. You called it a living, breathing, ravenous energy that nearly destroyed Grace."

"I said it feels like that. It's energy, pure and simple, which means I can control it."

"Do you even realize how crazy you sound?"

"Sure, but—" He cut himself off because he'd been about to defend the Golden Power, to claim it didn't feel that bad inside him and maybe they could use it to their advantage. "Jesus, I'm poisoned with it."

"Shake it off."

"Not sure I can."

"I'm sure." She hesitated, her mouth tight, then marched up to him and slanted her head back to meet his gaze. "You are strong and good. You can shake off this poisonous power. Do it, Sean. Do it quick before the Golden Power gets too deep inside you."

He needed to do it. Wanted to do it. But he could think of only one way to burn out the infection.

Get this crap out of you by any means necessary.

"Dammit," he hissed.

Sean hauled Kira into him and crushed his mouth to hers.

A riot of sensations flooded over him. The warmth of her lips. The softness of her skin. The womanly scent of her that enveloped him. The heat of desire, hers mingling with his. A sweet, gentle feeling of...belonging. The sensation swelled in his chest, a blooming warmth that spread outward into his entire body while the soft yet solid core of it remained rooted in his chest, over his heart.

In his heart.

His pulse sped up at the realization, though he couldn't comprehend what it meant, not consciously. He slipped his tongue inside her mouth, reveling in the taste of her, the slick softness of her tongue as she answered his movements with her own. She opened wider for him, and he took more, took as much as she would give, drowning in the pleasure of their kiss.

The sliver of oily power, shaved off the ultimate source of psychic energy, crumbled away in the presence of her.

Sean broke the kiss, breathing hard, but couldn't make himself let go of her or pull back. Their mouths lingered a hair's breadth apart. She gazed up at him with a dazed expression, her blue irises burning with a preternatural fire and the pupils large and black, a door to the unknown recesses of her soul, a place he'd gladly dive into without reservation.

A lazy smile curved her kiss-swollen lips. "You're looking at me like I'm the answer to your prayers."

You are, he thought but couldn't manage to say. His voice wouldn't cooperate. That he wanted to say those words, that he understood the truth of them deep in his soul, raked a shiver down his spine. Not a chill. Not really hot, either. The shiver embodied something in between, something indescribable.

He brushed his fingertips down her cheek, awed by this incredible woman who, for some reason he couldn't comprehend, wanted him. Trusted him. Saved him.

"It's gone," he finally said, his voice rough. "The sliver of the Golden Power that got wedged inside me. It's gone."

She'd gotten inside him and obliterated that sliver. Had his shields popped a leak? The thought spiked cold through him until he took a second to inspect his mental vault and realized it was intact. He hadn't slipped up. She had penetrated his shields because he'd let her inside them, expanding them to protect her. And because she could get to him when no one else could. His surrogate family, Grace and David, they'd tried to get through to him, but he hadn't listened. Then Kira blasted into his life, and he couldn't ignore her.

More than her powers got to him. She made him feel again, whether he'd wanted to or not.

He hadn't wanted to, but now, he couldn't imagine not feeling this way.

She smiled again, her eyes sparkling. "I'm glad it's gone. You don't need that nasty power to get the job done. We can do it together."

He nodded, because he couldn't figure out how to explain what she'd done to him—or how much he needed it. Needed her.

Kira touched her lips to his, the kiss feather-light and achingly sweet.

"It's time," he said. "Let's take down those bastards."

A FIELD OF INKY DARKNESS SURROUNDED THEM, SPRINKLED WITH white stars, pinpoints that marked someone or someplace within the universe. Kira hung suspended in the crossroads with Sean, unable to see him but sensing him close by along with the strange feeling he was holding her hand. In the real world, they both sat on the porch swing of a stranger's house, eyes closed and hands linked. Here in the metaphysical world, they were joined in a different and far more intimate way.

Their powers had become one.

She sensed it but couldn't explain the feeling. Connection. Belonging. Even those words failed to describe it.

A star pulsed, and they rocketed toward it.

Down the tunnel they sped, bursting out into a dimly lit space.

Their astral bodies had landed inside the bunker in the room where they'd found Caleb last time. Now, the barrel-roofed space stood vacant.

A chill scraped along her nerves. *Something's off,* her intuition warned, but she had no idea what precisely she'd detected. Not a smell, not a sound, not a physical sensation.

"You feel it," Sean said, "don't you?"

She nodded. "Not sure what *it* is, though."

"For me, it's a feeling. Kind of dark and squiggly, cold but spiked with heat."

Yes, that described what she was experiencing rather well. Realization tingled through her. "I know what it is."

He glanced at her, a question in his eyes.

She swallowed against a lump in her throat. "Foreboding."

"Yeah, you're right." He assumed a posture and an expression of acute alertness as if observing and analyzing everything. "I'd say it's more like impending doom."

"That's what happens if we fail. Let's not do that."

He gave a sharp, decisive nod.

Then he took hold of her astral hand—would she ever get used to having no body but seeming to have a body at the same time?—and guided her toward the door to the isolation room. He ducked his head through the door just enough to peek inside.

"Nobody in there," he said.

They checked the file-cabinet area but found nothing there either.

"Must be another door," she said. "One we missed the first time."

Sean led her around the room's periphery, but they discovered no other entrances or exits. When they circled back around to the isolation-room door, Sean glanced at it, glanced away, then focused on it again and swallowed visibly.

He exhaled a long breath through his parted lips. "Guess it's through there, then."

Anxiety rolled off him in psychic waves.

She squeezed his hand. "We could go through one of the walls and see what's on the other side. We don't have bodies after all. Walls don't limit us."

"Might be solid rock on the other side, or solid dirt." He shook his head. "Flailing around blindly isn't the answer. The most expedient method is to follow the doors we can see."

He was right, of course, but she knew he didn't want to go into the isolation room. Her heart hurt for him, for what he'd endured in the past and for what he had to do now. She admired his tenacity in going through with this, despite his fears. He was brave and selfless, not at all the arrogant jerk she'd taken him for when they first met.

In her defense, he had been kidnapping her at the time.

Bygones. She understood him now, understood his motivations and fears.

They marched through the closed door into the isolation room. Lights flashed on the equipment banks. Hard drives whirred. A chilly draft wafted over them from the ventilation system. On the opposite side of the room, a door hung open.

She flashed back to the guards dragging Nathan through that door. That could've been her brother. It still might be.

"Let's go," Sean said, and they hurried through the other door.

It took them into a corridor with cracked and worn linoleum floors, gray walls, and bare white bulbs affixed to the ceiling at regular intervals. The odor of disinfectant permeated the space.

She tried not to think about why they'd needed to disinfect the corridor.

Head turning right and left, Sean screwed up his mouth. "Which way?"

"Take a guess. Let your intuition guide you."

"Maybe we should listen to yours, not mine."

She exhaled a frustrated noise. "Fine. This way."

With her hand around his, she headed left down the corridor. No doors except the one to the isolation room. No signs indicating…anything. Had she really expected a literal sign? Red-painted letters with a big red arrow next to them announcing "bad guys this-a-way"?

Maybe not an actual sign. But a psychic one…

Kira halted.

Sean gave her a confused look.

"Is there a way," she said, "for us to look around and see if anybody's here? And if so, where they are?"

"Grace can do that. I tried, but I couldn't pull it off."

"Let's try now."

"We're not Grace."

Kira growled in frustration this time. "Jeez, you really have an inferiority complex about Grace, don't you? We've got the power of two psychics to work with. If she could do it alone, we can do it together for sure."

One side of his mouth kicked up. "You're a real can-do person, aren't you?"

"Better than being a doomsayer." She raised her eyebrows. "You were all 'la-dee-da, everything's cool' when you had that piece of the Golden Power influencing you. If I'd suggested this then, you would've jumped at the chance. Probably would've fist-pumped and told me 'we are the awesomest and we can do anything,' but now you're back to thinking Grace is the only one who can do anything."

"Awesomest?" He shook his head. "I would never say that. I might say 'we rock.' I wouldn't fist-pump either."

"Not the point." She took his hands and looked straight into his eyes. "Help me create psychic radar."

"If we're looking for people, it'd be more like thermal imaging."

She threw her head back and growled again.

He chuckled softly. "Let's do this."

Their gazes locked, and power sizzled between them. She focused on the task, creating a visual means of detecting human bodies, zeroing her psychic senses in on the idea like a laser sighting in on a target. Sean's eyes glowed bright green, rims of fire around his dark, shrinking pupils. In those ever-narrowing disks of blackness, she spied a reflection of her own eyes blazing blue.

Energy poured into them from the crossroads, not the bad kind, but the good and necessary kind that fueled their powers. They hadn't traveled back to the crossroads, but she felt the latent connection to that place like a power line funneling electricity. This line surged with psychic energy, imbuing them both with what they needed to accomplish this feat.

Find human bodies. Living, human bodies, she amended.

No, she did not want to find the corpses of innocent people these villains had murdered.

Something shifted inside her like a switch flicked to the "on" position. She tore her gaze away from Sean to scan the corridor.

Everything looked different. Walls came through as dark slabs, and though they stayed in focus, with a tiny release of power she could peer through the walls and then zoom back out to see them again. She noted pipes in the walls and shimmering white lines that must've been electric wires as well as the chasms of ventilation shafts.

"Are you seeing this?" she asked in a hushed voice, amazed at what they'd done.

"Yeah," Sean said, his voice equally amazed. "We did it."

Holding his astral hand in hers, she towed him down the corridor.

Wait. They were holding hands? On their previous excursion, they couldn't touch each other. Something had changed between them.

"Sean," she said as they kept moving down the corridor, "how are we touching each other?"

He slowed his pace, his brows knitting together, and glanced at their hands. "Not sure. Our shared power has gotten stronger, I guess."

"But why?"

"Don't know. Don't care right now."

A lot of things had changed since they'd first met. They'd experienced each other's powers, they'd had sex, and they'd bonded on a deeper level because of it and also because of the secrets they revealed to each other.

But Sean was right. They had more important concerns at the moment.

They wandered past yard after yard of walls with nothing behind them. Nothing under the floors, either. Above, she saw ventilation shafts and wiring and pipes. If there was another floor above this one, she couldn't see through to it. Wall, wall, wall after gray wall. She observed nothing else.

Kira turned her gaze to the end of the corridor.

And stopped dead.

"I see it too," Sean said.

Human-shaped blobs—revealed in shades of red, yellow, and blue—moved around somewhere beyond the wall. Pipes and vents and wiring obscured her view, but she recognized those shapes as human. She ran to the wall, running her hands over its surface in search of any indication of a doorway but finding nothing. Another corridor began where the first one ended, shooting off to the right.

"Door must be down there," she said, and without waiting for Sean, she sprinted down the corridor.

Their footfalls slapped on the linoleum floor. She wondered briefly how astral feet clad in nonexistent shoes could make any noise, but she'd realized a while ago trying to make mundane sense of psychic stuff was pointless. She'd give herself a headache but gain no insight.

Another corridor branched off this one, so Kira swerved left down that path.

Sean grabbed her shoulders from behind, forcing her to halt.

"Slow up," he growled in her ear. "You're not paying attention. Look, you can see them right there."

He raised one arm to point to her left a few feet ahead of where they stood.

The hairs on her arms lifted and her skin prickled. Beyond the wall, human-shaped blobs moved, glowing like infrared footage she'd seen in movies. Sean was right. This ability was more like thermal imaging than X-ray. Four blobs held motionless, posted in a semicircle around another person who seemed to be sitting in a chair, though her human-only infrared couldn't show her the furniture. The other three blobs shifted this way and that, bent down, gesticulated. One person threw his or her hands up as if frustrated.

"Ready to go in?" Sean asked.

"Yes."

He took her hand, leading her straight through the wall.

They emerged inside a laboratory. Unlike the isolation room, this room featured no electronic equipment. It held medical paraphernalia, everything from devices to measure vital signs to an open cabinet full of hospital gowns—and of course, tools. Scalpels. Needles. Blood pressure cuffs. A small saw.

Kira's attention stalled on the saw. What were they cutting with that thing?

Sean noticed her staring at the serrated implement and murmured, "Tesler thought he could mine powers from people's brains by cutting them out."

"Cutting out their brains?" Her voice was barely a whisper. She couldn't fathom how anyone could do such a horrific thing.

"Yeah," Sean said. "He wanted to cut out Grace's brain."

Oh God, she prayed Dr. Ferrell hadn't tried that.

Kira tore her attention away from the saw to peruse the rest of the room. Four guards stood sentinel in a semicircle around a chair identical to the one in the isolation room, guarding the man strapped into the chair. Nathan had his eyes closed, his muscles slack as if he slept or had been drugged unconscious. In front of their prisoner, Ferrell and two lackeys loitered, all dressed in lab coats. Ferrell drummed the toe of one sensible shoe on the linoleum floor, arms crossed over her chest and one finger tapping, as she watched her underlings scurrying around to gather tools.

"Hurry up," she hissed. "He wants the contingency in place before the retrieval begins."

Kira wanted to ask Sean what a retrieval was, but she didn't want to miss anything Ferrell said or did. Everything seemed important, even the way she snatched a ballpoint pen from her breast pocket and twirled it between her fingers. Any little thing might provide a vital clue.

Right. Like Kira Magnusson was a crack detective. Sherlock Holmes with boobs.

One of the lackeys, the one she'd called Watkins earlier, cast a wary glance at Nathan. "We've tried this before, but he always resists the process. Can't we do without the contingency?"

"No." Ferrell strode up to the lackey, towering over the short, lanky man. "Watkins, you disappoint me. And our leader will be severely disappointed in your lack of commitment to the cause. Should I call him in here so you can explain why you refuse to activate the contingency?"

Watkins' skin turned a shade paler, and he flapped his head meekly.

"I didn't think so," Ferrell said, and she stalked to the chair. She tilted her head side to side, examining her prisoner with dispassionate interest, the scientist mulling her specimen. After a moment, she sighed and planted one hand atop Nathan's arm. Leaning her weight into his flesh and bone, she raised her other hand and smacked his cheek. She struck him hard enough to redden the skin. "Wake up, Nathan. I know you're only pretending to sleep. Your boy is almost here, and soon he'll be in our custody. How does it feel to know you've lost? After so many years of protecting your son at the expense of your own freedom?"

Nathan's lips warped into a grimace. He opened his eyes, spearing Ferrell with a glare as hot and sharp as a steel spike thrust into a smelting furnace.

"You don't have him yet," Nathan said, his voice calm but laced with something dangerous. "If you did, you wouldn't be making vague threats and talking about your beloved contingency plan."

"He's nearby, darling." She leaned more weight into her hold on his arm, earning a wince from Nathan. "Thanks to David Ransom, we know they're coming here and that they'll find a place not far away to hunker down. They plan to breach this facility. We will be ready for them."

What did Ferrell mean about David? Had they bugged David's phone and overheard him talking to Sean earlier?

Kira had no time to puzzle out the answer because the rest of what the scientist had said penetrated her mind at last. They. Ferrell spoke of more than one person. And she said "they" were hiding close to the bunker intending to breach…Her thoughts trailed off as a cold realization shuddered through her.

Ferrell was talking about her and Sean.

She sensed the truth sinking into Sean's mind too, a detached but no less disturbing shiver of understanding. Nathan's son…

"That's right," Ferrell said like she'd read Kira's mind, though she was speaking to her prisoner. "Nathan Vandenbrook will finally be reunited with his son."

A bolt of shock erupted from Sean to slam into Kira. She gasped, whirling toward him.

His face had gone ashen, and his jaw was slack. Not blinking, he gaped at the man strapped into the chair. His father.

Chapter Eighteen

S EAN STOOD PARALYZED, HIS ASTRAL BODY COLD AND STIFF, HIS heart hammering with such force his chest hurt. He couldn't breathe. Couldn't think. This man was his father? No, no, his dad took off for no good reason, abandoning him and his mom without so much as a goodbye. Mom never talked about it, but Sean deduced the truth from the anguish in her eyes whenever he'd asked about his dad. For her to be that broken up about it even years later, the bastard must've done something awful.

Nathan angled his head the slightest bit, and for the first time, Sean got a clear view of the man's eyes. The green irises gleamed in the light of the sterile bulbs suspended from the ceiling.

Green eyes. His mom's had been gray-blue. His grandfather, Tesler, had dark-brown eyes.

No, no, no, no. Sean scuffled backward a couple steps, suddenly breathing hard, almost hyperventilating. This man couldn't be his father. If he was, that meant Tesler had abducted his dad, ripping him away from his family and imprisoning him for seventeen years. Why? Sean swallowed hard, his breaths shortening into staccato gasps. His ears rang. His face tingled with numbness. Why do this to his father? Why?

Kira's hand slipped into his. She threaded their fingers, clasping his hand.

"You'll never get him," Nathan told Ferrell. "Sean is brave and smart. Sophie was a good mother, and even after everything Tesler put him through—" Nathan's voice broke, but he pulled in a breath and fortified his tone. "Even after the torture and the drugs, Sean grew into a strong and good man. He'll fight you, and he'll win."

Strong and good? This man, his supposed father, couldn't know anything about him. Tesler had held Nathan hostage, presumably in a different facility from Sean, for seventeen years. Sean had never seen his father, much less spoken to him. This man wasn't present when sweet Gramps beat and burned and cut Sean, then injected him with enough of JT's poison serum to make him half mad. Somehow, Sean had survived those trials without going totally nuts, but he wasn't normal either.

Not strong. Not good. He'd screwed up too many times to qualify for either adjective.

Kira brushed a lock of hair from his forehead, and he marveled at the fact they could touch in astral form. Why they could this time, he had no clue. This connection with her, it was more than psychic or sexual. He recognized that, but he didn't understand why it should be.

And he didn't deserve her tenderness or the bond they shared.

"The contingency," Ferrell said, leaning in to glower at Nathan from inches away. "You will implement it, or Caleb Magnusson dies."

Nathan gritted his teeth, his lip curling with a hatred Sean understood. He'd hated Tesler that much.

Kira's hand clutched his.

They had to rescue Caleb first before they tried to take down Ferrell and whatever psycho she called her boss.

Ferrell had said "thanks to David Ransom" they'd found where Sean and Kira had hidden. Whether her goons really had found them, he didn't know. David had no knowledge of their hideout, and he wouldn't betray them, anyway. Unless Ferrell threatened to hurt Abby. Or unless they'd tapped David's phone.

Someone had abducted Grace and Abby. It must've been Ferrell and her cohorts.

He and Kira needed to find Grace and her daughter too.

"You know what we want," Ferrell said. "Do it now."

Nathan spat in her face. "Fuck you."

Sean pulled Kira tight against him. "We have to get Caleb now. Then we need to find out where Grace and Abby are."

"But your father—"

"Can obviously handle himself. We'll come back for him."

Sean prayed getting some distance from the man would ease the deep-down itch inside him, the unease that made him so antsy he thought he might pop out of his own skin. But when they materialized in the barrel-ceilinged room, the itch got worse instead of better.

Caleb slouched on the overstuffed couch. He looked so small and helpless perched on the big cushions, knees drawn up, hugging himself while—

Oh jeez. The kid was crying.

With a glance, no words required, he and Kira agreed on a plan. They made themselves visible to her brother.

Caleb's head shot up, his bleary eyes wide. "Kiki?"

Sean couldn't even manage a sarcastic comment about the nickname. Yeah, things had gone beyond bad straight into horrifying.

Leaping off the couch, Caleb ran to Kira and tried to hug her. His arms passed right through her. "Kira?"

"It's me," she said, kneeling before her brother. "I don't have time to explain right now, but it's really me. I need you to trust me and do what I say. Can you do that?"

The boy bit his bottom lip and nodded.

Kira raised a hand as if to touch him, then lowered it. "This is my friend, Sean. He's going to help us get you out of here."

Caleb nodded again, biting his lip harder.

"We have to move," Sean said.

Kira rose. "I know."

"You'll need to do something about that door." He pointed toward the sealed entrance to the isolation room.

She lifted a hand, clamped her fingers tight, and shot them straight.

The door exploded open, thwacking into the wall inside the other room and bouncing back to a halfway-closed position.

Sean moved toward the door. "Follow me. And watch out for bad guys."

With Sean in the lead, they wended their way through the bunker facility single file with Caleb between him and Kira. The kid had serious mettle. Despite being kidnapped and having his life threatened, Caleb marched down the corridors as fast as his legs could go, no longer crying, not even complaining about the breakneck speed of their escape. Nathan had called Sean brave, but that was crap. He'd crumbled under pressure more than once. Tesler had stormed into his life when he was fifteen. Caleb was only eight, but he evinced an inner strength Sean had never achieved.

Though she'd blown open the first door, Kira dialed it back after that, releasing the locks and then engaging them again after Caleb got through the doors. The psychic thermal imaging he and Kira had created let Sean check for enemies before they led Caleb through any doorway or into any new corridor. How much time did they have before Ferrell and her cohorts discovered Caleb was gone? *Not enough.*

A clock ticked in Sean's head, counting down the seconds until all hell broke loose. It was a clock with no hands, no digital readout. He had no clue how long they had.

They reached a door that looked different from the others. It was dark-gray metal with a lever handle and clearly thicker than the other doors they'd breached. Sean thrust his head through the door—and sunlight blinded him. Through the brilliance, he spotted trees.

Sean pulled back into the building. "This is the exit. Take Caleb and find him a spot where he can hide until we come for him."

"What about you?" Kira asked.

"I'll hang back to keep watch and scan for more warm bodies. You go with Caleb."

She watched him for a moment. "Okay. But I'm coming back as soon as he's hunkered down."

"Fine." He'd known it wouldn't be that easy to get rid of her, but he also knew he had to do it. His messed-up life would not hurt anyone else.

Kira unlocked the door and eased it open with her powers, raising her hand palm out to nudge it. She exited first, with Caleb close behind.

The kid paused to look back at Sean, then followed Kira outside.

Once Kira had shut and locked the door, Sean flew back to the room where Ferrell held Nathan. He was slumped in his chair, eyes glassy, mouth open.

The doctor patted Nathan's cheek. "I knew you'd see reason. The serum always makes you more pliable."

Serum. Sean tensed, his nerves bristled by the word. By what it meant. Ferrell must've employed the drug developed by Jackson Tennant, which he'd called a serum. The drug Tesler had given Sean.

Burning agony. His mind on fire. Muscles cramping with convulsive force.

And Ferrell had done that to his father how many times? *Seventeen years.*

"It's time," Ferrell said to Nathan. "Activate the contingency."

A wave of searing energy shot through Sean, shattering his astral body, obliterating his connection to Kira.

He hurtled back into his physical body with the force of a skydiver slamming into the earth because his chute hadn't opened. Bones shattering. Skull fracturing. The agony of a thousand shards of glass gored him from head to toe.

And he screamed.

His entire body throbbed. His vision was blurry and wobbling like his eyes had turned into vibrating jelly. The paralysis lasted a few minutes that seemed like hours, but gradually, he regained movement in his fingers, then his arms, then his legs. His vision settled and swam back into focus.

Gasping for air, he gaped at the wood ceiling above him. The cabin. The porch.

Kira.

He rolled onto his side, realized he was lying on the porch floor, and heaved himself into a sitting position with more effort than it would've taken to lift a one-ton rock. His muscles burned and ached. He blinked rapidly, focusing in on the lump on the wooden swing.

Sean scrambled closer.

Kira lay in a heap on the swing, her feet dangling over the edge, her eyes shut. With shaking fingers, he checked her wrist for a pulse. There it was, strong and steady. He nearly collapsed from relief but forced himself to stay upright. He stroked her cheek, swept hair from her face, and closed his hand around one of hers.

"Don't move!"

Sean swung his head to the right and tightened his grip on Kira's hand.

Men dressed in camouflage outfits and wielding big guns had surrounded the cabin. One of them stood at the bottom of the porch steps, his weapon trained on Sean.

"You can't get away," the man hollered, louder than necessary. "Come quietly, or we will shoot you. Not dead, but it'll hurt like hell. Either way, you're coming with us."

Sean tried to tap into his powers, any of them, but he met a yawning vacancy in his own mind. No remote viewing. No healing, though he desperately tried to use that power on Kira. No empathic sensing either. He had zilch.

The lead commando clomped up the steps. "I'm sure you've realized by now your powers are gone. You can't fight us. If you try, your girl will get hurt—and we'll take you both anyway."

What could he do? He had no weapons, not even a big stick. He was powerless.

Sean got to his feet, hands raised, and spoke the words he'd sworn never to utter. "I surrender."

Chapter Nineteen

THE GROUND TREMBLED BENEATH KIRA, ROUSING HER FROM A DEEP and groggy slumber. A rumbling accompanied the shaking. An earthquake? Did they have those in…Where was she? Montana, that was it. She and Sean had flown to Montana on Gabriel Amador's jet and…What had they done here? Everything was fuzzy.

Kira peeled her lids apart, wincing at the brightness of sunlight in her eyes. Her cheek rested on fabric—denim, she realized. She was lying on her side with her head propped up on…someone's thigh. She blinked repeatedly to clear her vision, and the surroundings came into focus. She was in a vehicle. In front of her, two large seats bracketed a center console, and two large men occupied those seats. They wore all black and stared straight ahead with a purpose and resolve indicative of men following orders.

An arm draped over her with one big hand resting on her elbow.

Warmth sifted through her. Sean's thigh pillowed her head and his hand cupped her elbow. The protectiveness of the posture softened her unease, but only a smidgen, because the memory of what happened flared in her mind. Scorching energy had slammed into her, disintegrating her astral form and plummeting her back into her body at the cabin. The agonizing force of her ejection from the bunker had knocked her unconscious.

She pushed up into a half-sitting position, held up by one straight arm. Sean's hand slid down to her hip, shifted by her movement. His body faced forward, but he'd turned his head toward the window, hiding his expression and eyes from her. Though his hand on her hip seemed relaxed, the rest of his body was strung taut.

"How are you feeling?" he asked without looking at her, his voice flat.

"Okay." She swung her legs off the bench seat, her feet coming to rest on the floor of the bulky SUV. It was black, of course, with a dark-gray interior. "How long was I out?"

"Ten minutes, eighteen seconds."

An awfully specific length of time. He didn't wear a watch.

Kira wriggled to get situated on the seat close to Sean, their thighs touching.

He lifted his arm to accommodate her, then settled it around her shoulders.

She studied his profile, wishing to hell he'd look at her. "How do you know the minutes and seconds?"

Moving only his index finger, he pointed toward the front, into the gap between the passenger seat and the door. Kira leaned over his lap to squint into the space. The black-clad guard seated there had his right elbow braced on the door's armrest with his hand raised, fingers tapping the glass. On his wrist, he wore a big digital watch. The numbers glowed green.

"I can count," Sean whispered, "and that guy's had his hand like that the whole time."

Ah. At least that explained how he knew the specific length of time she'd been out. But she had another question about that.

Leaning back into the seat, into the sanctuary of Sean's arm, she asked, "Why were you keeping track of exactly how long I stayed unconscious?"

At last, he swung his head toward her and speared her with a look of such intense longing it made her throat constrict. "Because I needed to know."

His voice was intense too, rife with things she didn't dare consider right now.

They had bigger problems than whether he…had feelings for her. Or vice versa.

"Are they taking us to the bunker?" she asked.

"I'm guessing yeah." He tugged her closer. "We have no powers."

"What?" *Not possible,* her logical brain insisted. But when she flicked her fingers toward the man in the passenger seat, intending to shove his seat forward, nothing happened. She got a faint zing of psychic energy, but then it fizzled out and flicking her fingers again produced nothing. No zing. No fizzle. Just a yawning emptiness where her powers should've been. "What do we do?"

"Nothing, for the moment. Wait for an opening or something." He pulled her tight against him and dipped his mouth to her ear to murmur, "Caleb?"

"Safe, for now," she said sotto voce, speaking out of the corner of her mouth in case the guards up front could read lips in the rear-view mirror. These days, nothing seemed impossible. "I got him hunkered down before—What the hell happened to us? It was like I got torn out of remote-viewing mode and stuffed back into my body."

"More like a bomb detonating in your psyche, I'd say. That's what I felt, anyway."

Though he sounded calm, she perceived the dark tension in him and didn't like it one bit. His demeanor reminded her of the night they'd met, when he'd been hell-bent on punishing the person who set off the bomb at the cafe. He couldn't bring himself to hurt her, though. She had a sick feeling he might lose those compunctions when confronted with the mastermind of this terror spree.

If he tapped into the Golden Power again…

Dread shuddered through her, cold and viscous.

She rested her head on his shoulder and winced at a soreness on her scalp. "Must've hit my head when I passed out. Got a sore spot."

His arm around her stiffened. "Are you okay? Do you feel any dizziness or pain?"

"No, I'm fine."

Though his arm slackened a bit, he gusted out a sigh. "I can't even heal you."

"I'm fine." She found his other hand, the fingers of which he'd bent into his thigh, and took hold of it. "How could we lose our powers?"

"No frigging idea." He exhaled a slow breath. "Electromagnetic fields tuned to a particular frequency can dampen psychic abilities, but even that can't erase them altogether. David said his powers are gone. These people must've used the same method on us, to cancel out our abilities."

"You think our powers are gone for good?"

"Don't know." He slid his hand up and down her arm, caressing tenderly. "Dr. Ferrell kept talking about a contingency plan. Maybe this is it."

"Knocking out our powers? I guess that would solve the problem of us remote viewing their bunker, but so far, they've wanted us to use our powers to do things for them." She picked up his hand, sandwiching it between both of hers. "Why would they suddenly want us de-powered?"

"No idea."

The vehicle crested a hill, and the driver steered it off the road and onto a two-track. The dirt road sloped downhill, heading into a forested area. Shadows closed in around the SUV, plunging the interior into a false twilight, the sudden gloom making Kira clasp Sean's hand more firmly. Her pulse accelerated more the closer they got to wherever they were being taken. The bunker, she knew that. She'd exited the place and glimpsed its exterior, but having the powers ripped out of her mind had turned her flight with Caleb into a blurry rush. She remembered getting her brother settled into a hiding spot in the woods. Everything else had become hazy.

Concrete steps. Yes, she recalled that. The door had opened into a concrete stairwell that led up to ground level. Trees, she remembered that too. Lots and lots of trees.

The SUV rolled to a stop.

Kira straightened and peered out the windshield, but she couldn't see anything.

Bushes, she abruptly remembered. Right, there had been bushes concealing the stairwell.

Damn, some seriously paranoid weirdos had built this bunker. She couldn't see any hint of it, even when the guards ushered them out of the vehicle. A second SUV had followed them, a fact she hadn't noted until they climbed out of the vehicle that had brought them here. The second one must've trailed close behind, since it arrived at the same time.

Four guards piled out of the second SUV. They joined the first two to shepherd Kira and Sean toward a clump of bushes. Only when they drew up parallel to the steps did she notice the yawning maw of the concrete stairwell. Trees shielded it from overhead viewing.

Seriously paranoid people, for sure.

The two guards from the first SUV tromped down the steps to the door hidden under a concrete overhang, masked by shadows. Keys jangled. A lock chunked.

A door swung inward.

"Bring 'em in," a guard said.

His four buddies nudged Kira and Sean toward the stairwell. They descended into the shadows, through the open doorway into a lighted corridor. This was the way she and Sean had brought Caleb on their flight from the facility. Now, they were being herded into its bowels. Powerless. Captive.

Fear shot through her. When Sean had kidnapped her, she hadn't feared for her safety. With these lunatics, she had no idea what to expect. They tortured people. Orchestrated bombings. Would they kill too? Yes, her intuition warned. Yes, they would.

Kira lost track of how many times they turned into a different corridor. She lost track of everything, her mind reeling from the sequence of events that led her to this moment. How had these maniacs found her to begin with? How had they taken Caleb? She'd gone to pick him up after school only to find him missing, and minutes later, she'd received the first call. *Wait for instructions*, they'd said. *Tell no one or your brother dies.* She'd obeyed, too stunned to think of what to do. Then came the tests, the practicing, and after that...

The cafe. Sean. The movie theater. Sean. Healing David. Flying to Montana. Those brief moments of bliss with Sean, followed by finding his long-lost father and freeing Caleb only to have their powers stripped away.

Why had any of this happened? What did it all mean?

So much didn't make sense. Terrorists claimed responsibility for their attacks. These people hadn't. They'd left the world wondering how and why these tragedies occurred. The first bomb had no trigger, nothing to clue police in to the origins of the device. The second one had a trigger and had detonated without a psychic push. The villains must've guessed she and Sean would try to find the second bomb and dispose of it without causing an explosion. They'd built a failsafe into the device that time, so they could set it off remotely.

And still, they hadn't claimed responsibility.

The guards unlocked a door and ushered Sean and Kira inside a room.

Kira gulped back a gasp. The isolation room.

Sean had gone stony, his body taut and his gaze glued to the chair at the room's center.

Nathan was strapped to the chair with leather restraints and shackles, the double bindings a clear sign these people feared him. Or feared his powers. They must've brought him back to this room so they'd have the added protection of the dual restraints.

But Sean said he couldn't sense any psychic energy in his father. Something else that didn't add up.

Dr. Ferrell stood by the banks of equipment, her hip braced against the wall, arms folded over her chest. She observed the newcomers with detached interest, once again the scientist examining her specimens.

Her assistant hovered nearby, his eyes large, hands clamped over his belly, fingers scratching his skin.

Jeez, how badass was Nathan to inspire this kind of anxiety?

Unless…they feared someone else.

The assistant had his gaze nailed to a single person, the same individual Ferrell's scientific interest had settled on.

Sean.

But he had no powers anymore. *Right now,* he didn't. Maybe they knew he'd regain his abilities soon.

God, she prayed he did. She prayed her powers came back too. Together, they could stop these lunatics.

The door to the barrel-ceilinged room pivoted open, and a figure strode into the isolation room.

Kira froze.

Gabriel Amador smiled. "Welcome to my sanctuary."

S EAN STARED AT AMADOR, HIS BRAIN STRUGGLING TO COMPREHEND what he saw. It couldn't be. As much as Sean disliked Amador, he never would've thought the guy could become the mastermind of a terrorist organization bent on…doing things that made no sense. Yeah, that fact alone should've made him suspicious Amador was involved. The guy had a handful of screws loose inside that skull of his. They must've jangled whenever he shook his head.

No, this was impossible. Amador lacked the coherence to mastermind his own life, much less a bizarre plot of this magnitude.

Then again, Amador had founded and helmed an international venture capital firm. He'd gotten rich that way and kept the company going even after his son and wife died and he'd descended into revenge-driven madness.

Amador had seemed almost happy about David being in a coma—and disappointed when Sean and Kira healed David. Amador had stayed by Grace's side, offering a smarmy kind of comfort. The guy had kindled a torch for her ever since they'd met five years ago, though Grace swore he'd gotten over those feelings. *Yeah, right.* A fruitcake didn't shed its fruit.

He should've seen this coming.

Right, he should've guessed the nutjob who adored Grace would get hold of his long-missing father and orchestrate a nefarious plot to do crazy things that seemed to have no purpose.

Sean's gaze tracked from Amador to Nathan. His father stared up at the ceiling, his breathing heavy, his body limp. What had Amador done to Nathan?

"You are curious," Amador said, one hand in the pocket of his gray slacks. He wore a crisp white dress shirt, long-sleeve, with gold cuff links that glinted in the light of the bare bulbs suspended from the ceiling. "You wonder why I've done all of this."

Sean snorted. "No shit."

"The world needs to understand. I am showing them."

"Understand what? How whacked-out you are?"

Amador's mouth curved in a creepily satisfied smile. "They need to understand psychic faculties exist. Only when they accept the existence of such powers will they comprehend the danger posed by the individuals who possess them."

The guy had to be kidding. Insane-o dude on the loose, remember?

"Let me see if I've got the gist of this," Sean said, trying for the calmest tone he could muster, which wasn't real calm. "You kidnap and torture psychics, then blackmail Kira into setting off bombs as part of a plan to convince the world we're the bad guys? You set off the second bomb, not us. You abducted a little boy, and I'd bet a trillion dollars you took Grace and Abby too. Why would anyone believe a word you say? Nobody's going to accept psychic powers made a bomb go off." Sean shook his head, so baffled he couldn't think of words for a few seconds. "I thought you wanted Grace to, you know, fall for you or something. She's a psychic, bonehead. If you vilify all of us, you vilify her too."

"She will understand," Amador said, "once my plan is fully executed. She will be grateful I saved her from a life of constant fear of discovery and constant anxiety about the Golden Power."

"Jeez, Gabe, that's—" No other word for it, so Sean plowed ahead. "That's crazy, man. Like, one-hundred-percent bonkers, nutcrackers insane."

Amador sighed like a man forced to exercise extreme patience with a slow child. "Sean, you fail to see the wider picture. Sometimes violence is the only action that will gain the world's attention. Only when forced to see the truth will they do so."

"The truth? You're showing the world you're a terrorist." Sean stopped as a realization struck him. "But nobody's taken responsibility for these bombings. Nobody knows how they were done either, which means nobody realizes this has anything to do with psychics. Your plan is toast."

"We begin the final phase shortly." Amador strolled over to Nathan's chair, resting his hand on the back next to the other man's head. "Once that begins, everyone will know the truth. And the final phase begins with you."

Sean jerked his head back. "Me?"

"Actually," Amador said, "this begins with your father and ends with you."

Sean couldn't wrap his mind around anything Amador had said. He shook his head dumbly.

"Your father was the key to entrapping you," Amador said. "Now that we have you, the rest of the plan may be enacted."

Sean glanced at Nathan.

His father raised his head and focused on Sean. "I'm sorry."

For what, Sean wanted to ask. His voice wouldn't cooperate.

Amador patted Nathan's head. "Your father is a null."

Sean felt his forehead wrinkle as his brows cinched together. "A what?"

"He's one of a rare breed known as nulls." Amador circled behind the chair, trailing his fingers along the top of its back. "Other psychics can't detect a null's power, but more importantly, a null has the ability to cancel out the powers of another psychic. This is how we captured you and Kira, and Grace and Abby. Nathan sent out a nullifying pulse aimed specifically at the Ransoms, eliminating Grace and David's powers. Later, he fired off another pulse directed at the two of you."

Amador gestured at Sean and Kira.

Nullifying power? That...wasn't...possible.

Was it?

"You have never heard of this ability," Amador said, "have you? I'm not surprised. It is rare, and few have seen it, much less studied it. Buried deep in Tesler's records, which Grace permitted me to examine over the years, I discovered a one-paragraph statement about nulls. The only scientist to have studied one died in nineteen twenty-three, but he left behind tantalizing clues about these rare and coveted individuals."

Sean could do nothing except shake his head again.

"Tesler never realized your father had this ability," Amador continued. "Dr. Ferrell, though once his protégé, had taken control of an ALI facility here in Montana. She began secret experiments to determine if any of the travelers in her domain might be nulls. Tesler had taken your father to study his known psychic talents, but his powers were too weak to be of much value. This was before Jackson Tennant developed the power-enhancing serum. Since Nathan seemed useless, Tesler sent him to Ferrell. She was to keep him in custody until Tesler could get you transferred to his aegis."

Custody? Aegis? Sean stared at Amador without blinking. "I don't get—I mean, why would Tesler want me? I didn't come into my powers until I was fifteen, long after my mom ran away from her father because he was such a scumbag."

"No, Sean. You evinced paranormal abilities long before then." Amador laid his palm atop Nathan's head. "That is why your mother fled with you and hid from her father. Tesler had witnessed your nascent powers and wanted to study you, but your mother at last realized what 'study' meant to her father. She would not allow him to harm you, so she and Nathan fled with you and tried to hide." Amador smiled wistfully. "But Nathan made the mistake of returning to your former home to retrieve your favorite toy. Tesler's men were lying in wait and captured him."

His father had gotten caught because of him. Sean rocked back on his heels, his mind spinning with colliding thoughts. It was his fault. His fault.

"Unfortunately," Amador said, "your father managed to call your mother just before Tesler's men apprehended him. He'd sensed someone following him and feared for the safety of you and your mother, so he instructed her to run. She did. You were only five at the time. Sophie did an excellent job of hiding you both, that is why Tesler couldn't find you for years."

Sean didn't want to know, but he couldn't stop himself from asking. "How did he find us?"

"Ask your father."

Nathan dropped his chin to his chest, his shoulders caving in.

"What do you want from me?" Sean asked Amador.

The bastard rolled his shoulders back and lifted his chin. "You will become the face of the movement, the one who forces the world to recognize the reality and dangers of psychic phenomena."

"How the hell do I do that?"

"By taking responsibility for the attacks."

CHAPTER TWENTY

HE FACE OF THE MOVEMENT. SEAN STILL COULDN'T MOVE ANY PART of his body except his mouth, which he couldn't seem to shut up. Amador meant Sean would become an avowed terrorist. So far, the bombings hadn't killed anyone, and the second event hadn't resulted in any injuries, but the sinking feeling in the pit of Sean's stomach warned him Amador wasn't done yet. Did this wacko actually believe terrorism would make the world believe in psychic powers?

"Your plan sucks," Sean said. "Even if I do what you want, it won't have the effect you're hoping for. Nobody's going to believe in the paranormal because we claim to have set off a bomb with telekinesis."

"You will demonstrate for them. In the video you will make and we will distribute."

"Sure, because everybody knows videos can't be faked. Totally convincing." No point in arguing, Sean realized. Amador would never give up his crazy plan. So, he asked the question he'd been wondering about since Amador made his grand entrance. "Why did you keep telling me not to investigate? Sounds like you wanted me here to play patsy for you."

"I do, and it was my plan from the start. David's injuries would push you to hunt for the perpetrator, I knew this because you crave vengeance the same as I have."

"But the first bombing could've injured or killed me."

The whackjob shrugged one shoulder. "A risk worth taking. If you had died, I could have easily made Kira the face of the movement."

Blame whatever psychic was handy. *Awesome.*

Sean straightened, determined to appear strong in front of his nemesis—and that's what Amador had become, his enemy. "You said your master plan starts with my dad. Tell me how."

Amador shrugged, his attention wandering along with his gaze.

"Wake up," Sean growled, snapping his fingers to regain the man's attention. "I talked to David a while ago. I know Grace and Abby have been kidnapped." Sean fisted his hands, then forced himself to loosen them. Calmness and strength, that's what he needed to convey. "You took them, admit it."

"Yes, I have them," Amador said, "or I soon will. They should arrive any moment. Four psychics with no powers have less than no chance of besting me. Once you accept you have no other recourse, Sean, you will do as I command."

He could've pointed out no one could have "less than no chance" of anything, but logic no longer held any sway over Amador.

"You seriously think," Sean said, "I'll claim responsibility for the bombings."

Amador wagged one finger like a metronome. "More than that, I'm afraid. You will also take responsibility for the worst act of terrorism in recorded history."

Cold swept through Sean, and a steel ball of dread solidified in his gut. His fingers crooked into his palms, the nails digging into his skin. "What are you talking about?"

He knew it would be bad, whatever Amador had cooked up for his final phase. It would be really bad. Colossal. But he couldn't have imagined how terrible until the man voiced his scheme.

"It's quite simple," Amador said as if discussing a football game. "Malmstrom Air Force Base is not far from here. The base houses intercontinental ballistic missiles with nuclear rockets inside them. You will launch one of these missiles and destroy a significant portion of the eastern seaboard of the United States."

Sean stumbled backward a step, unable to blink or breathe. He shook his head. His brain had gone into its own little nuclear meltdown as he struggled to comprehend Amador's words. ICBM. Rockets. Launch. Destroy.

Amador wanted to nuke the East Coast. To get revenge on psychics, he'd sacrifice millions of innocent people.

His son had been psychic. The single thought broke through the melee in Sean's mind. Why would Amador punish others like his son? *Think, man, get a grip fast. No time for panic.*

Sean glanced at Kira. Wide eyed and pale, she met his gaze head-on, and he knew. They couldn't let this happen. If they had to die in the effort, they must stop Amador from enacting his plan.

Without letting on they were sabotaging him.

Kira nodded as if she'd heard his thoughts or guessed them. Two people shouldn't know each other this well after a couple days, but they did. Circumstance had forced them together, but something else linked them. Something he didn't have time to consider.

To Amador, Sean said, "Your son, Evander, had psychic abilities. How can you hate all of us when your son had the same kind of powers we have?"

"Do not mention my son. Do not speak his name." Amador's face turned crimson, his lips warped and quivering as he snarled his words. "Powers killed my son. If he had been a normal child, Karl Tesler would never have taken him, and he would never have died. My wife and son would still be with me."

"Okay, but—"

"Stop speaking!" Amador roared. "You are the grandson of the man who tortured and murdered my child. Tesler stole my son's life, but he let you live. You do not deserve the life you have been given, do not appreciate it, believe you have suffered more than anyone else. You have no conception of what suffering truly is. Only I know!"

The last three words thundered through the contained space, reverberating off the walls and vibrating in Sean's ears. Amador had gone so far off the deep end he must've sunk straight to the bottom of the ocean. Sean had never claimed he suffered more than anyone else. Maybe he hadn't appreciated what he had as much as he should, but that didn't make him evil. The weirdest part of this whole experience was that it had shown him he deserved the life he had, the loved ones he had, the powers he had. Kira proved all of that to him.

Amador had no clue about anything.

"I will have my vengeance," Amador hissed, raising his fists to shake them in the air. "Innocent blood must be spilled to convince the world of the true danger."

"What exactly do you think will happen if you nuke the East Coast?"

"Everyone will believe. Everyone will see the truth."

"Then what?"

Amador's fury dissolved into a blank expression.

"You don't know," Sean said. "If the final phase of your plan is launching an ICBM, that means you have no clue what to do after that. Nuke the East Coast, blame the psychics, and that's the sum total of your plan."

"I need no further actions after that," Amador said with a confused expression. "I will have made my point."

"Don't you realize the authorities will start an all-out, no-holds-barred hunt for the terrorists who murdered millions of people? They'll come for all of us, you included."

"They will come for you, the one who confesses to these crimes."

"And I'll give you up." Sean scratched his neck, unsure how to proceed when Amador wouldn't admit to the lunacy of his plan. Take another tack, he decided. "I'm not doing jack for you. Cancel your statement to the world because I will not be the face of your crazy movement."

"Will you watch Kira and Nathan suffer and die?"

Of course he wouldn't, but Amador absolutely would hurt them to hammer his point into Sean's brain. The point being "I'm a nutjob bent on destruction." Sean needed a plan of his own, but so far nothing had come to him. Refusing to do Amador's bidding hadn't worked.

Should've gotten a degree in psychology, not math.

"Let me talk to my dad," Sean said. "Alone."

"You may speak to him, but only in my presence."

"Uh-uh. I talk to him alone or you can forget about Malmstrom and the East Coast apocalypse." Not that Sean would ever launch a nuke, no way, but he needed Amador to believe he might do it. He would die before he'd nuke an entire country or even a single acre of land. He had no choice but to reiterate his threat, channeling the anger that had simmered inside him before Kira showed him how to let it go. "Leave me alone with my dad or no dice. You can find somebody else to launch your ICBM, and I'll watch you torture Kira and Nathan. I mean, I don't even know my dad. And Kira, well, I kidnapped her because she blew up my best friend. Do you really think I care what happens to them?"

Amador pursed his lips, his gaze narrowed on Sean. "But you hold her hand."

"To make sure she doesn't run away." Sean hesitated. "It's not like I can use my powers to escape with my daddy. I've got no mojo, thanks to the nullifying trick. I'm as harmless as a kitten, right?"

Even kittens had claws and sharp teeth, though.

Amador huffed. "As you wish. But you will have five minutes, not one second more."

"Fine." Sean waved toward the sweet lady doctor. "And take Ferrell and the goons with you. Kira stays."

Kira looked surprised but stayed silent.

Amador squinted at Sean. "If you don't care for her, why do you wish her to stay?"

"Because I do." Damn, he really sucked at this manipulation crap. Luckily for him, Amador was too screwy to realize it. "Do what I say if you want your doomsday to happen."

Lips squashed into a sharp line, Amador nodded. "You are not to remove Nathan's restraints. We will be watching on the monitors in the control room across the hall."

He gestured for the others to follow him, and they trooped out of the room into the corridor, shutting the door.

Alone with his father, Sean suddenly had no clue what to say. He clomped up to the chair, itching to tear off the restraints, but Amador would be watching. Sean had to leave the restraints in place.

"It's all right," his father said. "I know you can't set me free, not with Amador keeping an eye on you."

"Can you read my mind?"

His father laughed without even a hint of humor. "No, I wouldn't even if I could. But I can't, anyway. You were staring at the restraints, so I assumed you wanted to free me."

Sean glanced at the leather straps and metal shackles again. The heat of anger swelled in his chest, and he couldn't tamp it down. Nullifying his powers seemed to have stripped away his natural ability to repress emotions, and the calm Kira had imbued into him had been tapped out when he had to pretend he'd let Amador butcher her and his dad. He'd relied on his empathic ability to keep his emotions in check. He didn't know how to repress without paranormal assistance.

He'd have to feel it. Push through the anger and pain, and somehow, get through this ordeal.

Dead or alive.

Kira came up beside him and slipped her hand into his. The simple gesture evoked a storm of emotions inside him, things he couldn't sort out even if he had the time. Mostly good things. She'd gotten through his psychic defenses to make him feel again, so of course, she got through his normal defenses too. He couldn't hide from her.

"Mom never talked about you," Sean said to his father. "I thought you walked out on us. When I came into my powers, I figured you must've known I'd be a freak and you left because of me."

Nathan gave him a sad smile. "I never wanted to leave you or your mother. I loved you both. I never stopped loving you."

Sean's throat constricted, but he squeezed the words out. "It was my fault you got caught. You went back for my toy."

"It wasn't your fault. I should've known better than to go back there, but you were so distraught about leaving your favorite bear behind. After taking you away from the only home you'd ever known..." Nathan shut his eyes briefly. "I had to do one small thing to make it better for you. I made a mistake, Sean. You did nothing wrong."

Maybe not back then, but lately...Yeah, he'd messed up enough for one lifetime.

No more.

His father bent toward him as far as possible with the restraints holding him down. His expression and his voice conveyed wrenching emotion. "It's my fault, Sean, not yours. I betrayed you twice. I tried not to, but they have ways of breaking even the strongest person, and I was never the strongest. Not like you and your mother. They broke me, and I told them where to find you."

Tiny arcs of electricity sparked across Sean's skin, the physical manifestation of a shock too deep to repress, even if he'd had the capacity to do that. He knew of one surefire way to break the strongest psychics.

"JT's serum," Sean said. "The one they gave you earlier today. They've given it to you before, haven't they? That's how they broke you."

"Yes. I fought it as hard as I could…"

"Nobody can fight that poison." A memory barreled through his mind, of the searing agony and the mind-melting power of the serum. "I've had it. I know what it's like."

Nathan stared at him, eyes wide. He opened his mouth to speak but seemed incapable of piecing together words, his jaw working.

The horror and concern on his father's face triggered a hard pang in Sean's chest. All his life he'd believed his dad abandoned him and his mom—for no good reason, or else because of Sean's latent powers. He'd finally learned the truth.

Just in time for both of them to die.

Kira squeezed his hand, and he squeezed hers right back.

Then he spoke to his father. "Are my powers gone for good?"

"No, they'll come back."

"How long?"

His dad shrugged, wincing as the restraints bit into his muscles. "It varies. Six hours at most, based on past experience. Could be less, though."

Sean prayed it would be a lot less. They needed their powers back now.

What Nathan had said a moment ago resurfaced in Sean's mind. "You said you told Amador and his buddies where to find me. How did you know?"

A bitter smile tightened Nathan's mouth. "Traveling. I've been keeping an eye on you for as long as I've been a prisoner of Tesler and the ones who came after him. No one noticed. I found ways to disguise my activities by checking on you when they thought I was asleep or during scheduled excursions. My powers aren't particularly strong, but I have limited remote-viewing abilities. It was enough to let me keep tabs on you." He shut his eyes again, swallowed hard, and looked straight at Sean. "When Tesler got his hands on you, I tried to intervene. But I don't have that kind of power. I'm sorry, Sean."

He didn't know what to say to that or how to feel about it. Maybe his dad wasn't the prick he'd thought he was, or maybe this was an act instigated by Ferrell and Amador to trick Sean into doing things he would never do without coercion. They might've decided subtle coercion, of the emotional kind, would work better than blackmail or threats of violence.

With his empathic ability crippled, Sean couldn't get a read on Nathan. He'd have to trust his instincts about the man, but he was too confused to do that. He'd trusted Grace and David as soon as he met them, despite knowing nothing about either of them. His instincts urged him to believe in their good intentions, and he'd been right to take that advice. David had been a prisoner of Tesler and JT when Sean met him, and Grace had been on the run from the same two villains. Neither of them, however, had been a prisoner for seventeen years.

Could someone held for that long stay true to his own nature? Nathan must've been tortured, drugged, and who-knew-what else. What if he'd been worn down? Broken and then reshaped into whatever Tesler and now Ferrell wanted him to become?

What better weapon to use against Sean than his own father?

"You don't know if you should trust me," Nathan said. "I understand. You're smart to doubt me. I doubt myself sometimes, after all these years as a prisoner. But I've always tried to protect you the best I could, though I didn't always succeed."

Sean wanted to believe him so badly.

Despite knowing the answer wouldn't make him feel better, he had to ask. "How bad was it? The things they did to you, I mean. Being a prisoner for so long."

"There were unpleasant times, but I spent most of my days in fairly decent quarters reading or watching TV. I have an old photograph of you, me, and your mom. I'd look at it whenever I needed to remember why I'm fighting them." Nathan sighed, seeming older and more exhausted all of a sudden. "I assumed I'd never get out of here. The torture was occasional, but it's the drugs that bother me the most. I can withstand pain a lot better than chemicals that turn my brain to jelly."

"We'll get you out of here somehow."

Nathan shook his head. "Don't bother about me. Whatever happens, whatever they threaten, you cannot give them what they want."

"I know."

Sean would make sure Amador never got his way, no matter the cost. If Sean had to die to stop the madman, he'd make the sacrifice without hesitation.

CHAPTER TWENTY-ONE

A LOCK CLUNKED, AND THE DOOR SWUNG OPEN. KIRA BACKED away from Nathan, with Sean following her, as Amador and his cohorts marched into the room. The revelations so far had proved shocking, and she couldn't imagine what Sean must have been feeling right now. His father was alive. Nathan had never willingly abandoned his family. Kira was happy for Sean that he'd learned the truth, but she worried about what might come next. Amador was far from done with them.

She sensed it in a way she couldn't explain. The certainty rang in her soul.

Kira and Sean backed up to within ten feet of the door to the barrel-ceilinged room. Her hand found his, and she clasped it tightly. He returned the gesture, though neither of them looked at the other. Their gazes stayed trained on Amador.

The lunatic aimed a benevolent smile at Sean. "I permitted you to speak with your father. You should now realize the gravity of your situation. If you refuse to obey my commands, your father will suffer. Kira will suffer."

Sean glared at Amador. "They can handle it. I am not launching a nuke for you."

"Perhaps Kira can convince you."

Kira shook her head. "Forget it. I'm not telling Sean to kill millions of people."

"That's unfortunate. I had hoped to avoid this, but you leave me no choice." Amador waved to the guards. "Retrieve the surprise."

Two guards departed, and the door shut behind them with a *chunk*.

"Do you wonder," Amador said, "how we found you, Kira?"

She had wondered about that a lot, but suddenly she was sure she didn't want to know.

He told her anyway. "Your boyfriend wasn't the only witness to your display of psychic power. Onlookers not only watched but also recorded your outburst on their cellular telephones. Two of them posted the videos online."

Kira bit down on her lip but even the slight pain couldn't keep her focused. Videos? Online?

"None of them believed your display had been paranormal in nature," Amador said. "No, they thought it a prank instigated by one of those practical-joke shows on television. But the keywords they used when describing the incident attracted the attention of our search bots. When we viewed the videos, we knew you must have powers. One of the witnesses named you, even tagged you in the social media post. That is how we found you."

Tagged her? Kira didn't remember that, but then, she'd avoided social media after her boyfriend posted a rant about what an evil witch she was. The videos must've been posted after that.

Jesus. Videos. Social media ruined her life, literally.

The door burst open, and the guards ushered two people into the room. The prisoners had black hoods over their heads, but she could tell the couple included a man and a woman.

One guard shut the door while the other nodded to Amador.

He spoke to Kira. "You needed the proper motivation to undertake the tasks ahead of you. I gave you that motivation."

With a jerk of his head, he commanded the guards.

They whipped the hoods off the prisoners' heads.

Kira gasped, stumbling backward.

Her parents blinked rapidly as if clearing their vision in the sudden brightness. When they focused on her at last, they both began to cry. Her mom tried to rush to her, but a guard slung out an arm to bar her way.

"Kira, sweetie," Mom said, "are you okay? Where's Caleb?"

She couldn't speak for a moment, a span of a second or two when time seemed to have stopped. The room swayed around her once. She took a couple slow breaths and marshaled all her self-control to remain calm. "I'm okay. Caleb's okay too."

As far as she knew. She'd left him in the woods, tucked inside a hollow, dead tree trunk that had fallen to the ground. He would stay there because she'd asked him to, and Caleb was a good boy.

The start of tears pricked at the backs of her eyes. She breathed in through her nose, deep and slow, and blew the breath out through her mouth. No time for crying. She needed answers pronto.

"I thought you were in Africa," she said, hoping her voice didn't betray her bitterness. "You said that's where you'd be when you walked away without a second thought. When you abandoned your eight-year-old son."

Her father winced. Her mother looked stricken.

"Please believe us," her father said, "we never wanted this."

Don't hate us, we never wanted this. That's what their note had said.

Gabriel Amador sauntered up beside her parents, a smug smile on his lips. "They tell the truth, Kira. Your parents would never have left of their own volition, despite learning of your telekinetic abilities. I tried to convince them to come with me voluntarily, but they refused to leave their beloved children. They required a greater motivation."

Dread coiled in her chest like a snake about to strike, sinking its cold, razor-sharp teeth into her heart. She resisted the impulse to hug herself because she suspected Amador wanted her unsettled. No way in hell would she give him what he craved.

"I don't understand," she said in the calmest tone she could muster. "What did you do to them?"

"To them? Nothing." Amador cast his gaze on her parents, then focused on her again. "I merely told them if they wanted to prevent their children from enduring painful and extended torture, they must do precisely as I say. They agreed."

You evil, insane son of a bitch. Kira's fists clenched at her sides, and she fought with all her strength to keep from hurling her body at him and clawing his eyes out. She didn't give a damn what he'd suffered, what reasons he had for going nuts and tormenting others. Nothing justified the things he'd done.

"Now you see," Amador said, "what is at stake. I did this for you, Kira. The proper motivation is vital to completing the mission. I know from experience loss and pain are a powerful impetus for taking action most would consider immoral but which is crucial to changing the world, remaking it into a place free of criminals with unspeakable power."

Criminals? She supposed she was one after the things she'd done lately, but only because this man had forced her to do it. Not every psychic was a criminal, though. But why argue with the man? He was beyond reason, beyond logic, entrenched in a crazed fantasy that painted him as a hero. What he believed he was saving, she had no idea.

Amador was obsessed with Grace. Maybe he thought he was saving her. He had claimed she'd be grateful once he'd fully executed his plan.

"I don't get it," Kira said. "You went to all this trouble just to terrify the world into believing psychic phenomena are real. And you think Grace will want you after that? She won't be grateful you ruined her life and the lives of countless other people."

"All will become clear, eventually. I have what I need now—you and Kira and Nathan." Amador rubbed his jaw. "I do have multiple contingencies in case you require further motivation, but I would prefer you cooperate willingly."

Contingencies for what? Nathan had been a contingency, with his nullifying ability. Kira couldn't think about what else Amador might have up his sleeve. Too many other things to worry about, and besides, he might be lying. Crazy people liked to do that.

"You claim you got Sean involved on purpose," she said, "but you couldn't have known he'd go to that cafe."

"Of course I did." Amador clasped his hands behind his back, bouncing on his heels. "I've been watching Sean for some time, waiting for the moment when he would be at his weakest and most desperate. Only then would he insert himself into the plan. By urging him not to become involved, I ensured he would. I believe it's known as reverse psychology."

Sean looked as confused as Kira felt. "How did you know I'd be at the cafe?"

Amador reverted to his most patient tone. "I'd installed listening devices in Grace and David's home as well as in your apartment. The Ransoms and Edward McLean have become lax in their security measures, and they stopped sweeping their home for surveillance devices six months ago. They at last felt safe in their new home, which made this the perfect time to enact my plan. I overheard David speaking to Grace about his planned 'intervention' with you that morning and that the cafe was a fine place to talk."

"But..." Sean shook his head slowly, his brows drawn together. "You wouldn't have had time to plant the bomb and tell Kira to go there."

Amador smiled in that smugly satisfied way again, rocking on his heels. "One of my agents was watching you, and he had the device with him. The moment you and David left to walk to the cafe, a journey that takes ten minutes, my agent drove there to plant the device. At that time of day, the restaurant is busy. No one noticed another man dressed as a waiter. While my agent placed the bomb, another of my people called Kira to give her instructions."

Sean stared into space, his gaze distant. "But she would've had to be close by."

"They'd called me an hour earlier," Kira said, "and told me to wait in an alley. Turned out that was a block from the cafe."

She'd forgotten about that until now, what with her life being threatened every other minute and an apocalypse looming.

"At last, you see," Amador told Sean, "how perfectly I planned all of this."

"Oh yes," Kira said, "you're a bona fide genius. Congratulations on wounding all those innocent bystanders."

Amador's chest puffed up, clear evidence he hadn't grasped the snide tone of her comments. He really believed he'd done a good thing. Saving the world from psychics. Getting his revenge.

"Sean," Amador said, "it's time for you to speak to the world and take responsibility for these incidents. The final phase begins now."

CHAPTER TWENTY-TWO

Take responsibility for terrorist attacks that wounded innocent people? Sean gritted his teeth. No way. He would never do that. If he refused outright, Amador might hurt Caleb or Kira's parents—or Grace and Abby, maybe even David. What the hell was Sean supposed to do? He had no powers, no weapons, no way to fight back except with his big, snarky mouth.

And that didn't seem to be working. Not for him, not for Kira. No matter what they said, Amador wouldn't budge in his nutso conviction he was saving the world. The guy had sunk so deep into his delusions he might never crawl back out.

Much as Sean hated to admit it, he'd thought Amador got better over the past five years. Sure, for all these years the guy had wandered in and out of a psychiatric clinic. One particular clinic, actually. The one Amador had bought five years ago to help victims of Tesler's worst tactics, men who had been turned into mindless automatons, an army of zombie-like soldiers. Amador had also signed himself in to the same clinic and had spent a good part of the past five years in treatment there, off and on, seeming to make progress but apparently backsliding too. Why else would he have kept returning to the clinic as a patient?

His mind must've been too far gone for treatment to work. He'd endured losing his son to Tesler, a madman who abducted and tortured the twelve-year-old Evander Amador and finally slit the boy's throat when he served no useful purpose to Tesler's research. Then, Amador's wife committed suicide, and the man had no one left. No reason to keep going. No purpose in life except to seek vengeance.

That was how Grace had met Amador. He'd planned to use her as a tool in his quest for retribution. Sure, in the end Amador had helped Grace,

David, and Sean stop Tesler and his cronies. But he'd started out using Grace. Drugging her. Tormenting a teenage girl to coerce her into using her powers to stalk and terrorize Grace.

Karl Tesler had, ultimately, set in motion the events leading to this moment—to Amador's madness and the debacle it instigated. Sean's grandfather had created this monster.

A thread of knowing, too slender and ethereal to grab on to, flittered in Sean's mind. He must understand this. Right this second. The fates of so many people depended on it.

Sean took slow, deliberate steps toward Amador, halting an arm's length away.

The other man watched him with that bizarre calmness in his demeanor and that creepy little pleased smile on his lips.

Need those powers back. But Sean knew he couldn't count on them anytime soon.

"I want to understand this," Sean said. He fought through the shock and anger, determined to sound reasonable and give Amador no call to lash out. "Tesler—My grandfather was a monster. He did unspeakable things to men, women, and children whose only crime was having abilities most people don't have and can't believe exist. He killed your son. You want someone to pay for that, I get it. Maybe you really want the world to accept psychic phenomena as real because then they'd be accepting your son too, in a way. You want justice for Evander. Mass murder isn't the way to get it."

Amador's body snapped taut and ramrod straight. He narrowed his eyes, his lips tightening into a slash. "I told you never to speak my son's name."

"I'm sorry for what happened to you. Maybe I can't really understand what you went through, but I'm trying to understand you now. What is it you really want? Why was it so important to get me involved in all this? You said you want to punish me because Tesler let me live but he killed your son. I don't think that's the whole reason I'm here, though, is it?"

The question hung in the air like an invisible, fetid fog. Sean had the weird sensation if he took a single breath, if he heard the answer to his question, he'd ingest a toxin nothing could eradicate. The toxic cost of knowing.

Amador didn't move or speak, his features frozen in that expression of barely contained fury.

Silence blanketed them like the invisible fog Sean had imagined. It surrounded them and cloyed to their skin. He felt it on his flesh, chilly and sticky, raising the hairs on his arms.

"You are like me," Amador said coolly, speaking each syllable with the care of a man determined to make his thoughts known without any misunderstanding. "We share more in common than you realize, Sean. Your father was torn from you just as my son was taken from me. Tesler abused your father in much the same way he abused my son. Your mother died, and so did my wife. The difference, however, is that my wife chose to take her life. But they both died as a direct result of Tesler's actions."

"My mom died in a car accident."

The hard line of Amador's mouth softened the tiniest bit, kinking into the barest of smiles. "Yes, she died while in a car, but it was no accident. Your grandfather orchestrated it."

Sean's feet wanted to stumble backward, to carry him away from Amador, but he held his position. No way would he show any more fear or shock to this man. "The cops told me it was an accident. A tire blew out, she lost control, and the car hit a utility pole. She died instantly."

"No," Amador said with a pity-laden shake of his head. "Tesler ordered a traveler, one of his inmates, to destroy the tire in such a way your mother would lose control and strike that pole. He wanted her dead because she knew too much. Your mother had discovered the truth about her father's so-called research project, and she was horrified. She'd threatened to go to the authorities. Since she had evidence to support her claims, in the form of files she'd stolen from Tesler, he had to rid himself of her for good."

Sean stared at Amador. No, even Tesler couldn't have been that vile, having his own daughter murdered.

I did love her once. The thought pierced his brain, a memory of that recurring dream. This time when a fragment of the nightmare came back to him, the words were spoken in Karl Tesler's voice. Grace had believed Tesler cared about Sean in his own twisted way. Had the dream always been about Tesler? Why did he keep dreaming about his grandfather saying he loved "her"?

"We are alike in many ways," Amador said. "You abducted Kira just as I abducted your friend, Cari. What would you have done if I hadn't intervened and forced the two of you to work together?"

Not what Amador had done, Sean wanted to say. It would've been a lie. He couldn't claim he would've stopped short of hurting Kira because he'd been teetering on a desperate edge.

You wouldn't have hurt me, Kira had told him later. She believed it, believed in him.

"And of course," Amador said, still not shutting the hell up, "I betrayed Grace by alerting Tesler to her location. We have that in common as well."

"Who are you claiming I betrayed?" Sean asked.

"Grace."

What the frigging hell? Sean drew his head back. "I never did that."

Amador canted his head, eying Sean with a baffled expression. "You truly don't know, do you? I suppose Grace believed she was protecting you by not revealing your actions. While JT was still alive, Tesler tried to make David reveal the true identity of the traveler known only as Janet Austen. David knew the traveler was Grace and that her parents had secreted her away somewhere before their deaths. David would not be broken, though." Amador waved a finger at Sean. "You, however, required little coercion to comply. You exposed Grace and led Tesler and JT to her."

Now that he wanted to step away from this bastard, Sean's body refused to budge even one millimeter. He couldn't speak or think or look away from Amador. The man was lying. He had to be.

Yeah, someone had betrayed Grace years ago and led the bad guys to her. No one ever figured out who it was, or at least, no one would tell Sean if they did know. He'd sensed, thanks to his empathic ability, Grace and David kept something from him years ago when they told him Tesler was his grandfather. Since he'd had other things to worry about then, like getting a handle on his newly emerged empathic power, he'd decided to forget about it. Couldn't have been important, or else they would've told him what it was.

I did love her once.

The words catapulted him into a memory of the dream. No, not a dream. It had always been a memory of a real event, one too traumatic for his mind to hold on to, so his subconscious had repressed it. The truth emerged in fragments in a dream, pieces he couldn't tape back together.

Until this moment.

The here and now faded away as the past engulfed him.

Sean lies strapped to a chair in an isolation room, tears streaming down his cheeks, blood trickling down his forehead into his eyes. Cuts and burns, raw and blistered, have turned his arms into a red, seeping mess. The pain racks his body, his mind, too intense to let him think, let him understand. How could anyone do this to another human being? Why do they do this to him? He's never hurt anyone, but they demand answers he can't give.

An ALI technician hovers over him, lips pursed, scrutinizing Sean's face.

The door bursts inward, and Karl Tesler storms into the room.

Sean glimpses the scientist through a haze of blood-tinged tears. The two men speak to each other, but he can't focus on their words, can't focus on anything except the searing agony.

Tesler shouts at his underling, and the technician flees the room.

Sean sobs. He hates crying, but he's powerless to stem the tears.

Karl Tesler approaches the chair and leans in, his hand on the chair's arm way too close to Sean's arm. The man's hand floats up as if he might touch Sean's face.

He yanks his hand away, scowling at Sean. "I did love her once. You may not believe it, but I did. So very much. I wish this could be another way..." Tesler steps back, squares his shoulders, and his expression mutates into ice . His voice is equally chilled. "But there is no other way to deal with your kind. I need Janet Austen, and you will give her to me."

Footsteps. The technician returns and hands Tesler a syringe. "The serum, sir."

Tesler snatches the syringe from the technician's grasp and lowers it to Sean's arm. He hesitates, his brows pinched. With an annoyed sigh, he stabs the needle into Sean's arm, depressing the plunger.

Sean flinches at the burst of pain, but tears choke his voice. He can't beg for mercy even if he wanted to. Sean convulses as the serum scorches through his veins. His eyes bulge. He drags in one wheezing breath, his body ablaze with a new, deeper agony. His body slumps in the chair of its own volition.

Tesler bends near Sean's face. "Now, track David Ransom."

"Can't…" Sean's voice is slightly slurred. Why is Tesler asking him to do this? "Not my power."

"I just gave you more power than a weakling like you deserves. Track David Ransom."

Sean moans.

Tesler slaps him across the face.

His entire body jerks.

"Do it," Tesler hisses. "That's an order."

Sean has no choice. The serum warps his mind, his will, until he must do as he's told. He flies through the crossroads faster than ever before, spots a pulsing star, and races to the destination at light speed. He emerges inside a house. David is nearby, he senses it. Compelled by the serum and Tesler's command, Sean tracks David into the bedroom of the house where a woman lies on the bed, asleep.

Grace Powell.

Sean hesitates, afraid David will notice him, but his friend remains focused on Grace. David loves her, Sean knows. Sean loves her too, like a mother or a sister, and remembers all the times she talked with him about his powers and helped him accept what he is. Now, she doesn't remember any of it. David had told him Grace developed amnesia after her parents' deaths.

A thought explodes in his mind. He knows the answer to the question Tesler's lackey asked him earlier, over and over while cutting and burning him. He knows, but he cannot let Tesler know.

The serum melts away his resolve, but he must not tell.

Sean returns to his body, rousing in a groggy haze.

Tesler grips Sean's chin and wrenches his head. "Who is she?"

Sean clamps his teeth shut. He won't tell. He won't.

The serum scorches, weakens, annihilates.

"You. Will. Tell. Me." Tesler smacks him. Sean's head snaps back, and his mouth pops open. "Who is Janet Austen?"

"She… ahhh…" No, no, no, he will not say it.

"Tell me!" Tesler seizes Sean's shoulders and rattles him hard.

Sean's jaw quivers. Tears stream down his cheeks. He fights the serum as hard as he can, but it's not enough. His mind dissolves, his will dissolves, and a sharp sob racks him. "Grace Powell."

A sickening grin splits Tesler's mouth. His eyes sparkle with a dark glee. To his assistant, he says, "Make sure the boy remembers nothing."

The present reeled back into focus around him, and Sean staggered backward a single step. It was true. He betrayed Grace.

But that did not make him like Amador. A few days ago, he might've believed that. Today, he saw everything more clearly.

Amador reached Sean in one large step and grasped his shoulders. "We are the same. This is why I know you will do as I command and tell the world you orchestrated the bombings. You will also issue a warning about a far worse calamity to come. I have written a statement for you to read."

"Why would I do any of that?"

"Because like me you will do anything, no matter how heinous, to save the ones you love." He glanced at Ferrell. "Have they arrived?"

She brought out a phone and tapped its screen several times. "Yes. We've apprehended Grace and Abigail Ransom, and they've arrived at the facility."

Amador grinned. "You see? It all comes together. Soon, the world will see psychics the way I wish them to, and Tesler's true legacy will be exposed. Grace will understand even if you do not."

Grace would understand what?

Sean went stiff and cold inside as a dozen gears, once disassembled and scattered in his brain, clicked into position one by one.

Amador, unhinged as he was, had revealed the clues without meaning to. Little things he'd said shed light on his actions, his plans, his real purpose.

He'd hoped David would die in the first explosion. He'd been annoyed when Sean and Kira healed David. He believed Sean was just like him, driven by rage and a need for revenge too powerful to deny. Amador had dragged Sean into this cockamamie plot on purpose, and Sean saw only one reason for it.

Tesler's true legacy would be exposed, Amador had said.

And finally, Sean realized what this man wanted. He intended to kill David, convince everyone Sean was a madman like his grandfather, and probably kill him too. Like he'd already admitted, he would expose psychics as dangerous enemies. But he didn't want to convince the world. He needed just one person to believe.

Ferrell had said Grace and Abby had arrived at "the facility." She must've meant this underground bunker. Had Grace really lost her powers? Nathan said the nullification was temporary. Could she have regained her powers already? If she had, she would've escaped with Abby. Ferrell might've lied, and they might be safe.

If he had his powers, he'd know for sure.

He supposed this was what they called irony. He'd repressed his powers for so long, prayed they might just go away if he ignored them, and now he needed them desperately.

Sean had to know one last thing before he'd be sure of his realization. So, he looked straight into Amador's eyes and asked, "My father can nullify powers. You think you can use him to permanently strip a psychic's powers, don't you?"

"Yes."

Amador wouldn't strip Sean's or Kira's powers, not yet. He had one target in mind, the one person in the world he coveted enough to go to these outrageously insane lengths.

Grace.

Chapter Twenty-Three

THE FINAL PHASE. KIRA'S BRAIN HAD GOTTEN STUCK ON THAT phrase several minutes ago when Amador stated that "the final phase begins now." Whether he would really stop after nuking the East Coast was another question altogether. Who knew with someone as unbalanced as Gabriel Amador? In the past ten minutes, he'd shocked her and Sean with enough revelations to knock them off kilter for a good while. Exactly what he'd intended to do, of course.

Her gaze traveled to her parents for the umpteenth time. She still couldn't wrap her head around the idea they hadn't willingly abandoned her and Caleb. They'd surrendered to Amador to protect their children. Why had Amador taken them and left Kira to her own devices for sixteen months? The man seemed to have the patience of a snail, inching toward his goal one millimeter at a time, certain he would reach that goal one day, certain vengeance would be his.

Tesler was long gone. Punishing Sean probably seemed like the best alternative, to destroy the only living relative of the man who'd been responsible for his son's death. Amador kept insisting Sean was just like him, but he was dead wrong. When the choice came down to hurting her, he'd pulled back. Despite his desperation, Sean couldn't cross the line Amador had charged past a long time ago.

Did Amador really have Grace and Abby?

Kira glanced at Sean, standing beside her but his gaze distant. He'd gone stoic, and she couldn't blame him for that. Finding out your captor planned to force you to take the blame for terrorist attacks would turn anyone into a stone statue. If he had betrayed Grace like Amador claimed, that would explain the pallor of his face. She couldn't look away from him, wishing with all her mental might that she could sense his emotions and know if he was all right inside that stiff, stone-faced shell. She didn't have empathic powers, but with him she'd been able to detect some of his feelings as if they could share their powers. She needed that connection more than ever.

A tingling swept through her, light and brief but enough to raise the hairs on her arms and her nape.

What the…She just repressed a shiver as the sensation rushed through her again. No, it couldn't be, not yet. Then again, Nathan had said six hours at most and that it varied. She covered her right hand with her left, holding them in front of her casually, and flicked the index finger of her right hand against her thumb.

A spark snapped to life for a split second, then fizzled out.

Eureka. She fought the impulse to jump up and down pumping her fists in the air. Never in her life before today would she have believed she'd celebrate having her powers. She had to lose them to appreciate how much she needed, and yes, wanted them. They were a part of her.

She looked at Sean again. He was a part of her too, the part she'd been missing but never realized it until today.

With a slow breath, in and out, she relaxed into her returning powers.

Her mind touched Sean's. His only reaction was a faint widening of his eyes for half a second, followed by the briefest tightening of his lips. It had seemed like he was trying not to smile.

Maybe he'd figured out their powers were coming back online.

And then it happened. She sensed his emotions, or a taste of them, and her heart swelled with pride and…affection. What did he feel right now? Resolve, steady and sure. Yes, underneath she detected fear, anger, disgust, and a little bit of shame directed at himself. His overriding attitude, though, was an unbreakable resolve to find a way to stop Amador and thwart his plan. When she'd first touched his mind, he'd given off a hint of anxiety. Now, he believed with complete conviction they could succeed.

She clasped his hand, and power sizzled between them.

He locked down his shields, sealing them both off from prying minds.

Amador was in the corner with Ferrell, engaged in a heated discussion.

Nathan, slumped in the chair, suddenly swung his head toward Sean and Kira. His lips curved up for a heartbeat, then he covered his delight with a neutral expression. He knew their powers had returned. And he was glad.

Kira knew how he felt. She wanted to belt out a chorus of "Hallelujah."

Instead, she sank into the connection with Sean, into the power coursing between them through their linked hands. It hummed inside her, tingled through her, stronger than before. She wondered what they could do with this newly potent connection and decided to test it.

By sending a thought to him.

Can you hear me? She imbued the thought with the fervent energy of her hope. *If you can hear me, squeeze my hand.*

Sean gave her hand a light squeeze. His eyes rotated toward her, and at the instant their gazes intersected, she knew he'd heard her. It didn't seem to bother him in the least.

Do they really have Grace and Abby? she asked.

I don't know.

We need to check.

He aimed his gaze forward, so she followed suit, shifting her attention in the general direction of her parents. A phantom fist gripped her chest. She hadn't even been able to hug them.

Sean's hand tightened around hers, a gentle gesture of reassurance.

You check on Grace and Abby, he told her in her mind.

Me? I don't have a connection with them.

Through me, you do. We're connected.

And that didn't bother her at all either. She'd grown fond of this link with him, never having had anything close to it with anyone else. Close to it? No, nothing she'd shared with anyone else came within a million miles of this.

I'll try, she told him.

Eyes open, she soared out of her body and into the crossroads, rocketing through the tunnel in a nanosecond. Suspended in the field of stars, she let go of her thoughts and waited for a sign.

A star pulsed.

She flew toward it, straight through its brilliant light and down another dark tunnel. Her astral self popped out inside the bunker facility, inside a corridor she recognized because she and Sean had brought Caleb this way earlier.

Grace and Abby Ransom were being herded by two armed guards.

The men took them into a room furnished with a metal table and metal folding chairs. One guard waved for them to sit down, and they complied.

Grace looped her arm around Abby's shoulders. She was talking to the guards, but Kira couldn't hear the words. Floating nearer to them, she focused on sharpening her astral hearing.

"—could at least tell me where we are," Grace said. "Who are you working for?"

"You'll find out soon enough." The guard sneered. "You're the next surprise."

The guards exited the room. A lock chunked into position as they shut the door.

"What's going on, Mommy?" Abby asked, her blue eyes shining darker in the fluorescent lighting.

"It's okay," Grace said, kissing the top of her daughter's head. "Daddy will come for us, or Uncle Sean will. Everything will work out."

"When can we go home?"

"Soon, I promise."

A pain thudded in Kira's chest. She'd spoken the same words to Caleb, and she had yet to make good on them. She hadn't lied to her brother, and Grace was not lying to her daughter. Kira would make sure they both kept their promises.

"Why are we here?" Abby asked.

"I don't know, sweetie," Grace said. "I don't know."

Kira let out an explosive growl, the embodiment of her frustration. "You're here because Gabriel Amador is a goddamn liar and a lunatic."

Grace and Abby swiveled their gazes to Kira, their eyes wide.

Looking at her. They were *looking* at her.

Kira opened her mouth but couldn't make words come out.

Grace leaped up. "Kira."

"Amador is a liar," Kira repeated. "He's the mastermind behind this whole insane plot."

Grace's forehead wrinkled as if she could not comprehend Kira's words.

"David never trusted him," Grace said, "and I had my doubts too sometimes. But I never imagined...I mean, this is..."

She shook her head, and her mouth fell open then clapped shut.

"I know," Kira said. "Sean didn't like Amador, but he couldn't believe the man was capable of this either."

"What on earth is happening here?"

Faster than she'd ever spoken in her life, Kira spelled out the details she and Sean had learned from Amador. Well, almost everything. Two things she still couldn't decide whether to reveal.

Grace laid a hand on her forehead. "Oh dear God. Why didn't I see this before?"

"I don't see how you could have. It's total lunacy, and you're a sane person."

"Guess you're right."

"There's one more thing," Kira said. "Sean and I are in this building. And, um, I left something out when I told you about Nathan. He's—" Kira didn't know if she should be the one to tell Grace, but she suddenly realized the woman ought to know so she'd understand the full picture. "Nathan is Sean's father."

Grace stared blankly at Kira. "His father? Sean always said his dad ran out on him and his mom."

"That's what Sean thought. Turns out Nathan's been a captive for seventeen years, first held by Tesler, now by Tesler's protégé and Amador." Kira hesitated again, gnawing the inside of her cheek. This next bit, well, she still had no idea if informing Grace was a good idea. Once again, though, Kira decided the woman needed to know. "Amador told Sean he was the one who betrayed you to Tesler way back when."

"Oh Jesus," Grace said, shutting her eyes briefly. She flattened her lips, then sighed and relaxed as if she'd accepted an uncomfortable truth. "David and I knew. We found out five years ago, but we didn't tell Sean. He was still coming to terms with his empathic ability, and he'd just found out Tesler was his grandfather. Maybe we should've told him the rest, but we figured he'd never find out." Grace laid a palm on her forehead, rubbing the heel in the space between her eyebrows. "We never imagined we'd all get roped into another mess like this."

"Sean doesn't blame you for not telling him," Kira said, moving closer to the table. "He understands, and he forgives you."

And it was the truth. Through her connection to Sean, she perceived his feelings about the matter. He loved Grace and David like family, and he understood why they hadn't told him.

Grace straightened, lifted her chin, and with a steely glint in her eyes said, "We have to get out of here. Can you unlock the door?"

"Your powers haven't come back yet?"

"No. I feel an inkling of them, but not enough to work with."

Grace glanced down and raised her brows.

Kira followed Grace's eye movement down to her own foot. It tapped against the leg of the metal table. It *touched* the table.

"You didn't realize you're manifesting," Grace said. "I'm guessing this is the first time you've done it."

Speechless, Kira nodded. After a few seconds, she managed to say, "Sean told me only you can manifest. Other people need your help to do it."

Grace smiled with the exasperated affection of a mother. "Sean still underestimates himself, doesn't he? But this is all you, Kira, hey?"

"No." Kira gave a single, sharp shake of her head. "This is us. I can do more because Sean and I have a connection, it supercharges our powers."

Grace smiled again with a kind of knowing only someone older than twenty-two could achieve. "Guess there's a new power couple in town."

"Oh, we're not a couple," Kira said, "not officially. We haven't really talked about it. Anyway, I can bust the door open with a telekinetic shot."

Kira held up her hand and flicked her fingers.

The door popped inward with a *thwack*.

A guard jumped and spun around, waving his gun wildly.

With another flick, Kira zapped him with a jolt of electricity that bowled him over and sent him skidding across the floor. He lay dazed for a second before passing out.

"Nice," Grace said. "Wish I could do that."

"Better get moving," Kira said.

Grace and Abby followed her into the corridor. No other guards were in sight, but they needed to know for sure where everyone was.

"I'll scope out the facility," Kira said. "To check for bad guys."

She tried to zip back through the crossroads, to get into that thermal-imaging mode and scan the building for warm bodies, but nothing happened. She gazed down at her manifested body.

"It's anchoring you," Grace said. "Your artificially created body. You have to disperse it."

"Uh…What now?"

"Disperse it," Grace said with a faint laugh. "Let go of it. Your mind is holding on, keeping the molecules glued together. Release the manifestation."

"Sure. Piece of cake."

"You can do it, Kira."

The conviction in Grace's voice was genuine and unwavering. For a virtual stranger to believe in her…Well, Kira couldn't let Grace down.

She shut her eyes and exhaled, releasing her hold on everything with a whoosh of breath. The physical body she'd unwittingly created vanished, replaced by her astral form. Free of the anchor weighing her down, she opened up her senses and switched into thermal-imaging mode. Without any conscious decision to do it, she soared up through the ceiling to peer down on the facility concealed inside the hill. Blips of human shapes appeared in her vision. Most of them loitered in the isolation room, except for Grace and Abby—and several shapes she thought must be more guards. They waited in a space near the isolation room. In separate quarters distant from the isolation room and the guards, two individual blobs lingered.

Prisoners? Lackeys? She had no idea, but they were nowhere near the room in which Grace and Abby waited.

No one lingered in the vicinity of Grace and Abby, save for the unconscious guard.

Kira pulled back into her astral form, still inside the corridor with Grace and her daughter. "I can tell you how to get outside, so you can hide with my brother. I got him out of this place earlier."

"But you and Sean—"

"Please, Grace, we need to know you and the kids are safe. David's on his way, but I don't know when he'll get here. And his powers are gone too."

"They'll come back soon." Grace stood, and Abby got up too, wrapping her little arms around her mother. Placing a hand on Abby's shoulder, Grace said, "We'll find your brother and stay with him."

"His name is Caleb. Tell him Kiki sent you." Kira glanced at the open doorway. "I'll see you as far as the exit."

In silence, they hurried down the corridors to the door that led outside. Kira busted open the door and trailed Grace and Abby up the concrete steps to the outdoors. She watched until the mother and daughter vanished into the gloom of the woods. With her cool new thermal vision, she tracked them until they met up with Caleb.

She and Sean would stop this madness right now and free their loved ones, free the world, from the threat of impending cataclysm.

Unless they died. Of course, considering their powers, they might find a way to contact their friends and family even after death. *Not going to happen.* They would survive—and defeat their enemies.

They had to.

Kira released her astral form and flew back to the isolation room, settling into her real body with a surprisingly soft landing. Her actual eyes were still open, and her hand remained locked around Sean's. He didn't glance at her, though he must've sensed her return.

She beamed a single thought to him. Grace and Abby are fine and hiding with Caleb, which means Amador has two less bits of leverage.

He did dart his gaze to her then for the briefest moment. *Good. Time to stop Mr. Let's Nuke America.*

Kira held back the smile that itched to surface. *Got a plan?*

Yep. His lips ticked up at the corners, an expression so fleeting no one else would've noticed. *Let's kick his ass.*

How? My parents and your dad…

Sean twined their fingers, gripping her hand tight. *We're saving everyone. Right now.*

For a second, she wondered if the Golden Power had sneaked inside him again, fueling him with so much tainted power he believed he could do anything.

As if he'd read her mind, which he absolutely could have done if he'd wanted—hello, psychics here—he tugged her hand enough to draw her an eensy bit closer and whispered into her mind. *This is all me, not the Golden Power. We can do this if you believe it too.*

The truth rushed through her in a dizzying wave. *I believe it. I believe in us.*

Gabriel Amador ended his conversation with Ferrell and strode up to Sean and Kira. "It is time for your statement, Sean. It will be simulcast on television, radio, and the internet. Every signal will be hijacked, thanks to a certain traveler I have in residence here who turned out to be an accomplished hacker whose powers converge with his natural talents. Quite convenient, no?"

"Yeah, you really rock," Sean said. "Forcing more innocent people to do your bidding. How much did you torture this one to get what you wanted?"

A muscle jumped in Amador's jaw. He snagged the wrist of Kira's free arm, the one not currently held fast by Sean's hand around hers.

"Kira stays with me," Amador said.

Sean's eyes narrowed to slits, his nostrils flaring the tiniest bit. "She stays with me or you can forget this whole thing. You can't nuke anybody without our help."

"I have your loved ones. They will suffer if you fail to comply."

"Kira stays with me or this is over, and you can kill us all if you want."

What was he up to? Kira didn't have a chance to ask him telepathically because Amador released her wrist and said, "As you wish."

The man spoke words of acquiescence, but his expression conveyed pure arrogance. He believed he had them right where he wanted.

Amador gestured to the guards, and Kira and Sean were escorted out of the isolation room.

I hope you really have a plan, Kira told Sean through their link as they hurried down the corridor with guards surrounding them and Amador in the lead.

Sean's thought beamed into her, warm and full of assurance. *Today, we save the world.*

They crossed the hall to a room on the other side. The second they walked into the control room, Kira's stomach plunged downward with a sickening rush. A bank of black-and-white video monitors displayed various parts of the bunker facility. Many of the rooms were empty, but four contained human beings locked up in various kinds of cells. In one video feed, Nathan wriggled in his dentist-like chair, seemingly testing his bonds while a pair of guards observed without expression. Another feed showed her parents returning to their room, a slightly nicer version of a prison cell with a bed and bare-bones sofa as well as a Spartan bathroom.

A third feed showed a woman sleeping, or seeming to sleep, on a cot. The fourth monitor displayed images of a small room darkened by a false twilight, thanks to the weak, bare bulb suspended from the ceiling. A young man, maybe the same age as Kira and Sean, paced the width of the square cell, running his hand along the concrete wall.

These prisoners must've been the unknown blobs she'd spotted earlier.

Gabriel Amador pointed to the feed showing the young man. "This is Danny, our resident hacker. He has a talent for breaking into electronic systems, with assistance from his psychic powers."

"Why do you need me," Sean said, "if you've got this guy? He could launch your nuke for you."

"No, he can't." Amador tapped the video monitor. "Danny has never breached a network as highly secured as that of a nuclear facility. He tried once, with a site less secure than Malmstrom, and almost got caught. Without an electronic link to the target, his powers fail. We cannot risk that. You will handle this task for us."

Besides, Amador wanted to punish Sean for the crime of being related to Tesler.

Kira glanced around the room to note its other contents. Besides the monitors, it also housed equipment for recording video—a camera connected to a computer and equipped with a large, fuzzy microphone. A stool chair sat in front of the camera, and a blank wall provided the backdrop for Amador's video.

Sean's video. The loon was about to make Sean take the fall.

Without looking at him, she asked Sean in her mind, *What do we do?*

He clinched her hand tighter. *Zap their equipment.*

She sank her teeth into her bottom lip. Destroying the equipment would tick off Amador, and who knew what he'd do then. *What about your dad and my parents? Grace and the kids? And the other prisoners?*

Leave that to me.

Kira bit her lip harder, so hard pain cut through her flesh.

Trust me, Sean said in her mind.

With a rush of tingling awareness, she realized one vital fact. She did trust him. Completely.

She curled the fingers of her free hand into her palm and pulled in a deep breath. Energy crackled in her palm, silent and invisible yet palpable. With their minds connected and their hands joined, their powers had also become linked like a two-way electrical path coursing energy back and forth in a loop that supercharged their powers. The potency of it grew stronger and stronger, more than ever before. It fed into her enough strength to intensify the telekinetic energy contained in her palm, making it crackle and sizzle on her skin, under her skin, lifting every fine hair on her body.

She flung up her hand, fingers spread, and hurled the energy at the bank of monitors.

CHAPTER TWENTY-FOUR

SEAN CHOKED ON A GASP AS THE ENERGY OF KIRA'S TELEKINETIC blast tugged on his powers and crashed into the wall of monitors. The ball of electrical power erupted into miniature bolts of lightning that lashed out in multiple directions. The energy crackled and snapped, sizzled and hissed, diving deep into the circuits hidden within the electronics. Bolts lanced through the air to fry the video camera and singe the wire leading to the computer. The PC exploded, shards spewing through the room.

His veins burned with a heady rush of adrenaline and psychic power.

Mini bolts of lightning lanced the walls, seeking out electrical lines.

The lights went out.

Seconds. He had seconds to save everyone, or this was all for nothing.

Fueled by the double whammy of his powers and Kira's, Sean blasted through the crossroads, barely noticing the stars that blurred into elongated lines as he shot past them. He emerged in the isolation room, an arm's length from where his father sat in the torture chair. The emergency lighting painted the room in shades of blood red.

"You need to get out of here," Sean said. "We just pissed off a whackjob, and he'll be coming for you to punish me."

Nathan blinked once in slow motion, his lips parted.

"Hurry up," Sean said.

Nathan shook his head as if shedding the lingering memory of a strange dream and wriggled his hands inside the leather restraints. "I'm not going anywhere. Help the others."

No, no, no, he hadn't found his dad only to leave him behind in this hellhole. But he didn't have the kind of power necessary to shatter the restraints.

Or did he?

The energy surging through him carried with it the flavor of Kira's power. Telekinesis.

He threw open the floodgates of his mind, letting her power pour into him. Energy sparked on his skin, tiny explosions of kinetic power.

Nathan stared at him, unblinking. "I had no idea you could do that."

"Yeah, neither did I."

The energy gathered at his fingertips, shimmering and snapping.

Sean thrust out a hand, firing tiny bolts at the chair.

Metal buckles that secured the leather restraints popped open. The shackles burst apart.

"Did I hurt you?" Sean asked, his heartbeats thudding in his chest and in his ears.

"No." His father clambered out of the chair slowly like he couldn't quite believe he was free. Nathan faced his son, his smile evincing shock and pride. "Thank you."

A strange warmth radiated through his chest, but Sean had no time to figure out what it was. "Can you find your own way out? I have to hurry to help the others."

"I'll be fine. You go, save the world."

Sean hesitated for the briefest moment, staring at his father, over-whelmed by the bizarre but comforting warmth in his chest—around his heart.

Then he left.

He didn't need the crossroads this time. Somehow, he just...thought his way to his destination. He wanted to find Kira's parents, and zoom, he was in their room. The red light of the emergency bulbs provided minimal illumination, enough to move around with care. Sean didn't need to move, though. The Magnussons huddled in the corner, eyes darting, arms around each other.

Sean couldn't blame them for being afraid. They'd spent sixteen months in the tender loving care of Gabriel Amador. Who knew what the whackjob had done to them.

With a single thought, Sean made himself visible.

The Magnussons jerked in unison.

"It's okay," Sean said, holding his hands up, palms out. "I'm here to help. I'm Kira's friend, Sean. You saw me in the, uh, other room."

The torture chamber. Sean's stomach roiled at the memory, but he forced himself to stay calm.

Well, as calm as possible under the circumstances.

"Come with me," he said, "and I'll help you get out of this place."

"Where's Kira?" Mr. Magnusson asked.

"She's okay." Sean sensed her like a warm and steady breeze wafting over him, carrying with it the sweet scent of tropical things. He gestured for them to follow him. "Hurry, please."

I need more power.

The thought shivered through him. Kira's thought, not his own. He fired off his response even as he guided her parents into the corridor, flinging the door open with a burst of power borrowed from Kira. *You don't need to ask, just do it. This is our power now.*

A wave of heat rushed through him. It was like a steamy embrace from Kira, and it knocked him off kilter for one second too long. He stumbled, slapped a hand on the corridor wall, and fought for breath as a burst of vertigo whirled in his head. When it ceased, he heard a sound all too familiar to him.

The *ka-chunk* of a round being chambered in a large-caliber weapon.

Mrs. Magnusson shrieked.

Sean shoved away from the wall just as the solitary guard swung his weapon in Sean's direction.

"Don't move," the guy said, his voice slightly shaky. "I've got orders to take you alive, but I can shoot them if that's what it takes."

The guard swerved his weapon—an AK-47, maybe—toward the Magnussons.

Sean didn't want to hurt the guy. The guard's eyes were wide, and his whole body was shaking. He might've been forced to obey Amador, or maybe he'd signed on for the gig but didn't realize how totally nutso crazy his boss was until it was too late.

Either way, Sean preferred not to kill anybody unless he had no choice.

He tapped into Kira's power, and with his arms at his sides, he flicked one finger.

A mini bolt zapped the guard. He crumpled to the floor, his gun clattering on the linoleum.

Sean bent to check the man's neck for a pulse. It surged against his finger. *Thank God.*

He snatched up the gun.

Only then did he realize what he'd done.

A tingle rushed over his skin, awareness of the fact he'd failed to note until this very second. He'd manifested.

Holy smokes. He'd manifested all on his own, thanks to the boost from Kira's power.

Yeah, he felt like jumping up and down, hooting, pumping his fists. No time for celebration, though. He had to get these people out of here.

"Let's go," he told the Magnussons.

Kira's parents followed him without question, though they seemed kind of dazed. While he plotted out the best escape route in his mind, soaring out of his manifested body to view the network of corridors from above, he simultaneously shepherded the Magnussons through the facility. He had no clue how he managed the dual tasks, but he had no time to wonder or to marvel at it.

They rounded a corner.

A ripping noise inside the walls raced up the corridor. In its wake, black lines marked the singed electrical lines and cables buried in the walls. The black lines shot past them, around the corner, trailing the noise Kira's power created as she destroyed every last shred of technology in this place. Electronics not connected to the bunker's systems might've survived Kira's assault, but he doubted that would give the bad guys much to work with.

The emergency power might go soon too. Better hurry it up.

He mentally selected the fastest route out of the facility and urged Kira's parents to move faster.

The other prisoners.

Sean skidded to a stop, frozen by the thought. He'd forgotten about them. How could he forget? *Got to save them.* Adrenaline heightened his senses and coursed through his veins. He lost his grip on the overhead view of the corridors, lost his path to freedom for the Magnussons.

Get a grip, numbskull.

He couldn't do three things at once. Find the right corridors, guide the Magnussons, save the other prisoners. He would fail at all of it if he tried. And what about Kira? Amador might—

Fear zinged through him, cold and sharp and stinging.

Sean spotted a doorway and sprinted toward it, throwing the door open.

A supply closet.

Good enough for the moment.

He waved for Kira's parents to approach. "Hide in this closet. I need to check on Kira, but you should be safe in here."

Like he had even a shred of a clue if they would be. But he had no choice. Returning to Kira meant releasing his manifested body and his hold on this location.

The Magnussons hurried into the closet.

A cold weight settled in Sean's gut as he shut the door—and prayed he was doing the right thing.

He let go of the manifestation and slammed back into his body.

Gabriel Amador cradled his left arm, breathing hard. Sweat sheened his face.

The lunatic reached for Kira.

And got zapped big time by the glittering field of kinetic energy that surrounded her and Sean.

Sean glanced at her, and awe shimmered through his psyche. Her dark hair fluttered around her face in slow motion as if buoyed by static electricity. Her eyes glowed a deep and incandescent blue, like sapphires set ablaze.

The red emergency lights had gone out, but the shimmering white of her telekinetic power lit the room.

Amador stumbled backward, grimacing and bellowing at the burst of energy that had zapped him.

The guards had retreated into the corner furthest from Kira, faces pale, eyes bulging. Now, they bolted from the room.

Amador screamed at them in Spanish, probably a slew of curses. Nasty ones, by the tone of his voice. With his undamaged hand, he dug a phone out of his pocket.

Did you get them all? Kira asked through their telepathic link.

No. My dad's free, and I hid your parents in a closet. But I couldn't get the others. Not enough power.

Her anxiety filtered into him, tensing his muscles. She worried for her parents, he knew.

Amador fumbled with his phone.

What should we do with him? Kira asked.

Knock him out. Give us time to figure out the rest.

She lifted her hand, power sparking between her fingers.

"No!" Amador shouted, his eyes wild. "I have my finger on a button that will release a poisonous gas into this facility and kill everyone. If I cannot have my revenge on the world, I will exact it on you."

The whackjob hovered one finger over the phone's screen.

Kira curled her fingers, about to unleash a bolt.

Amador squashed his finger onto the phone's screen. "You are too late."

Chapter Twenty-Five

THE ROOM STANK OF SCORCHED WALLS AND FRIED WIRES. KIRA stared unseeing in Amador's direction, her mind spinning with thoughts that crashed into each other, shattering and reforming over and over while she fought to make sense of what was happening. Amador released poison gas. Into the whole facility? Into the cells where he kept his prisoners? Was he even telling the truth?

Her pulse raced faster than a hummingbird's heart. She felt lightheaded, her knees weak. This couldn't be how things ended. *Mom, Dad, please forgive me.*

No, no, no, this was not the end.

She glanced at Sean, but his grim expression matched her emotions. They'd expended a hell of a lot of energy on destroying the facility's electrical system and trying to rescue the prisoners. Even with their combined powers, they lacked the capability to stop the gas.

"In case you are wondering," Amador said, staggering backward to slump against the bank of monitors, "we will survive. The gas affects the guest wing, not the control room."

Guest wing? Seriously? Those people were prisoners.

We need more power.

Kira jumped at the sensation of Sean's words injected into her brain. She'd gotten used to sharing thoughts with him, but her nerves had been scraped raw. Everyone would die unless they did something. What? More power, they needed more power. Fast.

And she knew of just one way to acquire it.

She turned toward Sean, and as if he'd sensed her intention, he turned to face her at the same instant. They clutched each other's hands, forming a complete circle of psychic energy with their joined palms. This time, they spoke aloud.

"No," he said. "It's too dangerous."

"We have no choice. That lunatic—" She jerked her head in Amador's direction. The man had sagged to the floor, his expression dreamily crazed. "He's killing everyone. We have to do this, no matter the cost."

"The power will eat us alive."

She inched closer, her head tilted back to meet his burning green gaze. "You told me it acts like a living, breathing, ravenous thing, but it's not alive. It can't control us unless we let it. So, don't let it. We can fight together, for each other, for what we need to get this done. Trust me, like I trust you."

He stared into her eyes, the intensity of it shivering heat through her body. With a fierce determination she'd never heard from him before, he said, "I trust you."

Amador laughed, the sound almost hysterical. "It's too late for whatever you're planning. Too late, too long, too far."

The sing-song tone of the last bit made Kira cringe inside. The man had lost the last thread tying his sanity together.

Sean pulled her into his arms, hugging her to his firm, warm body. "If we hold on to each other, nothing will tear us apart."

It sounded silly, but she believed him. She wrapped her arms around his torso and nestled her face against his chest.

"Close your eyes," Sean told her. "And follow me."

Kira shut her eyes and held on.

Every other time, they had traveled as separate astral entities linked by their hands. Now, they soared up into the crossroads as one, their minds mingled, their powers merged, and broke out into the field of stars. She'd hardly noticed the tunnel. They hovered amid the blackness, surrounded by glittering points of light. They didn't seek a star, though, or the connection it might offer to a place or a person in the real world. No, they sought a far more elusive quarry.

They acted in unison, throwing out ropes of energy, hunting for their prey, lashing out into the furthest reaches of the crossroads. A barrier reflected their questing ropes back at them, and oily talons clawed at their minds, but they funneled everything they had into the barrier to punch through it. A concussion, like a blast of astral wind, pummeled them. They steeled themselves against it and dived through the gap they'd blasted open straight into the pulsating core of the ultimate power.

Energy. Glistening, golden energy.

It engulfed and infused them, fueled and emboldened them. The power surged into their minds with overwhelming speed and intensity, a tidal wave of the most potent psychic energy in the universe. It was the universe. It was the essence of power.

And it belonged to them.

The Golden Power shot through their astral bodies straight down into their physical bodies. It energized them with the heady ecstasy of an orgasm, but the climax of their union with the Golden Power had no physical effect. They imagined it did because it permeated their beings.

Kira exploded back into her body, ablaze with more power than she'd ever dreamed she could achieve, alive with an energy too potent to deny.

Sean's chest heaved beneath her head. His heart pounded under her ear.

He pushed her away just enough to grasp her shoulders and aim his blazing eyes at her. Shimmering green energy outlined his body, and when she glanced down at herself, she discovered the same green fire glittered around her.

"We did it," he said, breathless.

She nodded, struggling to catch her own breath. "Let's do this."

They shot out of their bodies once again, soaring through the walls of the facility to locate the endangered men and women trapped inside. They found her parents first, still hiding in the supply closet where Sean had left them. He hadn't told Kira where he left them. She just knew. The incredible power coursing through them both joined their minds like never before. She understood what he wanted without asking, knew what he knew without a word spoken—and vice versa.

Her parents startled when she and Sean materialized in front of them.

"Are you okay?" Kira asked.

"We're…fine." Her dad spoke slowly, his astonished gaze aimed at her. Mom looked the same, awestruck but not afraid of her or Sean.

"Hang on," Sean said.

Kira let him take them both out of their manifested bodies—an out-of-body-experience once removed?—to hover above the facility for a bird's-eye view. Instead of looking down on the surroundings, though, they gazed down on the interior of the underground building. The roof vanished, the ceilings of the rooms inside vanished, and they entered a kind of altered reality that revealed things invisible to the naked eye.

Streams of dark-gray smoke unfurled inside one section of the building.

No, not smoke. The tendrils of writhing, expanding grayness represented the invisible poison gas. The stuff emerged inside four rooms, spreading outward into the corridors.

Her parents and Nathan had escaped the gas so far, but inside two of the rooms, human-shaped blobs pounded on the doors of their cells. The rooms had filled with gas.

Are we too late? The thought, though her own, ripped into her soul.

No, dammit.

Had Sean thought that, or had she? The lines between them had begun to blur.

But the power, it infused them.

They raced to one of the rooms.

A tawny-haired woman sagged against the door, too weak to pound on it any longer. She sobbed and wailed, her cries suffused with anger and hopelessness. She wheezed, gagged, her eyes flaring wide.

Sean and Kira dispersed the gas with a burst of power, realigning the molecules until the poison became an inert gas. She had no idea how they'd done it, only that they had. The woman slumped to the floor, her face ashen, gasping for breath. Sean and Kira surrounded her, unseen and without form, ghosts embracing her with their power. White light enveloped the woman, and Kira sensed the damage to her body reversing, repairing, healing.

Before they left the woman, they opened the door for her and Kira whispered into the woman's ear the directions for getting out of the bunker.

They hadn't manifested or made their presences known, but the woman understood their instructions on a subconscious level. She hustled out of the room.

Next, they healed and freed the hacker-slash-psychic.

A quick overhead scan told them every last molecule of the poison had been eradicated, even the reserves Amador hadn't released yet. They also discovered Nathan had broken out of the facility and was ushering the other two prisoners out the door through which Sean and Kira had entered earlier. Amador's guards fled out another exit on the opposite side of the hill that concealed the bunker.

Gabriel Amador still huddled on the floor in the control room.

When they returned to the supply closet, dropping back into their manifested bodies, her parents no longer seemed shell-shocked. Instead, they wore looks of determination colored by exhaustion. She and Sean escorted them out of the building to meet up with Nathan and the others. They had no time for family reunions. Kira told Nathan where she'd left Grace and the kids, and he vowed to find them.

She believed he would do it. Though she'd just met both Sean and his father, she realized they shared the same stalwart conviction to help others and do the right thing. Just like Sean would've given his life to save someone else, Nathan would risk his own safety to find and protect Caleb, Grace, and Abby.

After quick farewells—not goodbye, but "see you soon"—Kira and Sean returned to their real bodies inside the control room. The green energy still glimmered around them like a body-size halo, but she didn't worry about that. She worried about their prisoner.

Gabriel Amador lay sprawled on the floor, his neck bent at a ninety-degree angle thanks to his head being lodged against the bank of monitors while his body lay perpendicular to the wall. Sweat slicked his face and matted his hair. His body trembled. The whites of his wide eyes shone a sickly color in the pale-green glow of the power halo around Sean and Kira.

Their halo provided the sole source of illumination.

Amador laughed weakly. "The world will know my vengeance."

Sean stepped toward the man, eying him with a pinched expression. "It's over, Gabriel. You lost."

"No, no, it's a setback only." Amador tried to push up off the floor but his arms gave out, and he crumpled again. "The ICBM. It will show them. Everyone will see."

With a gusty sigh, Sean knelt beside Amador. "No, they won't. You wanted everyone to know how dangerous psychics are, didn't you? Your son was one of us, so why would—"

"He was not one of you," Amador spat. "Evander had no powers until Tesler abducted him and pumped him full of drugs to induce psychic experiences."

"You told Grace your son had powers, and that's why Tesler took him."

"No, no, no!" Amador flung his body into a slouched sitting position, his arms dangling loose at his sides. "Evander did not travel. Tesler invented the story because he needed an excuse to take my child. He wanted younger subjects to study. I don't care what your grandfather said. Evander never traveled to the facility through remote viewing. He never sensed other psychics and went to them. It did not happen."

Sean threw Kira a confused look. She must've worn the same expression. The man before them, once cocky in his belief he had the upper hand, had dissolved into a lump of craziness.

"During my treatments at the hospital," Amador said, seeming unable to stop talking now that he'd started, "I had visions of the truth. The doctors called them hallucinations, but I knew the universe was gifting me with the truth. I realized Evander did not have powers after all, but that he was chosen for induction because of me. Tesler hoped to ransom him for the money he needed to continue his secret research since JT had never known about what he and Ferrell had planned. He did not even know Tesler and his cohort had abducted your father."

"But, uh," Sean began, rubbing his jaw, "did they ever ask for ransom money? I mean, I thought Evander was experimented on and then killed."

Amador sprang to his feet, roaring so loud it vibrated Kira's eardrums. "They would have ransomed him! I saw the truth!"

Oh jeez. The man had hallucinated the only truth he could accept—that his son had no powers and therefore was not like Sean or Kira or any of the others. Amador needed to believe his son had been taken for ransom, though the facts belied that belief.

Amador burst into sobs, doubling over, clutching his belly.

Sean strode back to Kira. "This guy has lost more than the plot. He's lost the whole frigging book and the library too."

"What do we do with him?"

"Lock him in one of the cells here and come back for him after we get everybody else to safety." Sean clenched his fists. "And we have to find Ferrell."

They half dragged Amador out of the control room, Kira holding one of his arms while Sean held the other. The man leaned on them heavily, his sobs mutating into moans. They dropped him off in one of the cells and locked the door, then headed out the same exit their families and the other prisoners had gone out of earlier.

Four guards awaited them, arrayed in a semicircle around the top of the concrete stairwell. Each man brandished a weapon that looked like an AK-47 but also had a pistol strapped to his hip.

Sean and Kira froze at the base of the steps.

The eyes of every guard went wide at the sight of the green halo around Sean and Kira, but each man held his position. Four guns stayed trained on them.

Well, they must've seen weird things before. They worked in a facility that held psychics.

Let's knock them out, Kira told Sean through their mental link.

He gave a sharp nod.

They stretched out their shared power, lashing it at the guards.

And slammed into a granite-hard barrier. The force of the impact flung their powers back at them and hurled them to the concrete. Stars burst in Kira's vision while pain webbed out through her skull. She winced, gasped, and lay there prone, paralyzed by the shock.

Sean groaned, pushing up onto his elbows, dazed.

Kira heaved her body up into a sitting position. Her head throbbed. She ached all over, but nothing seemed broken and she saw no cuts or abrasions on her or on Sean. What she did detect disturbed her far more than injuries might have.

She sensed a gaping maw of nothingness inside her, devoid of psychic energy.

And her connection to Sean had been severed.

Kira glanced at him, but his gaze had gone bleary and unfocused.

A slender figure pushed between the middle two guards at the top of the stairs.

"EM," Sean muttered. "She used..."

His voice trailed off, and he squeezed his eyes shut like he was struggling to stay awake.

"Yes," Ferrell said, "he understands. I've implemented another of our contingencies, an electromagnetic field tuned to the precise frequency of psychic powers. You have nothing."

Kira scrambled to her knees. "Only as long as you keep that field up. Since I destroyed the electrical systems in your facility, I'm guessing you got your EM field up and running with battery power. It won't last forever."

"Long enough, though."

Ferrell stopped at the edge of the top step. She'd shed her lab coat, but she clasped the handle of a canvas bag with a zipper closure. She waved a hand in the air.

The four guards moved aside. Behind, two more guards kept their weapons aimed at a group of prisoners.

Kira opened her mouth, but the gasp lodged in her throat. She recognized these people.

The guards watched over the two prisoners she and Sean had freed as well as Kira's parents, Sean's father, Caleb, and Grace and Abby Ransom.

"Congratulations," Ferrell said. "You failed."

CHAPTER TWENTY-SIX

"Y OU DON'T HAVE DAVID," SEAN SAID, BECAUSE IT WAS THE ONLY thing he could think of to say when he at last regained enough physical energy to speak and move. "David's a powerful traveler, and he'll be here any minute to clobber you."

In all the commotion, he'd forgotten about Ferrell. Hadn't looked for her at all. Made sure to keep track of Amador, believing him to be the biggest threat, but overlooked the deceptively pretty mad scientist. The face of an angel, the heart of a demon. That was Dr. Ferrell. Dear old Grandpa would be so proud of his disciple.

Sean had also forgotten about EM fields. *Idiot.* When he'd found out they used Nathan's power to cancel out his and Kira's, he'd stupidly assumed that was Ferrell's only trick. Amador had mentioned "multiple contingencies," but Sean hadn't realized what that meant.

He clambered to his feet and helped Kira up.

Ferrell surveyed her entourage—the guards and the prisoners—with self-satisfaction. "I have your father, and David's wife and child. You'll play your part to protect Nathan and these innocent bystanders. If David Ransom arrives, he'll do as I say too—unless he prefers to watch his family die painful deaths."

"You're as bonkers as Amador."

"Biel is right about you." She took half a step closer, a dark glee shimmering in her eyes. "You betrayed a woman you think of as a surrogate mother, leading her enemies straight to her and causing untold suffering. That makes you as twisted as Biel and as malleable too."

Malleable? Like hell.

She'd called Amador by his nickname, Biel. It had to mean something.

Acid ate away at his gut, giving rise to a gnawing dread, but Sean folded his arms over his chest and kept his chin up. "Don't you want to know where your boyfriend is?"

Ferrell's brows scrunched.

"Gabriel Amador," Sean said. "Your sweet Biel. He's gone way far over the edge, inches away from turning into a drooling idiot. His plans are toast, and so is his brain."

The woman's eyes narrowed, and her upper lip twitched. She shouted for her minions to bring Sean and Kira out of the stairwell, and two guards trotted down the steps to retrieve them. One man snagged Kira's arm and hauled her up the stairs roughly, making her trip twice. Sean clenched his fists, desperate to slug the creep for manhandling a woman. The other guard grabbed Sean's arm and tried to drag him in the same manner but didn't have the strength to do it. He settled for herding Sean up the stairs.

Once they were on the surface, across the little clearing from the other prisoners, Ferrell stalked up to Sean. "Where is Gabriel Amador?"

Sean considered lying, to make her believe he'd killed the guy, but decided that might piss her off to the point of being super dangerous. So, he told the truth. "We locked him up in one of the cells he used to imprison innocent people so the two of you could abuse them at your leisure. Seemed appropriate to confine the nutjob in his own prison."

"Which cell?" Ferrell spoke each syllable with exaggerated lip movements, her teeth clamped together.

"Don't remember."

What are you doing? Kira's question reverberated in his mind, but he didn't dare glance at her. He had a plan. Sort of. Right now, a half-assed scheme was the best option.

Follow my lead, he told her.

He sensed her anxiety, but she kept quiet, sending him a pulse of…He repressed a weird shiver. Kira had given him a taste of something sweet and warm and gentle. Affection? He wasn't sure he could recognize that emotion anymore. Yet his chest ached with a sensation not unlike what Kira had communicated to him without a word or a gesture, simply with her heart.

She was awesome. In her personality and in her powers.

Oh God. Did he—he couldn't—no way.

The realization he couldn't acknowledge, wouldn't acknowledge, got him choked up nonetheless. He gulped against the constriction in his throat, refusing to let Dr. Ferrell see any emotion, any weakness, in him.

Even if it had shown, Ferrell wouldn't have noticed. She was busy railing about her beloved Biel and how brilliant he was. Wow, Sean hadn't realized she actually had feelings for the loony-tunes guy. Maybe he could use that to his advantage.

Then she shattered his misconception.

Ferrell looked Sean straight in the eye and said, "Gabriel Amador is insane. You're correct on that point. If you think to hold him hostage as a means of getting your way, forget it. Kill him if you want."

"Thought the two of you were tight."

"We were lovers, yes, but only as a means to placate him. He is brilliant, but in the way of an idiot savant. Sex makes him easier to handle and more pliable."

Oh man. He got it now. Of course the crazy guy hadn't done all this on his own.

"You let him think he was in charge," Sean said, "but you were running the show. This nutso scheme to expose psychics as a threat to humanity was your idea. You used Amador's vengeance plot because it meshed with what you wanted. Nuking the East Coast must've been his idea, but the rest of it was you, right?"

"Most of it, yes." She stepped back, lifting the black bag. "I've brought some of my best tools. If you don't do as I say, I'll use them on your friends and loved ones."

Sean didn't point out he'd just met his father a few hours ago and hardly knew the man. Besides, Ferrell had Grace and Abby too, and Kira. He couldn't let this woman hurt anybody.

"What is it you want?" he asked.

"Essentially the same thing Biel wanted. You will make a public statement claiming responsibility for the bombings. Your statement, the one I've prepared for you, will make it clear psychics are a threat and are determined to take over the world."

Sean spluttered, trying not to laugh. He didn't feel amused, though. He felt dumbfounded and a little bit sick. Take over the world? Right, because all the psychics of the world had united into an army. Sheesh, would anybody believe that?

"You will, of course, offer proof," Ferrell said. "Gabriel's idea about launching an ICBM may be extreme, but it will get the job done."

Everything inside Sean went cold, doused with an icy bucket of reality. Ferrell was as crazy as Amador.

"Each ICBM," she went on, "carries multiple rockets. You will target various cities around the world and issue this threat in your broadcast. If the world's leaders accede to your demands, you'll disable the rockets."

"And what are my demands?"

"Ten billion dollars."

He spluttered again. Jeez, this woman had nerve. "Why would anyone believe this malarkey?"

"Because you will make them believe. You will kill the Vice President of the United States."

"Wh—How am I supposed to do that?"

Ferrell tapped her long fingernails on the canvas bag. "You and Kira clearly tapped into the Golden Power. Use that to enhance your own abilities and strangle the Vice President. He's currently giving a commencement speech at Vanderbilt University. Thousands will see it happen. Be sure to make it showy, so no one will doubt the attack is paranormal in nature."

Showy. Attack. Kill the VP.

No way in hell.

He needed her to believe he'd do this, though.

"Guess you've got me where you want," he said. "One problem. Your fancy control room is rubble now."

"Oh, you won't need that." She smiled, the expression not in the least friendly or happy. "You are going to commandeer Malmstrom Air Force Base."

Sean opened his mouth but couldn't make any sounds come out. Take over a military base? What, all by himself? "I need help to do that."

"You go alone."

"At least let Kira—"

"No."

"You'll have to take down the EM field."

"Nice try, but no," Ferrell said. "My men will escort you outside the field, but not before I dose you with my favorite serum. It will make you…cooperative."

The serum. Sean tried to swallow, but his mouth and throat had gone dry.

Ferrell gestured to the guard who stood beside Kira. When the man hauled her to the scientist, Ferrell extracted a syringe and a small glass vial from her bag. Setting down the bag, she filled the syringe and tapped out the bubbles, squirting a brief jet of liquid. Satisfied, she told the guard, "Restrain her."

The second the guard reached for Kira's wrists, she kicked out with one foot and landed a solid shot in the guy's groin. The guard doubled over, gasping.

Ferrell shouted, "Bring her to me!"

Just as Kira rammed her elbow backward into the guard behind her, another guard sprinted up alongside her and smacked the butt of his gun into her head. The *crack* of its impact echoed in the clearing.

Kira crumpled to the ground.

"No!" Kira's mother shrieked.

Sean's heart pounded so hard and fast he felt lightheaded. He started to run for Kira, but three more guards joined the one already posted beside him, swarming around him with guns aimed at his chest. He no longer had the capacity to stop them. His link to Kira was gone. The telekinetic power she'd shared with him had snuffed out when the EM field encompassed them.

No, no, no. He ground his teeth until his jaw ached, glancing around in a desperate search for a way out, something he could do, some way to get to Kira and make sure she wasn't…His jaw quivered. She wasn't dead. She couldn't be.

Between the guards' bodies, he spotted Kira's limp form on the ground.

If he ran for her, if he tried to get a weapon away from one of the guards, the others would shoot him. Maybe not dead, since that would blow up Ferrell's plans, but they'd make sure he couldn't fight anymore. A shot to the leg or the shoulder would do the trick.

Ferrell knelt beside Kira, feeling for a pulse in her throat. "She's alive. For now. But she won't be offering any aid to you, Sean." Ferrell jabbed the needle she still held into Kira's neck and depressed the plunger. "The strong sedative I'm giving her will make certain she'll be of no help even if the EM field goes down."

The scientist tossed the empty syringe aside. She brought out a fresh syringe and filled it with liquid from a small vial, then she strolled up to Sean.

"Maybe I'll just kill you right now," Sean snarled, "with my bare hands."

"You won't." Ferrell smiled again in that creepy way. "You don't have the power. Not psychically, not physically. Guns trump muscles, but the serum trumps everything."

Ferrell was right. Even if he could knock out the EM field, he wouldn't have the power. Not without Kira. She'd made him strong in more than his psychic abilities. She'd made him a stronger man, a better man, and he wouldn't let any harm come to her or the other prisoners. What could he do?

The EM field had dampened his powers to the point of being useless. But though the Golden Power had faded, its seductive energy simmered deep inside him. Even the dampening field hadn't eradicated it completely. If he tapped into it again…Without Kira to ground him, could he come back from it this time?

Grace had done it. But she'd also sworn never to use the Golden Power again, and she'd made Sean swear he wouldn't either. Now, he'd used it twice. Grace would rip him a new one for that alone. If he did it again, she'd kill him.

Dammit, he wasn't a kid anymore. He made his own choices. And Grace, as smart and powerful as she was, didn't know everything about the psychic world. The Golden Power hadn't consumed him this time, not with Kira beside him.

She was out cold. He'd have to do it alone. If it destroyed him, well, at least the others would survive and he'd take Ferrell down with him.

"You're right," he told Ferrell. "On my own, I don't have enough power to stop you."

But he could access more power. Though Ferrell had guessed he and Kira used the Golden Power, she clearly thought he couldn't access it inside the EM field. Good. *Powers dampened, not destroyed.*

Ferrell stabbed the needle into his neck, and searing acid scorched through his veins. It annihilated his willpower, his determination, everything that kept him from doing what she wanted. He fought against the serum even as it scoured out his mind and convulsed his muscles, refusing to collapse, refusing to give in.

The scientist got another syringe out of her bag and filled it from a different vial. "This will make Kira's heart stop beating instantly. One wrong move and she dies."

Yeah, the woman also thought only Kira could use telekinesis. *Keep underestimating me, you slimy, arrogant snake.*

Sean cleared his throat. "I need to RV the base to get the lay of the land. I've never seen pictures of Malmstrom, much less been there."

The woman squinted at him, angling her head. "All right. But remember, Kira will die if you pull anything—and should the serum fail for any reason, I can take your father outside of the EM field and have him nullify your powers at any time."

Sean glanced at his father. The second their eyes met, he knew—though he couldn't explain how—his father would never, ever again do that to him. No matter what Ferrell did or said.

Ferrell instructed one of the guards to retrieve Amador, then she told Sean, "No tricks, or Kira dies."

"I know."

The scientist studied Nathan, her gaze glinting with the light of keen understanding.

"Ah," Ferrell said, all but cooing the syllable, "I see I can no longer trust Nathan to do as I say. His fatherly instincts have gone into overdrive, haven't they? Well, I suppose you'll need a greater motivation."

"You've got Kira, and Grace and Abby. I'll do what I said."

If David showed up...Sean cursed himself silently for thinking his friend would arrive and save them all. This time, it was up to Sean.

"Best to be certain," Ferrell said. She rose and snatched the pistol from the holster of the nearest guard. "It's the scientific way."

She leveled the gun at Kira where she lay prone and unconscious on the ground.

A certainty of what was about to go down, almost a premonition, jolted through Sean. "No, you don't have to—"

Ferrell pulled the trigger. The shot detonated in the clearing, deafening and shocking.

Kira twitched. Red liquid oozed down her forehead from the bullet hole at its center.

Sean roared with a fury that scorched out reason, thought, intention—and the serum. It evaporated from his blood on a tide of his own healing power. He didn't give a damn that he'd finally healed himself and done it despite the EM field too. He surged forward determined to rip Ferrell's head from her body with his bare hands.

A guard punched the butt of his AK-47 into Sean's chest.

The impact slammed him to the ground backward. The breath exploded out of his lungs, and he couldn't suck in more air. Blackness dotted his vision. If he didn't regain his breath soon, he'd pass out—and be no good to anyone.

Kira. He could heal her. But when he tried, his mind slammed into a wall.

The fucking EM field. He could heal his own body but not hers? Dammit, he needed more power.

Don't let on the serum isn't working, he reminded himself.

He dragged in a wheezing breath, his lungs burning. And he glared at the bitch smiling down at him.

"Now you're properly motivated," she said. "Complete your task, and I will lower the EM field so you can heal Kira. Assuming you hurry. It's my understanding a healer can use his power only on a body whose soul hasn't departed yet."

Souls? He'd never considered that idea in relation to his power, but he had no time to think about it.

Two guards took up positions on either side of him, their weapons trained on him.

Ferrell wagged her finger. "Tick tock, Sean."

His gaze fell on Kira. The wound. The gunshot. His chest constricted, his heart seemingly squeezed by a phantom pressure. His jaw quivered from more than gritting his teeth. And in that instant, he realized exactly what he had to do.

Sean tried to fly out of his body, but the EM field ensnared him. *Shit.* He had to relax. Sure, with the woman he loved lying dead a few feet away. He loved her? Yeah, holy heaven, he did. The revelation rocked him, but he clung to the emotion, to the power of it, as he sought out the thread of the Golden Power that lingered inside him. He latched onto it. Tugged. Seized it with all his willpower and yanked.

A tiny hole, a pinprick, popped open in the EM field.

Power trickled into him. Not much, but enough.

He soared up into the crossroads and straight into the heart of the universe—straight into the purest, most potent energy that had ever existed.

And he devoured it all.

CHAPTER TWENTY-SEVEN

THE ENERGY FLOWED INTO HIM, AROUND HIM, IGNITING THE GREEN halo once more. The glow shimmered a millimeter above his skin, its energy tingling over his flesh even as its counterpart inside him crackled and suffused his psychic senses. The power wanted to overwhelm him—that seemed to be its natural tendency, like the way a deluge of rain would coalesce into a flash flood when it gushed down a hillside—but he refused to give the power an unimpeded path to his mind. He threw up dams, redirecting the flow to the place where he needed it to go.

He controlled the Golden Power.

Grace had been right when she said it was energy, nothing more, not a living thing that could seize control. The power could inundate a person's mind unless they seized it. Grace's fears had held her back and allowed the energy to consume her like it had him the first time.

When this was over, he'd show her how to take command of the power.

First, save Kira. Then, kill Ferrell.

Yeah, today he could commit murder no problem.

Sean dived out of the crossroads toward his body but halted above the woods, hovering there as an invisible spirit. He surveyed the landscape and the life-forms below. The bunker appeared as a small hill to the naked eye. He peered through the earth into the interior, searching the corridors for blips that would indicate life. One blip appeared, inside the cell where Sean and Kira had left Amador, while a blip outside the door indicated the guard Ferrell had dispatched to retrieve Amador.

Outside the bunker, he spotted the blips of the guards, the prisoners, and Ferrell crouched beside Kira where she lay prone on the ground.

Dead on the ground.

The weight on his chest grew heavier.

His astral form floated a few feet above the heads of the men and women congregated in the clearing.

Nathan veered his gaze toward his son, and Sean had the weirdest sensation his dad was looking straight at him, seeing him though he had no visible form. For anyone to see a traveler, they needed to share a connection. Sean had met his father earlier today. How could they have a bond? It was crazy.

And yet, his father was watching him. Nathan's lips kinked into a slight smile.

Sean glanced at Kira, but she still lay lifeless on the ground.

Ferrell, kneeling beside Kira, stood and marched up to Sean where he rested on the grass. It was weird to see his own body, his vacant expression. The scientist grabbed his chin and shook it but received no reaction. She pursed her lips, one hand fisted at her side, and slapped him with the other hand. Still no reaction. Sean sensed the slap, not as a physical sensation but as a snap in his psychic tether to his body.

The scientist glared into the vacant eyes of Sean's body. "If you don't come back soon, Kira will stay dead."

He summoned the power, gathering the diverging streams into a river of energy that obeyed his command.

Ferrell crouched beside Kira again.

Sean unleashed the torrent. Psychic energy poured down in a widening deluge no one could see but everyone experienced. The green power, sparkling with golden flecks, rained down on the group below, spreading outward from the center positioned directly over Kira and Ferrell. The scientist jerked, dropping the syringe. Her eyes went wide.

She collapsed, unconscious.

The guards crumpled next.

As the energy rushed outward, Sean redirected it away from the prisoners, like a sluice guiding the flow where he wanted. The power fizzled out at the edge of the woods and at the earth-covered wall of the bunker.

Next, he sought out the device generating the EM field. Though he had no clue where it was or what it was, he located it anyway. With a spurt of power, he disabled the EM field.

Kira is still dead.

The truth gripped him in its frigid claws. He'd done so much from outside his body, but to save Kira, he had to be in his physical form. He couldn't explain how he knew, but he understood what was required. Flesh and blood to restore flesh and blood.

Sean dropped back into his body. The switch from astral vision to the real thing made him dizzy for a second, but as his senses settled down, his gaze found Kira.

Peripherally, he noticed he'd knocked out all the bad guys.

His attention glued to Kira, he scrambled across the ground to her. He raised his shaking hands to her head, bracketing it with his palms over her ears. The green halo around him blanketed her. It crackled on her skin, poured into her through her nostrils, escalated until it enveloped them both in a blinding, sparkling veil of energy.

The power fled his body through his hands, streaming into her, healing the damage. The bullet emerged from the wound little by little as the tissues knit together in its wake. The slug rolled off her forehead and fell to the ground. Cells repaired themselves. Neurons reconnected. Her heart fluttered and thumped once, twice, three times, regaining its natural and strong rhythm. Blood coursed through her veins, enlivening and nourishing her flesh.

As the last iota of power vacated him, she opened her eyes.

"Sean," Kira said, her voice suffused with wonder, "how did you—"

He collapsed to the ground, and everything went black.

———

KIRA SPRANG TO HER KNEES. IN THE BACK OF HER MIND, SHE REALIZED something incredible had just occurred, but she had no chance to appreciate it. Sean lay slumped on the ground, out cold.

What had he done?

She pressed a finger to his wrist, praying for a pulse. Nothing. Struggling not to panic, she jammed her finger into his neck. Nothing. No, goddammit, he would not die in her place. Exchange one life for another? Like hell she'd let him get away with that.

"You're not leaving me," she said, tears pooling in her eyes, blurring her vision. "I won't let you do this, not for me."

She flipped him onto his back and laid her palms on his chest. Energy lingered within him, she sensed it. The energy of the Golden Power. That's what he had done to save her. He'd invited the ultimate power into his mind and body, not caring if it destroyed him.

For her. He'd sacrificed himself for her.

The EM field was gone. She recognized that fact. With every ounce of psychic energy inside her, she reached for the Golden Power within him.

And she tapped into his healing ability.

He wasn't dead, not quite yet. If she hurried…

So hurry, idiot.

Kira channeled his power through her own and back into his body, something she hadn't known she could do. Instinct took over, and she let it guide her powers. Her hands on his chest began to glow faintly green.

Sean moaned. His head lolled.

Relief gushed through her. She caught his face in her hands. "Wake up, you jerk. You don't get to leave me yet. We're stuck together, remember?"

His eyelids opened halfway, and he gave her a dazed smile. "You sure are bossy. I'm trying to die heroically here, and you can't stop telling me what to do."

Tears spilled down her cheeks. "Dying heroically is overrated. The people who love you, we'd rather you stick around."

"We?" He pushed up onto his elbows, his smile turning sexy. "You included yourself there. Guess that means you've got a thing for me."

"Shut up so I can kiss you."

Kira crushed her mouth to his in a quick, fierce kiss.

Nathan rushed up to Sean and Kira, his expression awed and proud at the same time. "You have amazing control, Sean. I thought you weren't very adept with your powers yet, but what do I know? I haven't seen you since you were five." He clapped a hand on Sean's shoulder. "Good work, son."

Sean's chest puffed up a little when his father called him "son." The dad he'd thought abandoned him had praised him for doing a good thing, and Kira understood the pride he must feel at knowing his father loved him after all. Until today he'd cursed his deadbeat dad, and she'd cursed her deadbeat parents. Maybe that's what Ferrell, and Tesler before her, had intended—to make them both weaker and more malleable by taking away their families, convincing them their parents hadn't wanted to be with them. But his father had fought every day for seventeen years, determined never to betray his kid. And her parents had made a desperate choice believing it would spare her and Caleb a horrible fate.

Their parents had done the best they could. She and Sean had done the best they could, and somehow, they'd emerged victorious.

"What should we do with them?" Nathan asked, indicating the guards and Ferrell with a sweep of his arm.

"I've got an idea," Sean said, "but I need Kira's help."

Sean raised a hand to cup her face. His skin was warm. His powers came alive, sizzling between them, awakening her own powers along with a damp ache between her thighs. She wanted him, yes. More than that, she needed him. She needed more than his powers and the ferocious potency of their merged psychic energy. She needed him, the man, the jerk who'd turned out to be a strong and caring person who'd taken her powers into himself despite not knowing her and despite the fact she'd tried to trick him repeatedly so she could escape. He trusted her even after that, and she'd learned she could trust him too. With her life. With her heart.

Crazy as it sounded when they'd known each other such a short time, she recognized the truth. She loved him, and the realization shivered through her, sultry and sweet.

With his palm on her cheek, he said, "We need to finish this. What do you say?"

"I'm with you. Whenever, wherever, whatever."

They both got to their feet. He brushed hair from her face, trailing his fingers down her cheek.

She glanced around, her brows lifting when she saw the unconscious baddies. Her gaze returned to Sean, and she touched his face. "You took out all the bad guys."

"Yeah, but it's not quite over yet. They're out cold, but not dead." He hooked an arm around her waist. "We have one more thing to do. It ought to set things right, but it won't be pretty."

"What are you talking about?"

"Ferrell and Amador were right about one part of their plan. Somebody has to take responsibility for the bombings, to close that case and let the world move on from it." He looked at the limp form of Dr. Ferrell and sighed. "It's the only way to make sure they're locked up for good, someplace they can't escape from."

Kira caught his face in her hands. "You're going to have to explain your plan to me."

"It's simple, really." He pulled in a deep breath. "We're going to manipulate their minds with thought projection. They are going to take responsibility for the attacks."

"First, we'd better lock up these guards."

"I'll do that," Nathan said.

Kira's eyes flew wide when her parents approached and announced, "We'll help Nathan."

Grace walked up then with Abby and Caleb in tow. "I should take the kids someplace less scary."

A horrible thought popped into Kira's mind, and she asked, "Did they see what just went down?"

"No. There were guards in front of us blocking our view."

Kira's shoulders slumped with relief. "Thank goodness for that."

Caleb rushed at her, latching his arms around her waist, forcing Sean to relinquish his hold on her. "Kiki! Kiki! Are you okay? I'm okay. Mom and Dad are here, did you see?"

"Yeah, kiddo, I saw." She tousled his hair. "They have to help me out for a little bit. Go with Grace and Abby, okay? Me and Mom and Dad will come get you soon, I promise."

"Okay," he said with the sort of annoyed tone only a child could make sound endearing.

Caleb ran to their parents and squeezed each of them in turn, his hugs fierce and quick. Their mom lifted him up into her arms for a fuller hug, kissed his cheek, and murmured to him. Dad chucked Caleb's chin and said something Kira couldn't hear. Her brother trotted back to Grace.

"Take them to the cabin," Kira said. "The one where Sean and I hid. It's a few miles away—"

"I can find it," Grace told her. She tapped a finger on her temple. "Psychic, remember? I'll scout the place with RV. We'll take one of the SUVs parked around the other side of the hill."

Everyone must have gotten their powers back. The EM field had been disabled several minutes ago.

Sean slung an arm around her waist again, tugging her close.

Grace went rigid, her gaze sharpening on a sight to the left of the bunker's recessed door.

Kira followed the track of Grace's gaze.

A blond man traipsed out of the woods.

"David!" Grace shouted.

She bolted for her husband, flung her arms around his neck, and lavished him with kisses hot enough to make Kira blush. David Ransom wrapped his arms around his wife.

Abby sprinted to her parents and clamped her little arms around her father's leg.

When his wife surrendered his mouth, David glanced around and said, "Looks like I missed the party."

"It was a dud, anyway," Grace said. "Amador didn't get his nuclear-fallout jamboree."

"Amador?" David said, seeming confused.

Grace patted his cheek. "I'll explain later. Right now, you should help Sean and Kira—and Sean's father."

David's brows shot up. "Father?"

"Explain later, honey. Help now."

Grace waved to Kira's mother. "Mrs. Magnusson, why don't you come with me and the kids? David will help wrangle the baddies. He's really good at that."

"I am?" David said with a faint smirk.

"Oh yes, honey, you are."

Kira's mom gave her a quick hug, then accompanied Grace and the kids to the rented SUV David had driven here. He'd hidden it in the woods a few hundred yards away, but they'd all agreed it was safer for Grace to take the rented car rather than the closer ones owned and operated by villains. Better to exercise excessive caution, he'd said. Everyone had agreed with him.

While the grumble of the vehicle engine faded away, David, Nathan, and Kira's dad gathered up the weapons belonging to the unconscious guards. Kira had asked to have one of the handguns, though she couldn't explain why she'd wanted it. Her intuition niggled at her, but she had no idea what it was trying to tell her. Sean took a pistol as well. Before rousing and corralling the guards, the other men took time to introduce themselves to the two prisoners Kira and Sean had freed.

Kira faced Sean, who had his back to the unconscious Ferrell. "How long will they stay knocked out?"

"Not sure." Sean tucked his gun inside his waistband. "Never knocked anybody out with my powers before."

A sensation shivered through her, cold and sharp like a blanket of needles pricking her skin. She curled her hand around the grip of the gun she'd commandeered, her finger hovering over the trigger.

"What is it?" Sean asked.

"Don't know." Kira stepped sideways. Ferrell still sprawled limp on the ground, eyes closed, but the sensation on her skin grew stronger. "Sean—"

"Ahhh!" a male voice hollered.

Kira whipped her head around to see a guard floundering to his feet, dazed, striking his fists out blindly. David landed a kick to the guard's gut, sending him tumbling to the earth again.

Something rustled behind Sean.

Kira swung her head toward the ground behind Sean.

Dr. Ferrell had clambered to her feet. She staggered forward with a scalpel in her white-knuckle grip. The scientist raised the scalpel, its blade targeted on Sean's neck.

"No!" Kira shouted.

She veered her gun up and pulled the trigger.

The shot boomed in the clearing. The bullet struck Ferrell smack in the chest. She jerked, eyes bulging.

Kira fired again and again.

Ferrell toppled to the ground, a lump of flesh, her eyes wide and vacant. Blood stained her white shirt, spreading outward.

Sometime between Kira shouting and when she'd fired the gun, Sean had whirled around to see what had frightened her. He stared down at the dead scientist without expression.

Kira dropped the gun. It plunked onto the earth. "I had to—She was about to—"

"I know." Sean pulled her into his arms. "You saved my life again. Thank you."

Despite the shock of killing another human being, Kira couldn't muster any regret for what she'd done or pity for the woman whose life she'd taken. Ferrell had shot Kira in the head. The woman deserved what she'd gotten. Besides, the so-called scientist had tortured God-knew-how-many innocent men, women, and probably children too.

The world was a better place without Dr. Ferrell in it.

From across the clearing, David called out, "What happened?"

"Kira saved my ass again," Sean said with a glimmer of humor in his green eyes.

"Oh, is that all?" David said, his voice rife with the same humor. "Not sure his ass is worth the effort, Kira."

"Man, you are not funny," Sean said, "no matter how hard you try. Stick to rounding up the bad guys. Your wife says that's all you're good for."

Kira peeked around Sean's thick bicep. David, Nathan, and her father had found zip ties on some of the guards, and now they used those very restraints to hobble the uniformed men.

"You're my hero," Sean said.

Kira rolled her eyes at him.

"I'm serious." He hooked a finger under her chin, urging her to meet his gaze. "You are an amazing, smart, and feisty woman. You talked back to me when I kidnapped you instead of playing the meek victim, and you believed in me when you really shouldn't have. I gave you no reason to trust me, but you did. You showed me my powers aren't dangerous, that I'm not dangerous unless I want to be. You made me feel human again. You made me feel, period. I owe you everything."

The way he was looking at her, she knew he meant all of it.

Footfalls clapped in the stairwell.

Sean and Kira swung their guns up and aimed them toward the concrete entrance to the bunker.

A solitary guard led a wild-eyed and haggard Gabriel Amador up the steps. When the guard noted his buddies tied up and the weapons Kira and Sean aimed at him, he dropped his gun and raised his hands in surrender.

Gabriel Amador laughed. Not arrogant laughter, either. Panicked, hysterical sounds.

"Okay," Sean said. "Time for Gabe here to confess in front of the world."

CHAPTER TWENTY-EIGHT

KIRA WATCHED SEAN AND NATHAN SET UP THE VIDEO EQUIPMENT in the clearing. Her telekinetic pulse had wiped out the electrical wiring and computers in the bunker—plus any devices connected to them. They'd found a backup camera and laptop computer in a storage room that hadn't been connected to the system and therefore hadn't been affected.

A few minutes ago, a realization had struck her, and she'd burst out laughing. Everyone had looked at her funny, but Sean had been the one to speak up.

"Why are you laughing?" he'd asked. "Did getting resurrected make you demented?"

"No." She shook her head, still chuckling. "I just realized I haven't even thought about lighting up a cigarette since we left that crappy hotel room in Kansas. I don't want one at all."

"Okay, resurrection didn't make you crazy. It cured you of smoking?"

She'd wandered closer to him to whisper so only he would hear. "Maybe it's you that cured me. I haven't craved a smoke since the first time we kissed."

At that, he'd grinned with supreme self-satisfaction.

Grace had called from the cabin to assure Kira her mom and Caleb were doing fine. According to Grace, Caleb and Abby were building a stick fort on the lawn. Both kids seemed to have shed all the weight of the trauma they'd endured lately. Children were resilient, though Kira hadn't realized how resilient until now. How amazing that under these circumstances a child could still have a good time.

Despite having spent seventeen years believing his father was a deadbeat, after less than a day with his dad Sean already looked at the man with a touch of hero worship in his gaze.

The men had locked the guards in separate cells inside the bunker and moved Dr. Ferrell's body into a storage room located inside the bunker next to the exit. Thanks to Ferrell's little bag of goodies, they'd been able to sedate Amador enough to keep him from trying anything. Not that the man seemed capable of causing trouble. It was a precaution, nothing more. Amador was too far gone to do much more than breathe. Kira and Sean hadn't bothered to secure the man with zip ties.

The two former prisoners had become part of the team. Danny, the hacker-slash-psychic, sat on the ground with the undamaged computer on his lap doing things he'd explained but that Kira did not understand. The woman they'd rescued, Eva, guarded the prisoners. She brandished a large gun and looked like she'd have no qualms about shooting any villains who might appear.

Kira's dad, never the hugging type before, seized her in a bear hug. "I can't believe you're here. This is a miracle, an honest-to-goodness miracle."

Her father had hugged her five times in the past twenty minutes. She didn't mind at all. In fact, she couldn't keep from smiling every time.

"All set," Sean called out to the group. "Danny, are you ready?"

"Good to go," the young man replied. "The funds have been moved, the feed is set up, and the documents are in place."

Sean had insisted they take a good chunk of Amador's fortune and allocate it to a bank account in the Cayman Islands. From there, once the dust settled, they'd distribute the funds to victims of the bombings and to psychics abused by Amador, Ferrell, and Tesler. Grace and David had found a number of those psychics over the past five years, and each deserved compensation. So did the bombing victims. They'd left Amador enough of a bank balance to make it plausible he could've funded a terrorist group.

Danny had also planted documents on Amador's computer system at his home, accessing it remotely from here in the Montana woods. Turned out Danny's powers supercharged his hacking talents just like Amador had claimed, letting him make brand-new files seem like they'd existed for years. The files planted on Amador's computer revealed his insane plot and his motivations, as well as Ferrell's complicity. In crafting the evidence, they had all agreed to omit Tesler's involvement—not to spare the dead man's reputation, but to spare Sean from becoming the grandson of an infamous madman. Sean had balked at the idea at first, though Kira had insisted on it. He'd relented when his father threw his support behind the plan.

He listened to his dad. It was sweet.

Sean hauled Amador to his feet, bracing the man with two strong hands on his slumped shoulders. Then, Sean used his healing power to eradicate the sedative. Amador blinked rapidly, his gaze clearing but his mind remaining addled.

This was the dangerous part. Amador needed to be clear of mind to make the video, which meant Kira and Sean had a brief window in which to manipulate his mind.

She knew Sean hated using thought projection. The idea bothered her too, but Amador had done much worse to so many people. This was justice.

Nathan and Eva stood behind Amador but out of range of the camera, guarding in case any of Amador and Ferrell's lackeys had escaped before they'd rounded up the lot of them.

Side by side in front of Amador, Kira and Sean linked their hands. Power crackled between them, and then they did it.

They reshaped a man's mind.

"I AND MY GROUP ARE RESPONSIBLE FOR THE BOMBS DETONATED IN THE cafe and the movie theater," Gabriel Amador said without a trace of remorse in his voice or his expression. "Jackson Tennant murdered my son, and the world allowed this to happen. I sought to punish everyone because everyone is guilty. I regret nothing. My path is just, exacting vengeance on a world that permits evil to exist provided the evildoers have money and power. It's not right, and we intend to stop the madness."

Amador paused, but his gaze remained fixed on the camera, unflinching and cold.

"Our next target," Amador said, "will be of global import. We will launch an intercontinental ballistic missile from Malmstrom Air Force Base in Montana. No one can stop us."

The television picture switched to a woman reporter standing outside the gates of Malmstrom.

"Earlier today," the reporter said, "Spanish billionaire Gabriel Amador was apprehended while attempting to break into Missile Command here at Malmstrom Air Force Base. Six coconspirators were also arrested at a defunct bunker in the mountains. They had apparently tried to destroy the bunker to cover their tracks but only managed to fry the electrical system. Amador claims to have psychic powers that allowed him to commit the attacks and that would've let his group launch an ICBM. However, authorities found a large amount of data on Amador's home computer that incriminates him and his coconspirators in a bizarre plot described as 'staggeringly unhinged.' The small terrorist cell helmed by Amador and the late Dr. Helena Ferrell, whom Amador admits to murdering, seems to have consisted of just six other individuals, all of whom are in custody and reportedly will testify against Amador. Evidence from Amador's computer reportedly shows how the cell members detonated the first bomb without using a trigger, but authorities won't share that information at this time."

The video changed to a scene of Amador, handcuffed, being shoved into a police car by men wearing FBI jackets.

The reporter said, "This audacious and ill-conceived terrorist plot has been disrupted with no lives lost. I'm Crystal Jones reporting from Malm-strom Air Force Base near Great Falls, Montana."

EPILOGUE

Three Months Later

SEAN LAY ON AN OVERSIZE BEACH TOWEL SURROUNDED BY GOLDEN sand with golden sunshine warming his skin. Since he wore only swim trunks, the heat of the tropical sun warmed most of his body. The sight beside him heated up the rest of him.

Kira sprawled across the other half of the towel wearing a skimpy bikini. The strings that held it together were tied in little bows. The way she reclined there made her breasts mound up. The bikini bottoms accentuated her hips. The outfit and the pose showed off every one of her lush curves to best effect and made his groin ache. Her dark hair sprayed over the towel and onto the sand while sunglasses concealed her eyes.

Her lips curved into a satisfied smile. "I like the Caribbean."

"Me too." Sean rolled onto his side, braced on one elbow, and his gaze landed on the mouthwatering slopes of her breasts. "I also like that nobody's tried to abduct or murder us for three whole months. How long do you think the peace will last?"

"You worry too much." She splayed a hand over his cheek, her thumb rubbing the corner of his mouth. "I thought you'd learned to kick back and enjoy life."

"I backslide once in a while. Maybe I need a refresher lesson."

"Mm, I like giving you refreshers." She reached up to graze her fingers over his hair. "I like you as a redhead. You're not hiding from the past anymore."

Yeah, he'd made peace with the past, with the fact he couldn't change who his grandfather had been or what the man had done. None of that tainted Sean. Not anymore.

The sound of splashing drew their attention to the water. Caleb giggled as he jumped around in the knee-high waves. His parents had dropped to their knees to let their son splash them relentlessly. The three of them grinned and laughed, and Mr. Magnusson lifted Caleb above his head. The family had been reunited for three months, and though recovering from what had happened took time, they'd reforged their family bond quickly.

Sean glanced over his shoulder at his family. His dad lounged in a beach chaise alongside Edward, who sat in a matching chair. Grace and David relaxed on a beach towel while Abby played in the sand. David sat up to help her make a little tower for her sandcastle. Grace observed with a smile lighting up her face.

Everyone was happy these days. Their group vacation to Aruba had begun a week ago, and they had another week before they went home. Then, they'd continue their mission to find and help psychics who were abused by Jackson Tennant, Tesler, Ferrell, and Amador. Considering JT and his lackeys had created two dozen facilities around the world, this mission could take the rest of their lives.

Saving people was never a waste of time.

As for Gabriel Amador, he'd spend the rest of his life in a high-security mental institution. Nobody could save that man.

They'd each taken a bit of Amador's money. When Sean had asked if stealing from a crazy guy was immoral, David had told him, "It's not stealing. It's compensation for what he took from us. You and I were locked up and tortured in the Mojave Desert facility."

"But JT locked us up," Sean had pointed out, "and then Tesler after that."

"We can't get to JT's money. Amador abused a lot of people, including you and Grace. He used the same tactics as JT and Tesler. It's not wrong to make him pay for our pain and suffering."

Sean decided he could live with that. Besides, the bulk of what they'd taken from Amador had gone to the bombing victims and psychics abused by JT, Tesler, and Amador. Sean and his extended family took just enough to make life a little easier.

"Hey," Kira said, tickling his chin. "What are you thinking about?"

With a long, satisfied sigh, he told her, "How lucky we are."

"Yes, we are that." She sat up and stretched. "Ready for that refresher?"

"Absolutely." Sean jumped up, then bent to grab her around the waist and lift her up too. She squeaked when he set her feet down in the sun-baked sand. He kept his arm around her, and that lithe body pinned to his, when he twisted sideways to wave at his father. When his dad noticed, Sean shouted, "We're going for a walk."

Nathan Vandenbrook flashed a knowing grin. "Have fun."

Sean led Kira down a well-maintained path for a ways until he saw the smaller trail he'd scouted earlier. "Scouting" meant he'd RV'd the trail to find the perfect spot. They emerged from the trees into a clearing around a small waterfall. The pool at the base of the falls shimmered a crystalline blue.

"This is beautiful," Kira said, smiling broadly as she surveyed the surroundings.

He pulled her tight against him and kissed her, exploring her mouth with his lips and his tongue, diving deep to savor the taste of her and the way she responded with silken strokes of her own tongue. "The scenery's not as beautiful as you. Nothing could be."

"I love it when you shower me with compliments."

"Plan on showering you with something else right now." He stripped off his swim trunks, then fingered the bow of one bikini string. "Sorry, but nudity is required for this event."

A flush tinted her cheeks, though not from embarrassment. Her nipples pearled, jutting against the flimsy fabric of her bikini top, and her breaths shortened.

He untied the strings of her bikini one by one. The top fell off first, fluttering to the ground, followed swiftly by the bottoms.

"What now?" she asked, touching her fingertips to his chest.

"You'll see."

He swept her up in his arms, strode to the pool, and tossed her into the middle of it.

Kira shrieked as she plunked into the water with a big splash.

Sean leaped in after her, water shooting up around him. He caught her around the waist. "Time for grown-up water games."

He slid a hand between their bodies, gliding it down her belly and between her thighs. When he slipped his fingers between her folds, she gasped. When he began stroking her flesh, her eyes drifted half shut and her mouth fell open on a long, low moan. He caressed her until she was writhing against him, held in place by his arm, her moans becoming louder and hungrier. The second her body tensed, he devoured her mouth, swallowing her cries as she climaxed.

She sagged against him, her head on his shoulder.

"I have to ask you a question," he murmured into her ear.

"Huh?" She sounded dazed, which he took as a compliment.

Sean rubbed her back in slow circles and nuzzled her wet hair. "I said I need to ask you a question."

With an irritated little noise, she lifted her head to gaze at him. "Can it wait? We haven't gotten to the best part yet."

He nipped her chin. "We'll get there, trust me."

She crossed her arms, resting them on his collarbone. Her nose bumped his. "Okay, ask your question."

"Um…" Suddenly, he couldn't make the words come out. He brushed the backs of his fingers over her cheek, mesmerized by her jewel-bright eyes. "I love you, Kira. Will you marry me?"

The wattage of her smile could've powered the lights for an entire city. "Yes."

He grinned. "Thank you."

She laughed. "You don't have to thank me for saying yes to your proposal."

"But I'm grateful." He placed a light kiss on her lips. "The ring is in our room at the hotel. I was going to hold off asking until later, but I couldn't wait a second longer."

She wriggled her hips. "Show me how grateful you are."

He took hold of her hips, and she wound her legs around him. The water lapped around them as he plunged inside her with one smooth thrust. Tiny waves splashed against their bodies while he took her slowly, sweetly, relishing every sensation. He fit inside her like she'd been made for him, and he knew they'd been made for each other. Psychic energy sizzled inside them and on their skin. He glided in and out, in and out, her soft wetness welcoming him, his hard-on throbbing with a mounting need to spill himself inside her. She clung to him, panting into his ear, her fingers clawing at his scalp. He thrust harder, faster, lost in the rapture of taking the woman he loved.

Her sheath tightened around him, and her body went rigid.

The moment her climax hit, he surrendered to the sensations, his release pulsating out of him and into her, melding their bodies even as the glittering, tingling energy of their powers merged. He let out a hoarse cry.

She kissed his neck and his cheek, her lips feathery on his skin. "I love you, Sean. Can't wait to marry you."

"Neither can I. We should do the deed before you start classes again." He combed his fingers through her drenched hair while her drenched sex stayed snug around him. "I'm proud of you for going back to college."

"It's not an amazing feat. I filled out some paperwork, that's all."

"After what you've been through, it takes guts to get your life back in order."

"You're the brave one." She ran a finger over his lips. "You went through way worse things than I did. I'm in awe of your strength and determination."

Right then and there, he knew he would love this woman forever.

He squeezed her ass with both hands. "Whatever happened to that refresher course in relaxation?"

She pushed away from him, swimming backward while crooking a finger at him. "Follow me."

He would follow her anywhere, even into the heart of the universe.

And for them, that wasn't a metaphor.

Did you love

Visit
AnnaDurand.com

to subscribe to her newsletter

for updates on forthcoming books
&
to receive exclusive content!

ANNA DURAND IS A BESTSELLING, MULTI-AWARD-WINNING AUTHOR OF contemporary and paranormal romance. Her books have earned bestseller status on every major retailer and wonderful reviews from readers around the world. But that's the boring spiel. Here are some really cool things you want to know about Anna!

Born on Lackland Air Force Base in Texas, Anna grew up moving here, there, and everywhere thanks to her dad's job as an instructor pilot. She's lived in Texas (twice), Mississippi, California (twice), Michigan (twice), and Alaska—and now Ohio.

As for her writing, Anna has always made up stories in her head, but she didn't write them down until her teen years. Those first awful books went into the trash can a few years later, though she learned a lot from those stories. Eventually, she would pen her first romance novel, the paranormal romance *Willpower*, and she's never looked back since.

Want even more details about Anna? Sign up for her newsletter to get exclusive content and updates on forthcoming books.

VISIT ANNADURAND.COM TO SIGN UP.

www.ingramcontent.com/pod-product-compliance
Lightning Source LLC
Chambersburg PA
CBHW050521190726
48284CB00003B/892